GOLGOTHA

Created by Matt Hawkins

PUBLISHED BY TOP COW PRODUCTIONS, INC.
LOS ANGELES

GOLGOTHA

Created by Matt Hawkins

Writers // Matt Hawkins & Bryan Hill

Artist // Yuki Saeki

Colorist // Bryan Valenza

Letterer // Troy Peteri

Editor // Elena Salcedo

Design // Vincent Valentine

Direct Market Cover Art - Raffaele Ienco

Kickstarter Cover Art - Joe Jusko

For Top Cow Productions, Inc.
For Top Cow Productions, Inc.
Marc Silvestri - CEO
Matt Hawkins - President & COO
Elena Salcedo - Vice President of Operations
Henry Barajas - Director of Operations
Vincent Valentine - Production Manager
Dylan Gray - Marketing Director

To find the comic shop
nearest you, call:
1-888-COMICBOOK

Want more info? Check out:
www.topcow.com
for news & exclusive Top Cow merchandise!

GOLGOTHA. JULY 2017. FIRST PRINTING.

Published by Image Comics, Inc. Office of publication: 2701 NW Vaughn St.,
Suite 780, Portland, OR 97210. Copyright © 2017 Matt Hawkins & Top Cow
Productions, Inc. All rights reserved. "GOLGOTHA," its logos, and the likenesses
of all characters herein are trademarks of Matt Hawkins and Top Cow Productions,
Inc., unless otherwise noted. "Image" and the Image Comics logos are registered
trademarks of Image Comics, Inc. No part of this publication may be reproduced
or transmitted, in any form or by any means (except for short excerpts for
journalistic or review purposes), without the express written permission of Matt
Hawkins, Top Cow Productions Inc., or Image Comics, Inc. All names, characters,
events, and locales in this publication are entirely fictional. Any resemblance
to actual persons (living or dead), events, or places, without satiric intent, is
coincidental. Printed in the USA. For information regarding the CPSIA on this
printed material call: 203-595-3636 and provide reference #RICH-750682.
ISBN: 978-1-5343-0320-1.

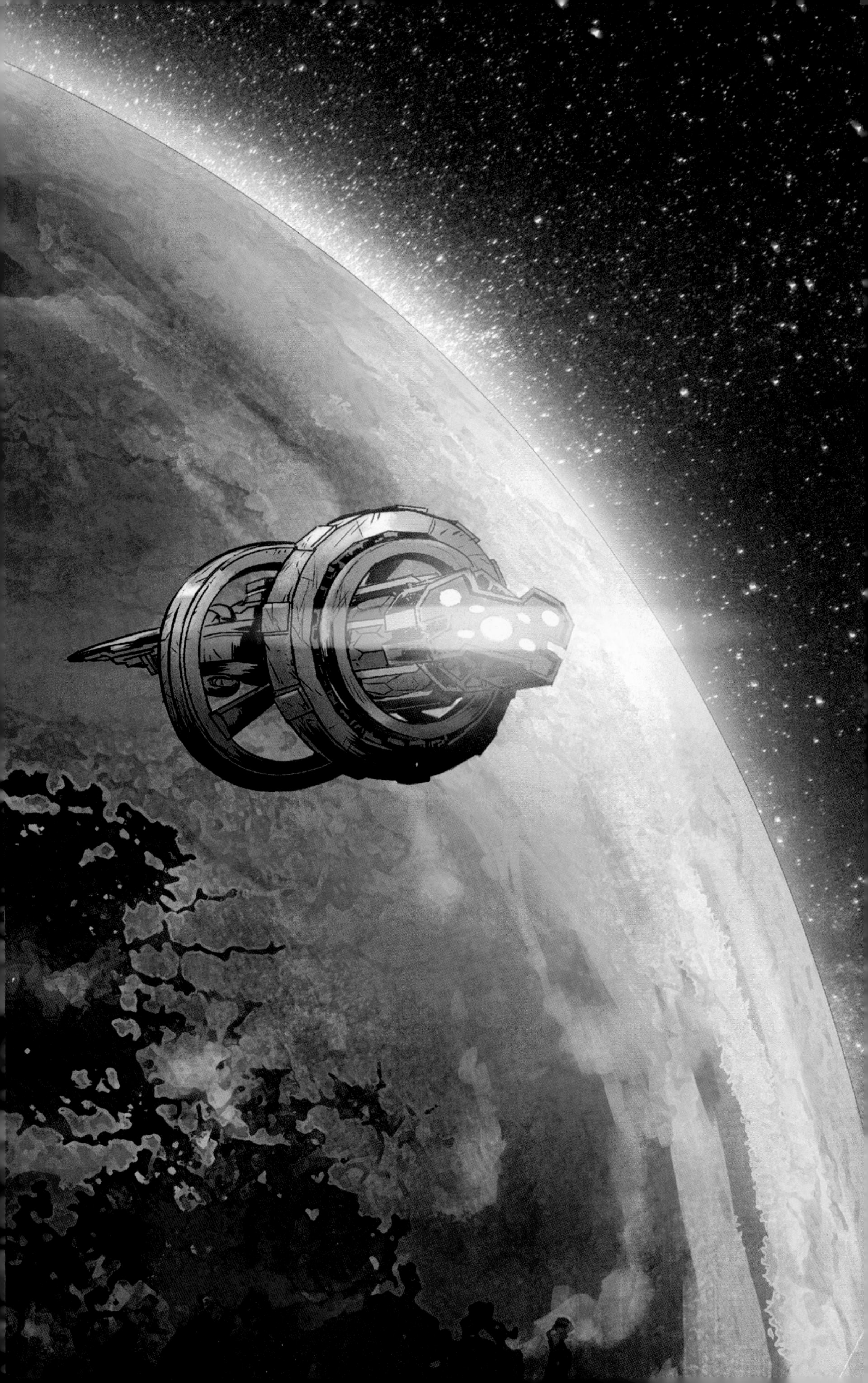

CHAPTER 1

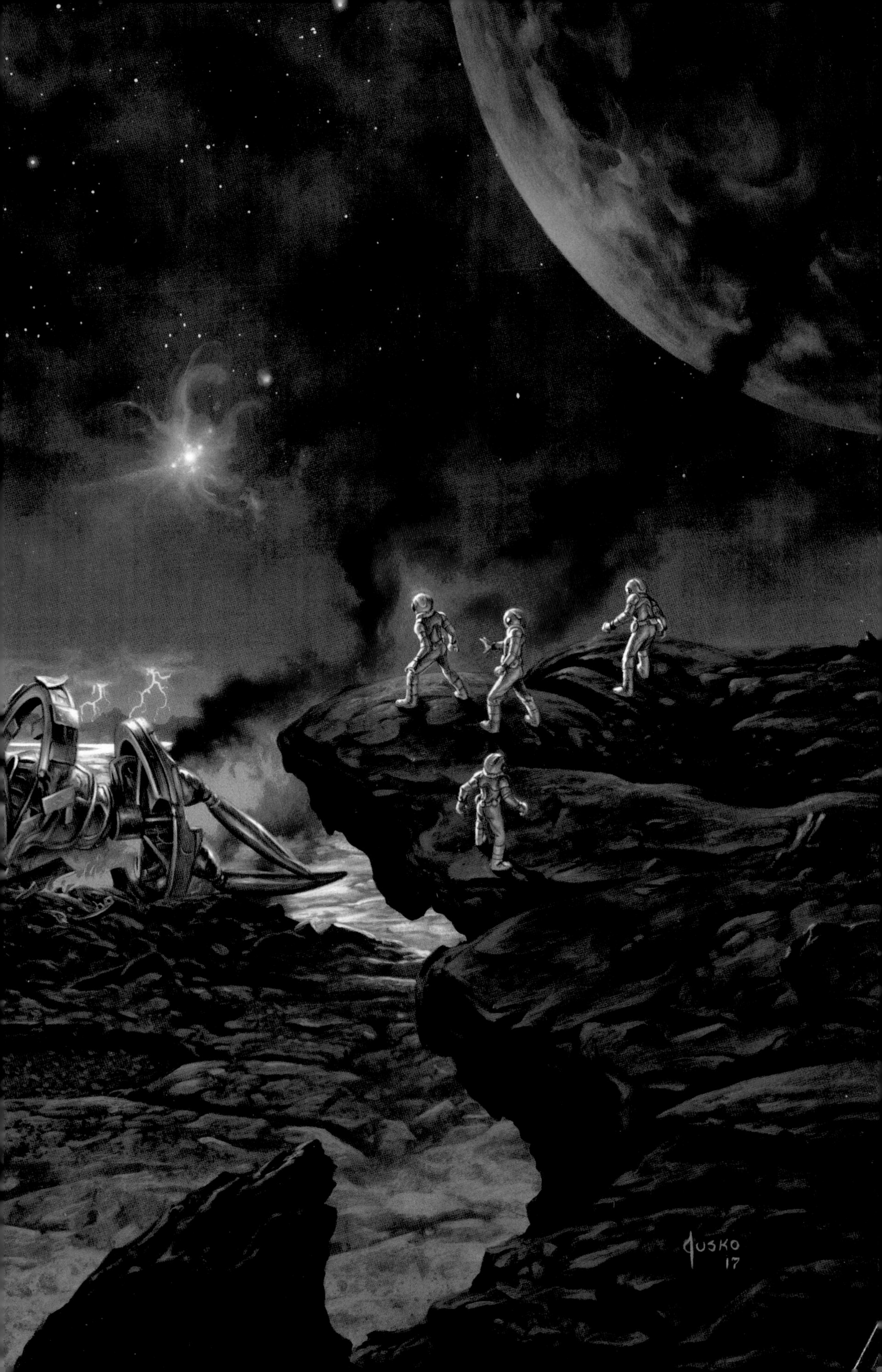

JUSKO
17

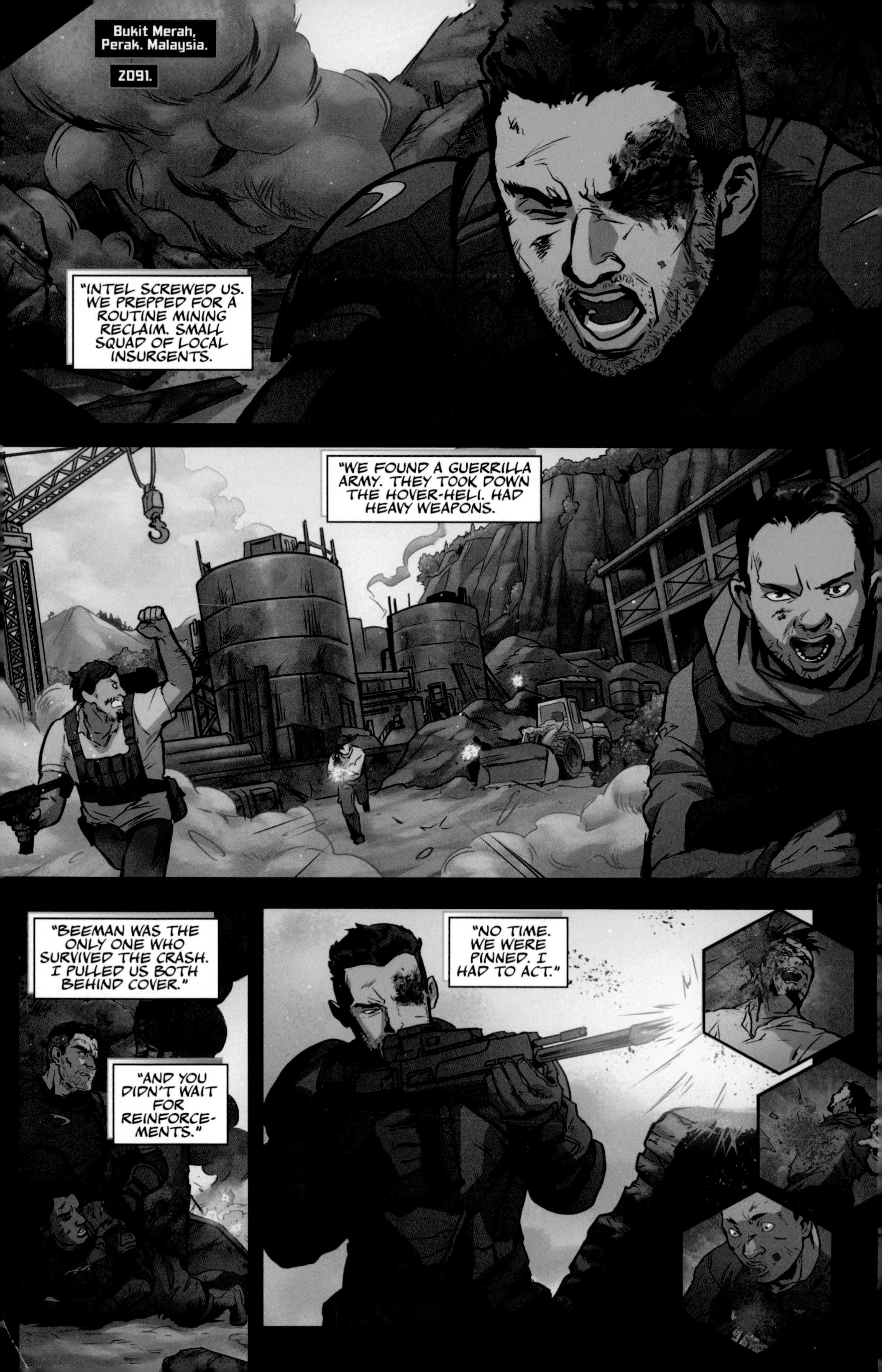
Bukit Merah, Perak. Malaysia.
2091.
"INTEL SCREWED US. WE PREPPED FOR A ROUTINE MINING RECLAIM. SMALL SQUAD OF LOCAL INSURGENTS.
"WE FOUND A GUERRILLA ARMY. THEY TOOK DOWN THE HOVER-HELI. HAD HEAVY WEAPONS.
"BEEMAN WAS THE ONLY ONE WHO SURVIVED THE CRASH. I PULLED US BOTH BEHIND COVER."
"AND YOU DIDN'T WAIT FOR REINFORCE-MENTS."
"NO TIME. WE WERE PINNED. I HAD TO ACT."

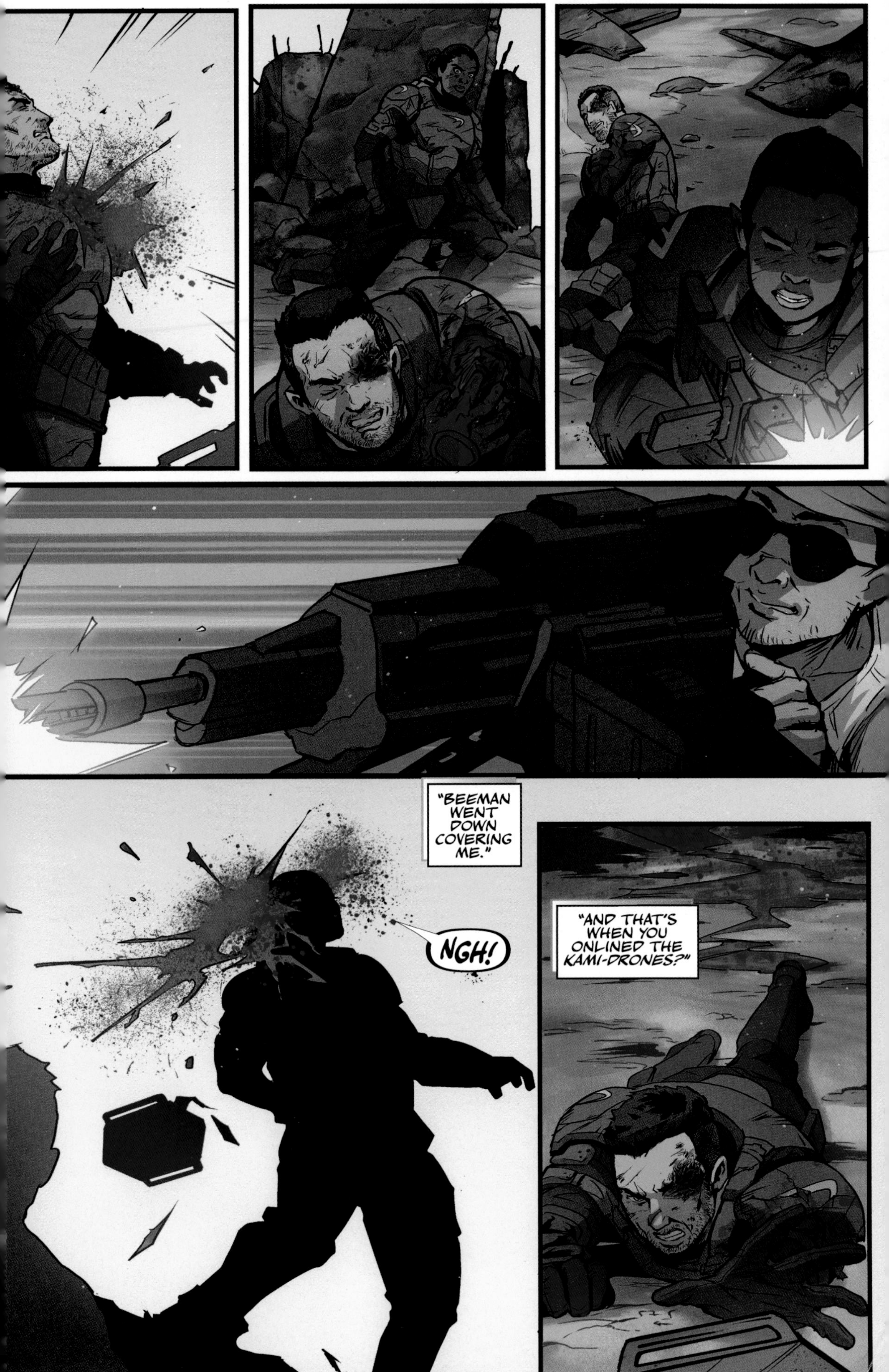
"BEEMAN WENT DOWN COVERING ME."
NGH!
"AND THAT'S WHEN YOU ONLINED THE KAMI-DRONES?"

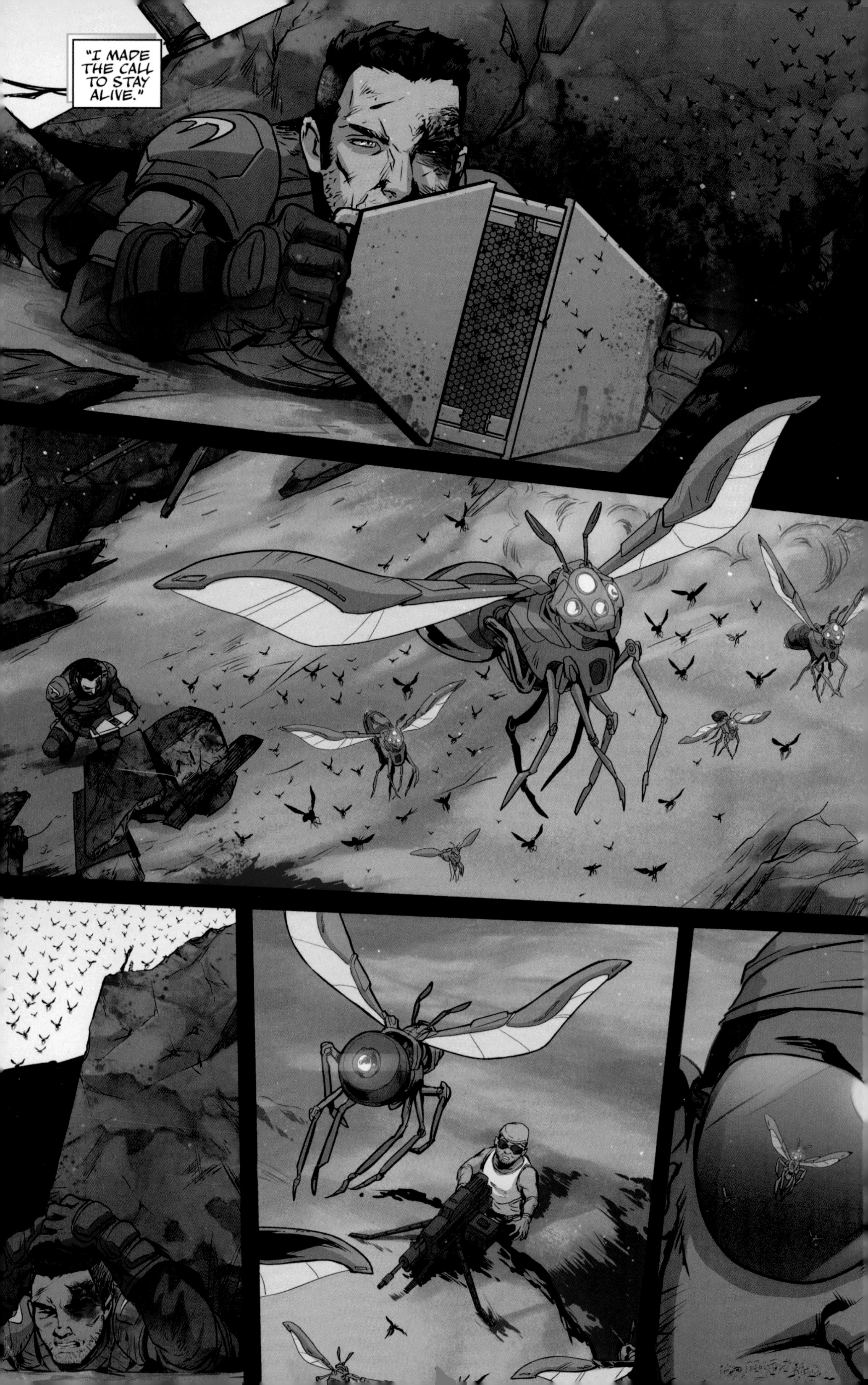
"I MADE THE CALL TO STAY ALIVE."

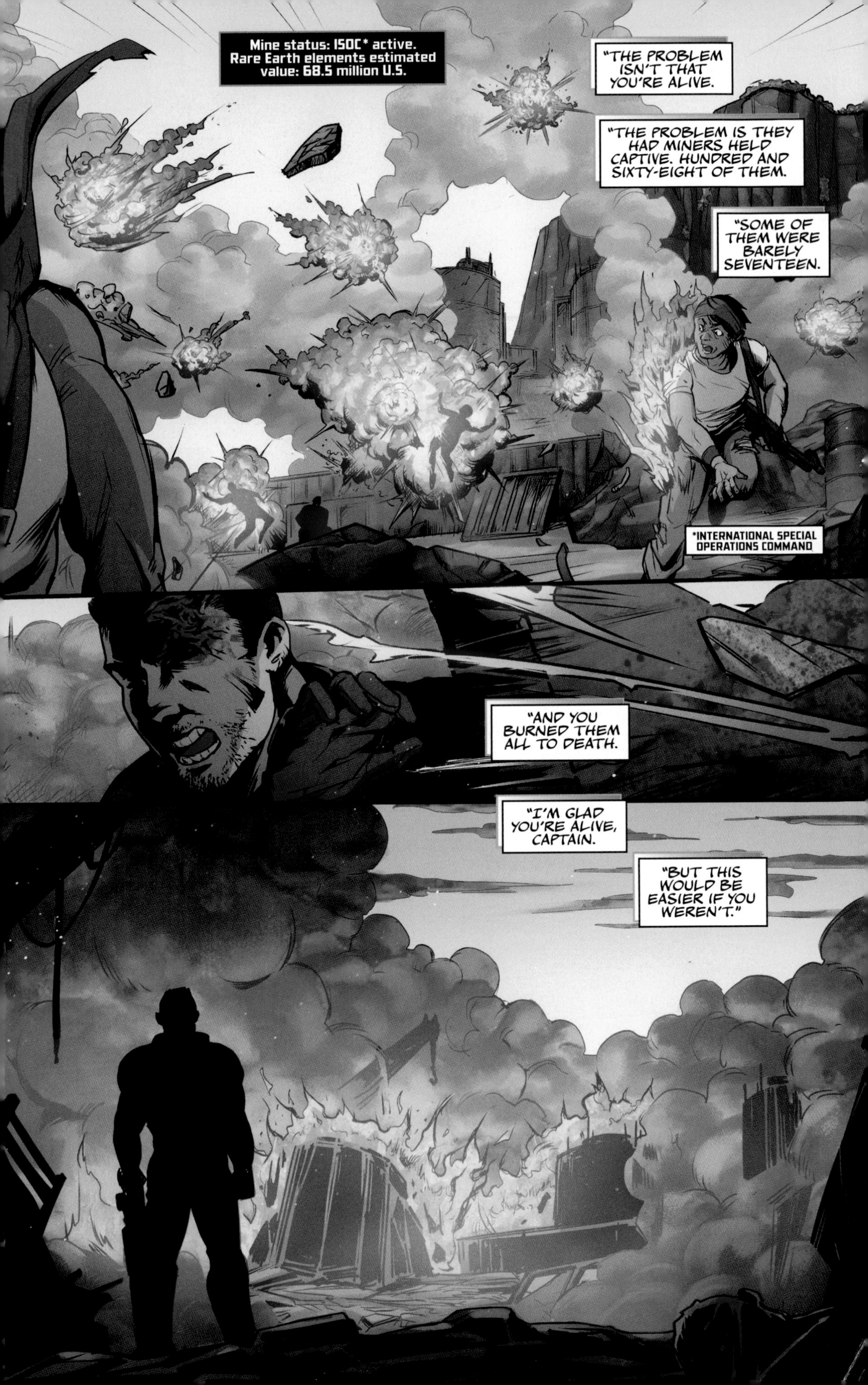
Mine status: ISOC* active.
Rare Earth elements estimated value: 68.5 million U.S.
"THE PROBLEM ISN'T THAT YOU'RE ALIVE.
"THE PROBLEM IS THEY HAD MINERS HELD CAPTIVE. HUNDRED AND SIXTY-EIGHT OF THEM.
"SOME OF THEM WERE BARELY SEVENTEEN.
*INTERNATIONAL SPECIAL OPERATIONS COMMAND
"AND YOU BURNED THEM ALL TO DEATH.
"I'M GLAD YOU'RE ALIVE, CAPTAIN.
"BUT THIS WOULD BE EASIER IF YOU WEREN'T."

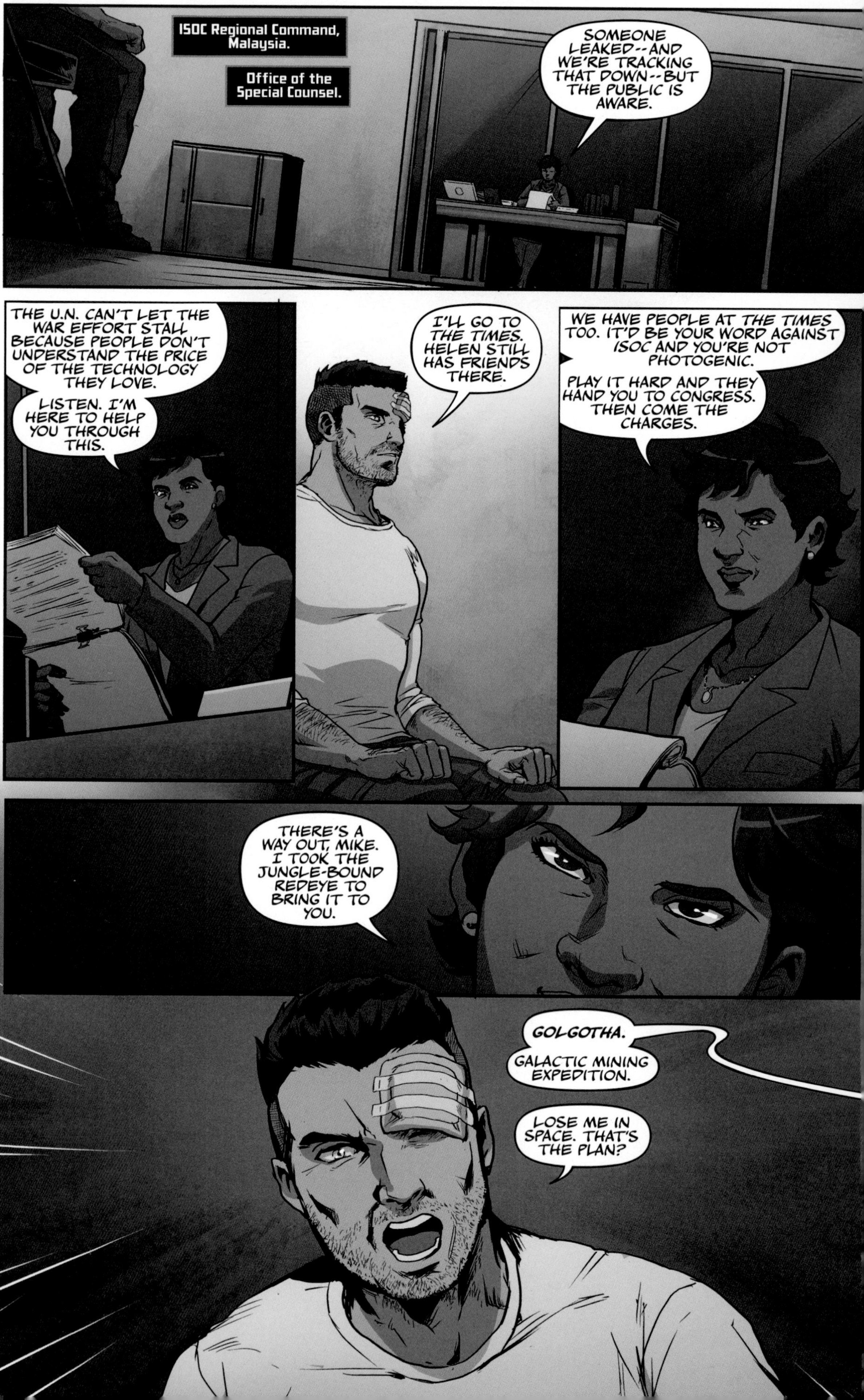
ISOC Regional Command, Malaysia.
Office of the Special Counsel.
SOMEONE LEAKED--AND WE'RE TRACKING THAT DOWN--BUT THE PUBLIC IS AWARE.
THE U.N. CAN'T LET THE WAR EFFORT STALL BECAUSE PEOPLE DON'T UNDERSTAND THE PRICE OF THE TECHNOLOGY THEY LOVE.
LISTEN. I'M HERE TO HELP YOU THROUGH THIS.
I'LL GO TO THE TIMES. HELEN STILL HAS FRIENDS THERE.
WE HAVE PEOPLE AT THE TIMES TOO. IT'D BE YOUR WORD AGAINST ISOC AND YOU'RE NOT PHOTOGENIC.
PLAY IT HARD AND THEY HAND YOU TO CONGRESS. THEN COME THE CHARGES.
THERE'S A WAY OUT, MIKE. I TOOK THE JUNGLE-BOUND REDEYE TO BRING IT TO YOU.
GOLGOTHA.
GALACTIC MINING EXPEDITION.
LOSE ME IN SPACE. THAT'S THE PLAN?

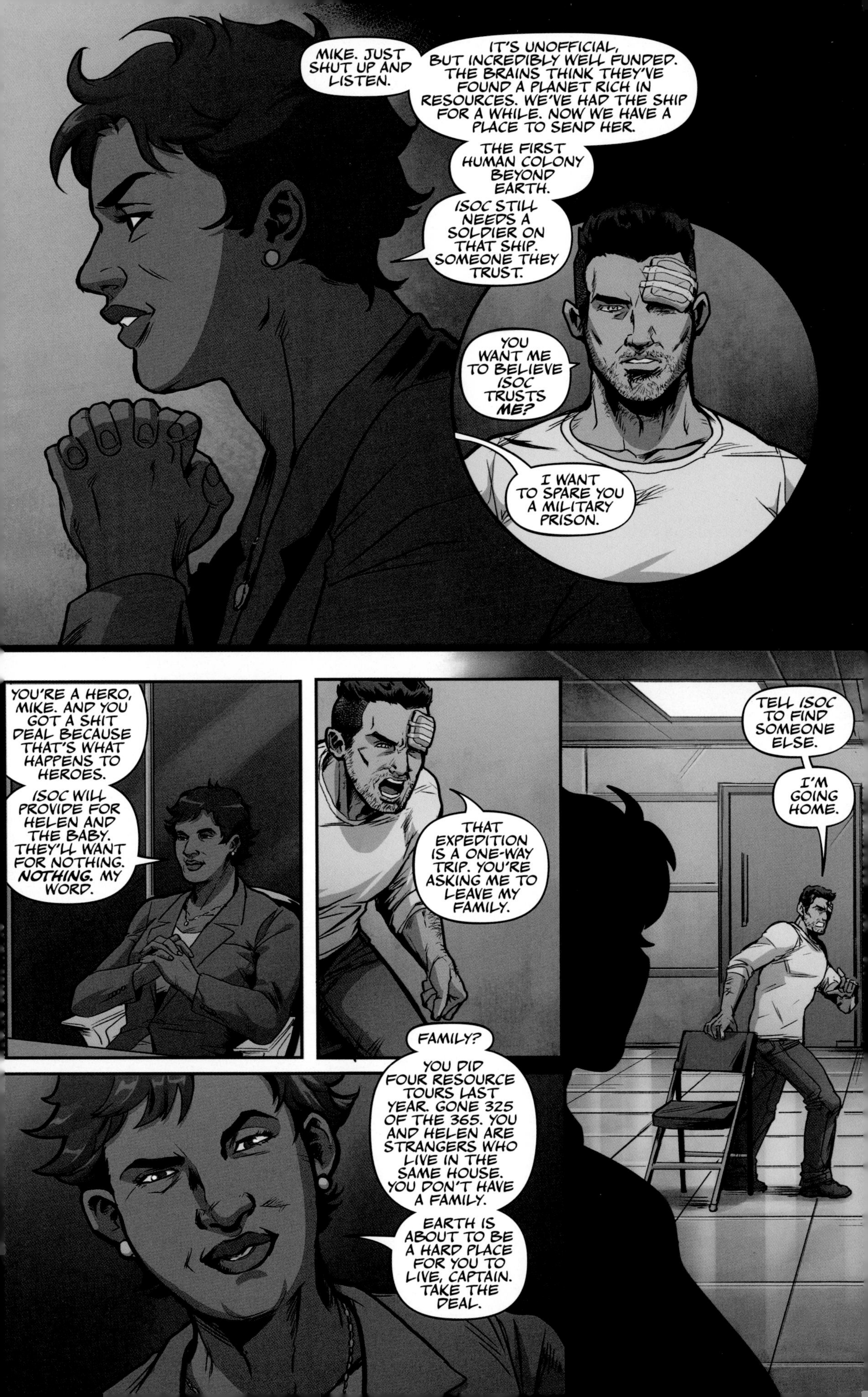
MIKE. JUST SHUT UP AND LISTEN.
IT'S UNOFFICIAL, BUT INCREDIBLY WELL FUNDED. THE BRAINS THINK THEY'VE FOUND A PLANET RICH IN RESOURCES. WE'VE HAD THE SHIP FOR A WHILE. NOW WE HAVE A PLACE TO SEND HER.
THE FIRST HUMAN COLONY BEYOND EARTH.
ISOC STILL NEEDS A SOLDIER ON THAT SHIP. SOMEONE THEY TRUST.
YOU WANT ME TO BELIEVE ISOC TRUSTS *ME?*
I WANT TO SPARE YOU A MILITARY PRISON.
YOU'RE A HERO, MIKE. AND YOU GOT A SHIT DEAL BECAUSE THAT'S WHAT HAPPENS TO HEROES.
ISOC WILL PROVIDE FOR HELEN AND THE BABY. THEY'LL WANT FOR NOTHING. ***NOTHING.*** MY WORD.
THAT EXPEDITION IS A ONE-WAY TRIP. YOU'RE ASKING ME TO LEAVE MY FAMILY.
TELL ISOC TO FIND SOMEONE ELSE.
I'M GOING HOME.
FAMILY?
YOU DID FOUR RESOURCE TOURS LAST YEAR. GONE 325 OF THE 365. YOU AND HELEN ARE STRANGERS WHO LIVE IN THE SAME HOUSE. YOU DON'T HAVE A FAMILY.
EARTH IS ABOUT TO BE A HARD PLACE FOR YOU TO LIVE, CAPTAIN. TAKE THE DEAL.

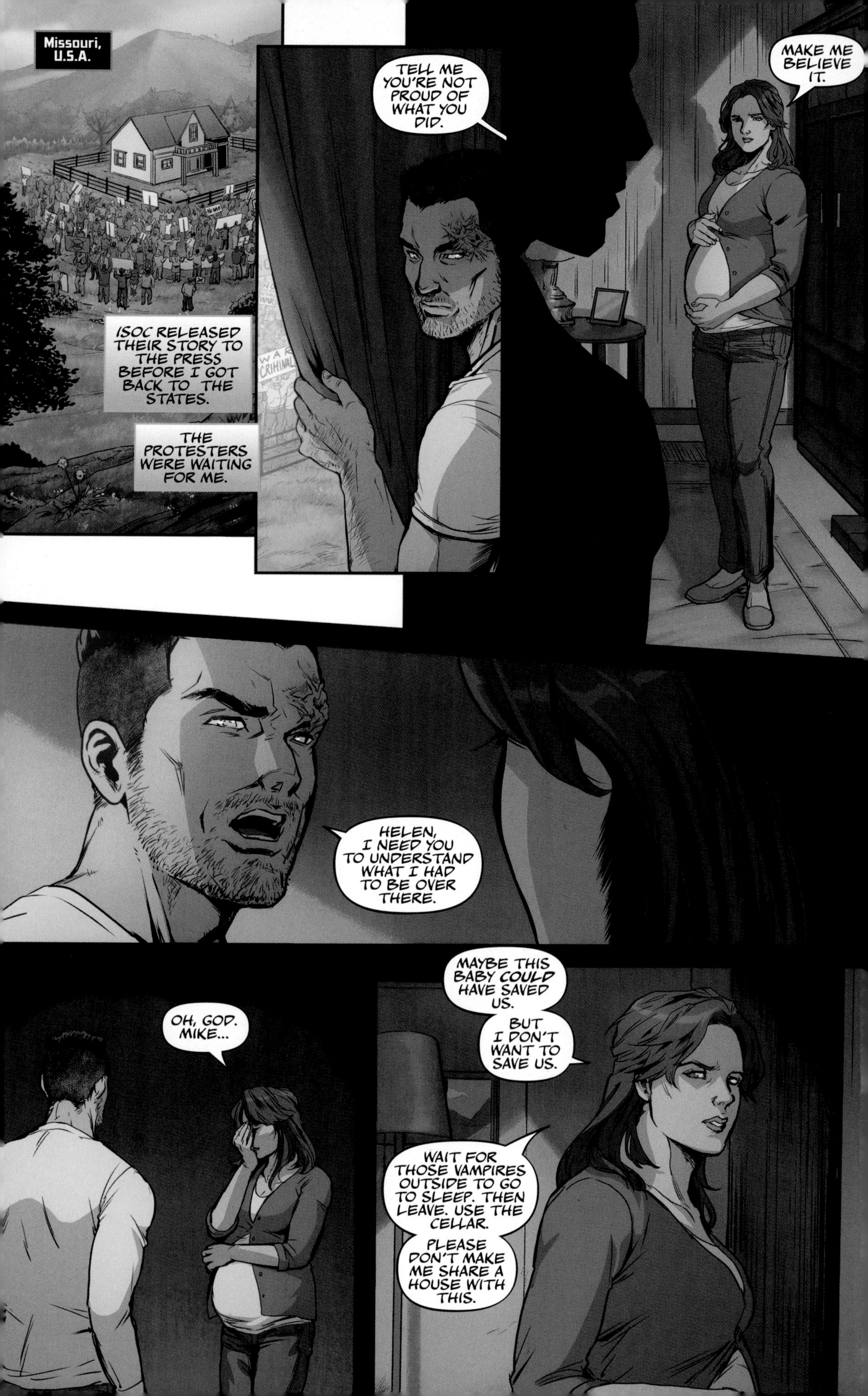
Missouri, U.S.A.
ISOC RELEASED THEIR STORY TO THE PRESS BEFORE I GOT BACK TO THE STATES.
THE PROTESTERS WERE WAITING FOR ME.
TELL ME YOU'RE NOT PROUD OF WHAT YOU DID.
MAKE ME BELIEVE IT.
WAR CRIMINAL
HELEN, I NEED YOU TO UNDERSTAND WHAT I HAD TO BE OVER THERE.
OH, GOD. MIKE...
MAYBE THIS BABY COULD HAVE SAVED US.
BUT I DON'T WANT TO SAVE US.
WAIT FOR THOSE VAMPIRES OUTSIDE TO GO TO SLEEP. THEN LEAVE. USE THE CELLAR.
PLEASE DON'T MAKE ME SHARE A HOUSE WITH THIS.

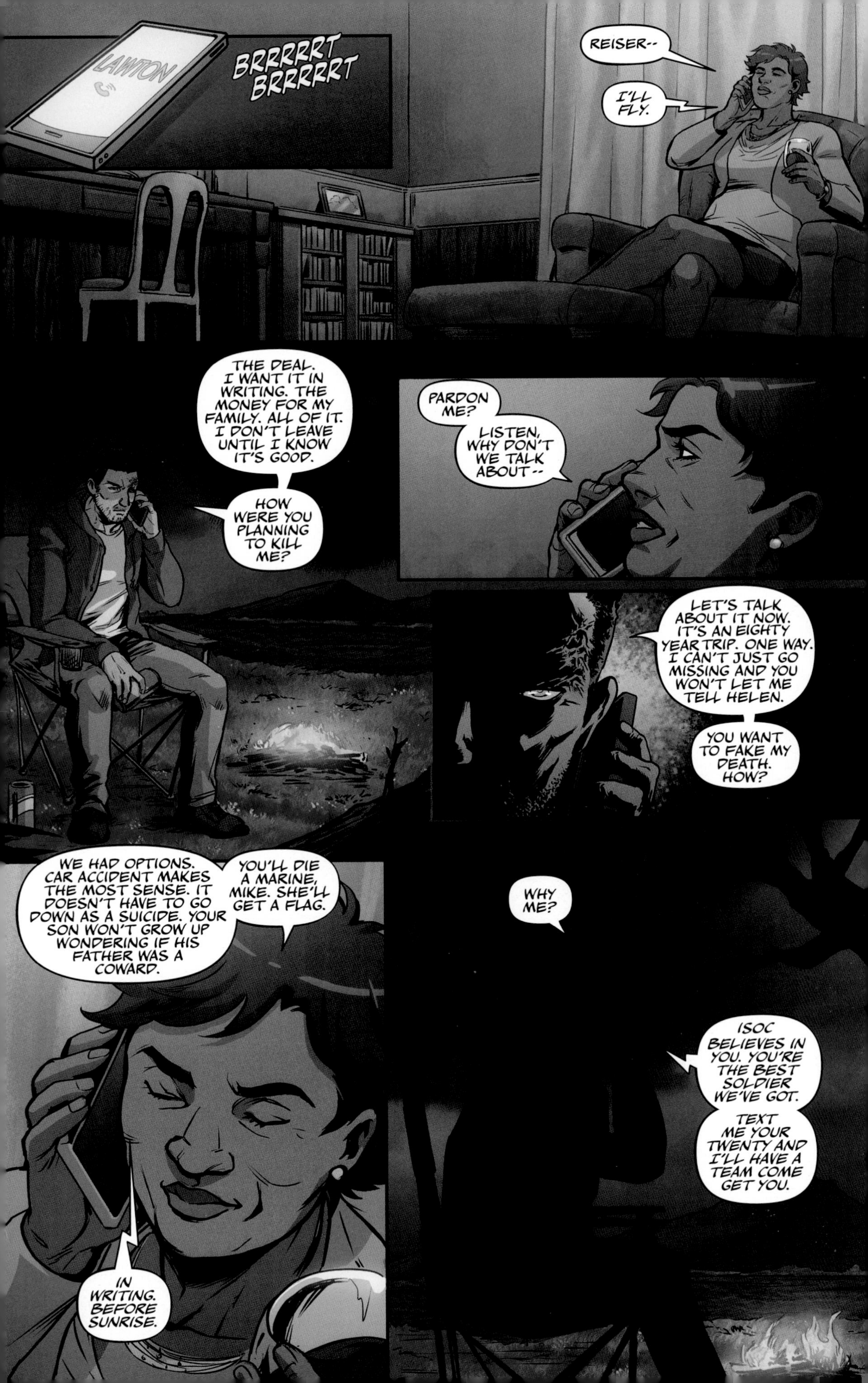
LAWTON
BRRRRRT BRRRRRT
REISER--
I'LL FLY.
THE DEAL. I WANT IT IN WRITING. THE MONEY FOR MY FAMILY. ALL OF IT. I DON'T LEAVE UNTIL I KNOW IT'S GOOD.
HOW WERE YOU PLANNING TO KILL ME?
PARDON ME?
LISTEN, WHY DON'T WE TALK ABOUT--
LET'S TALK ABOUT IT NOW. IT'S AN EIGHTY YEAR TRIP. ONE WAY. I CAN'T JUST GO MISSING AND YOU WON'T LET ME TELL HELEN.
YOU WANT TO FAKE MY DEATH. HOW?
WE HAD OPTIONS. CAR ACCIDENT MAKES THE MOST SENSE. IT DOESN'T HAVE TO GO DOWN AS A SUICIDE. YOUR SON WON'T GROW UP WONDERING IF HIS FATHER WAS A COWARD.
YOU'LL DIE A MARINE, MIKE. SHE'LL GET A FLAG.
WHY ME?
ISOC BELIEVES IN YOU. YOU'RE THE BEST SOLDIER WE'VE GOT.
TEXT ME YOUR TWENTY AND I'LL HAVE A TEAM COME GET YOU.
IN WRITING. BEFORE SUNRISE.

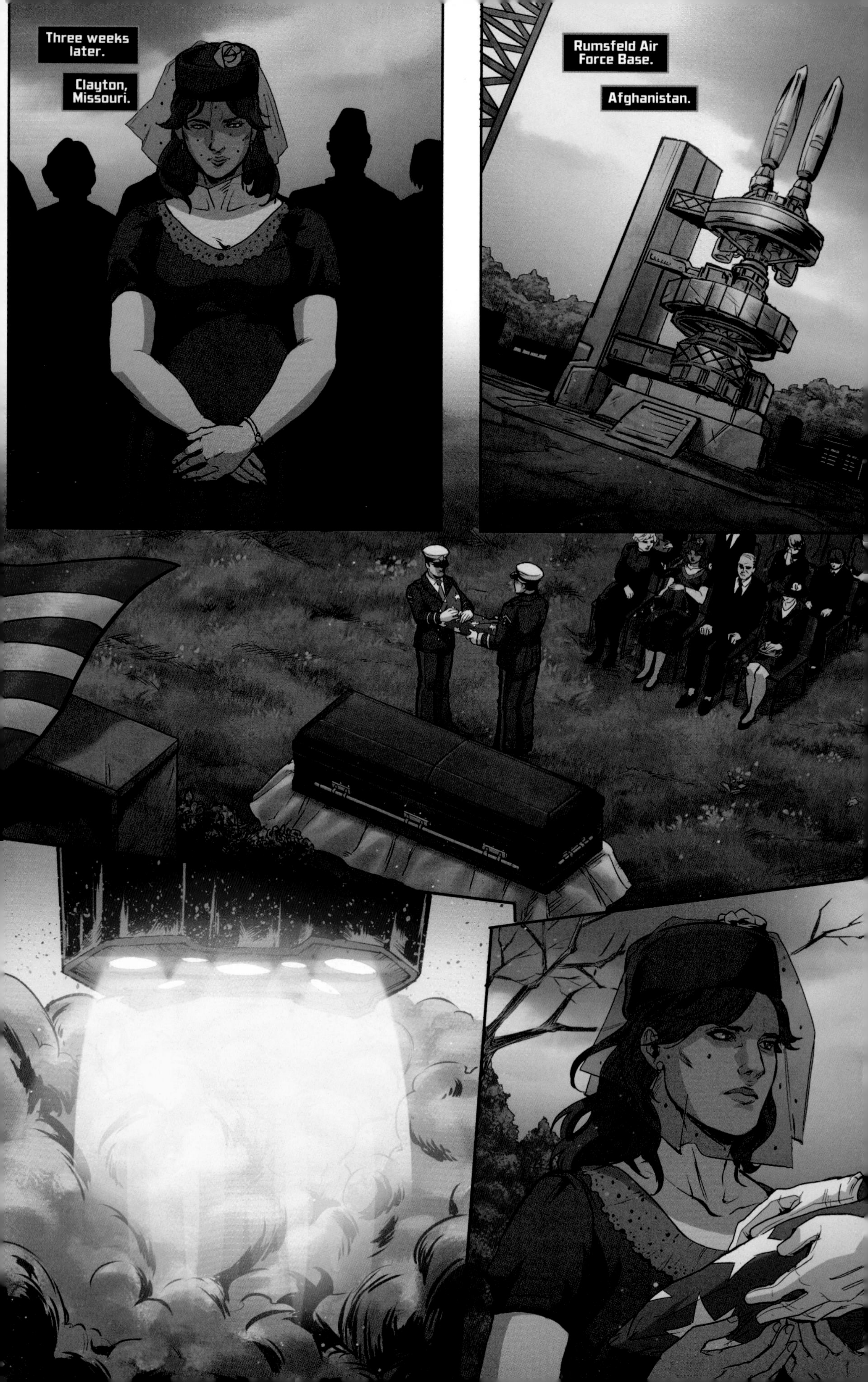
Three weeks later.
Clayton, Missouri.
Rumsfeld Air Force Base.
Afghanistan.

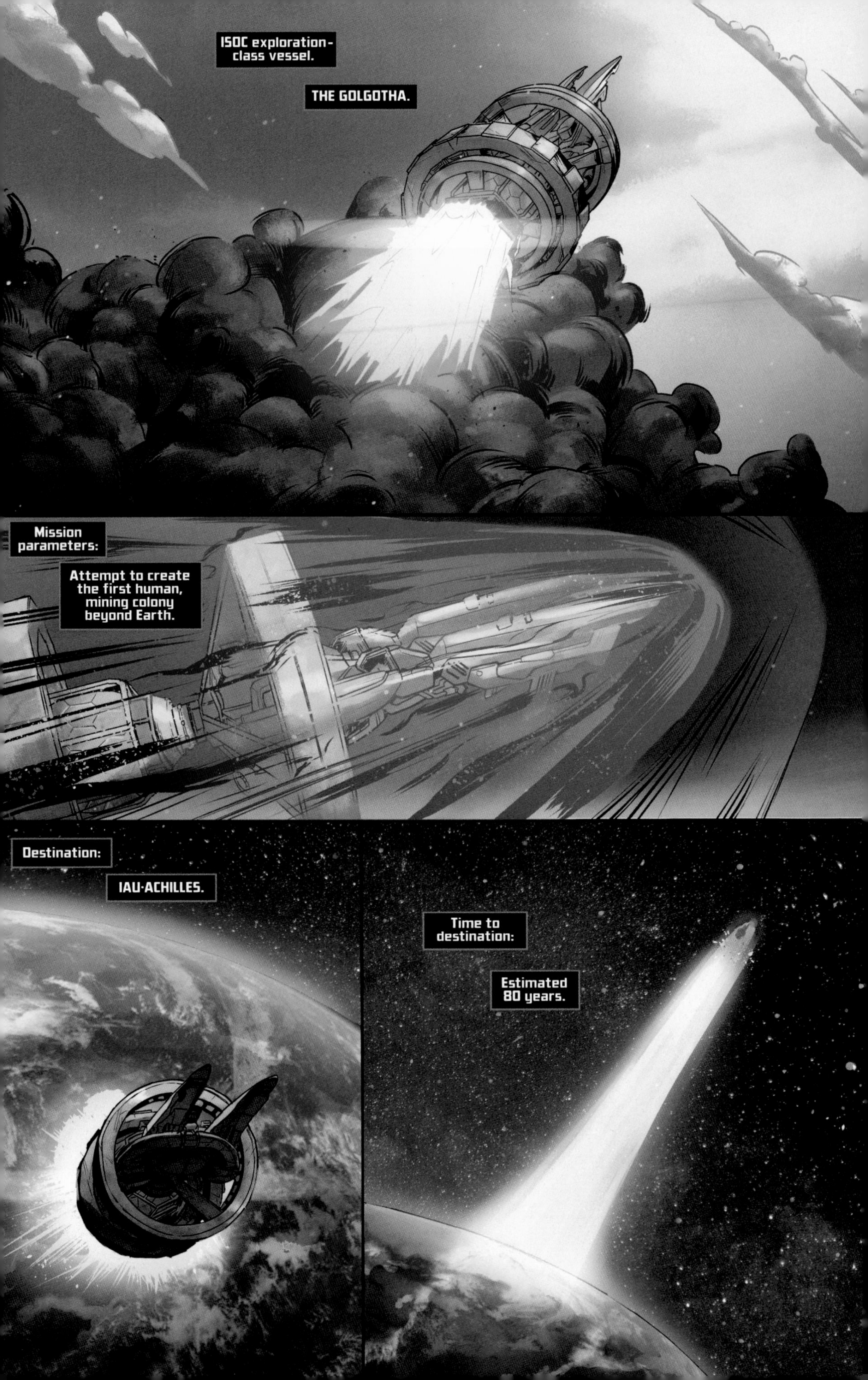
ISOC exploration-class vessel.
THE GOLGOTHA.
Mission parameters:
Attempt to create the first human, mining colony beyond Earth.
Destination:
IAU-ACHILLES.
Time to destination:
Estimated 80 years.

Essential crew:

CARILLO, Anabelle. AEF. HUM-INT backup pilot to automated ship system.

MEAD, Lancaster. Engineer.

LIPPENCOTT, Charlene. PhD. Agrophysics.

GAFANI, Abdul-Ghafaar. Imam. AEF.

CHENG, David. Chaplain. AEF.

ROSENTHAL, Moshe. Rabbi. AEF.

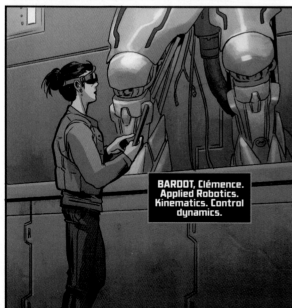

BARDOT, Clémence. Applied Robotics. Kinematics. Control dynamics.

LAWTON, Michael. Cpt. 31st Special Forces Group. JSOC.

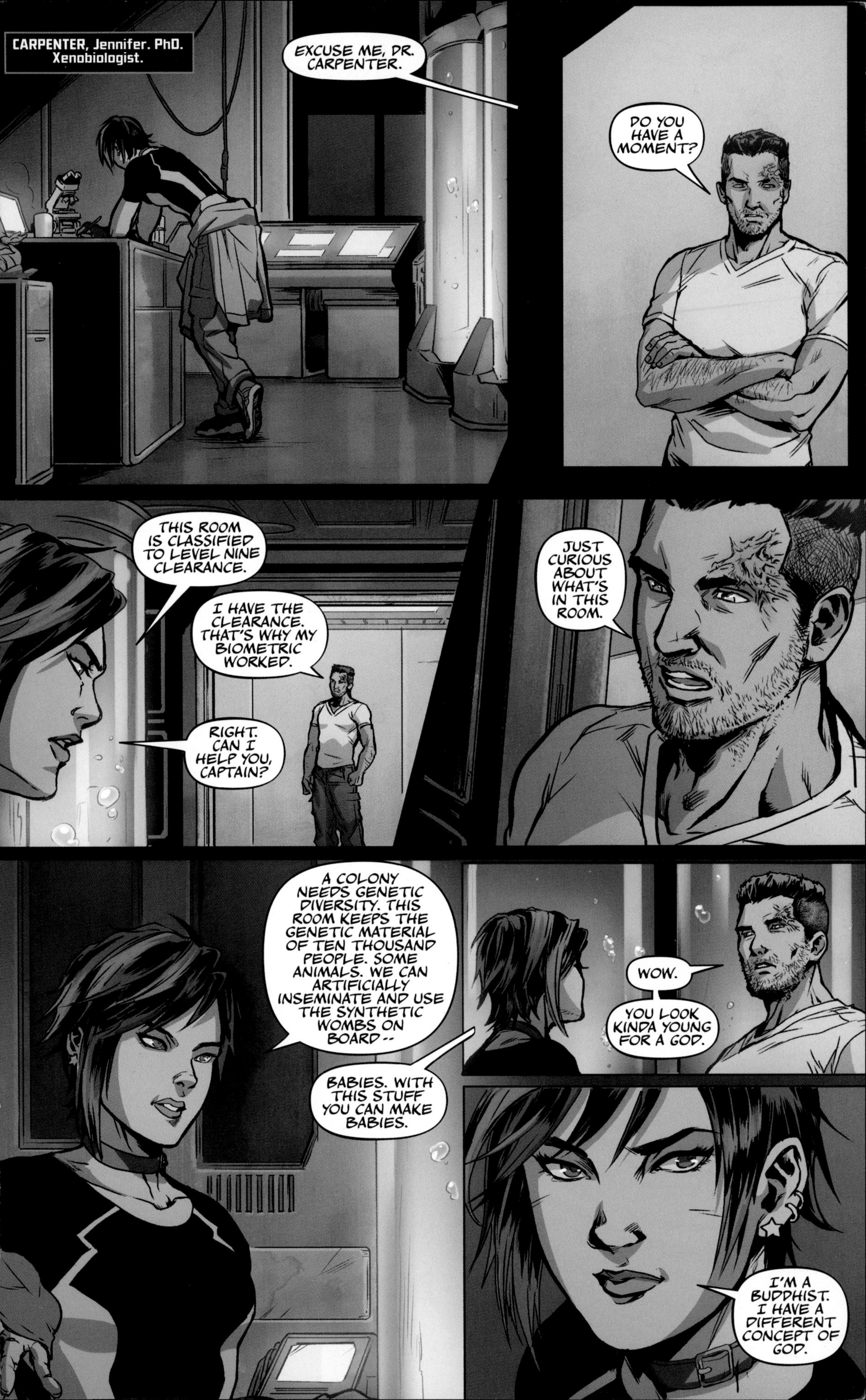
CARPENTER, Jennifer. PhD. Xenobiologist.
EXCUSE ME, DR. CARPENTER.
DO YOU HAVE A MOMENT?
THIS ROOM IS CLASSIFIED TO LEVEL NINE CLEARANCE.
I HAVE THE CLEARANCE. THAT'S WHY MY BIOMETRIC WORKED.
RIGHT. CAN I HELP YOU, CAPTAIN?
JUST CURIOUS ABOUT WHAT'S IN THIS ROOM.
A COLONY NEEDS GENETIC DIVERSITY. THIS ROOM KEEPS THE GENETIC MATERIAL OF TEN THOUSAND PEOPLE. SOME ANIMALS. WE CAN ARTIFICIALLY INSEMINATE AND USE THE SYNTHETIC WOMBS ON BOARD --
BABIES. WITH THIS STUFF YOU CAN MAKE BABIES.
WOW.
YOU LOOK KINDA YOUNG FOR A GOD.
I'M A BUDDHIST. I HAVE A DIFFERENT CONCEPT OF GOD.

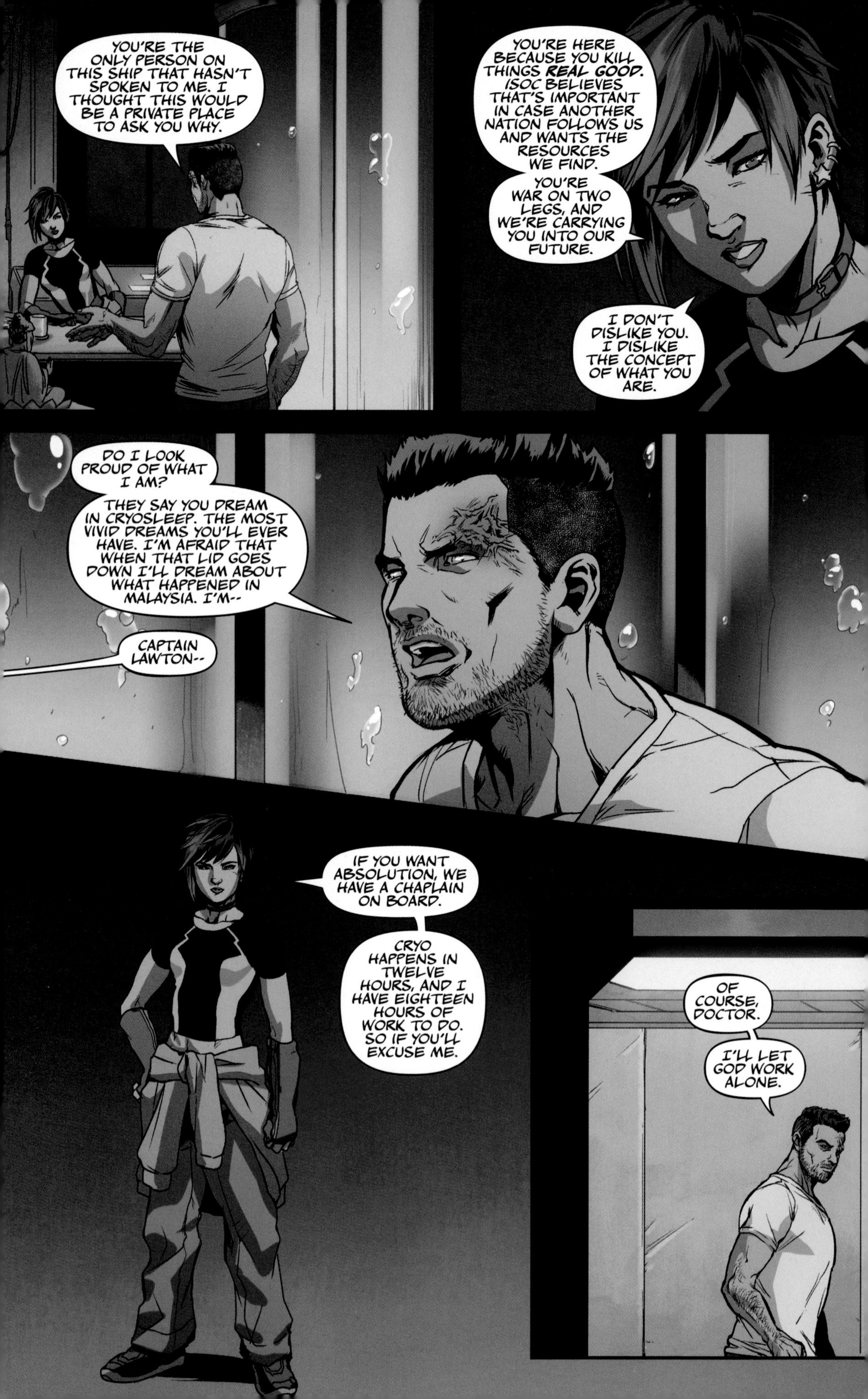
YOU'RE THE ONLY PERSON ON THIS SHIP THAT HASN'T SPOKEN TO ME. I THOUGHT THIS WOULD BE A PRIVATE PLACE TO ASK YOU WHY.
YOU'RE HERE BECAUSE YOU KILL THINGS REAL GOOD. ISOC BELIEVES THAT'S IMPORTANT IN CASE ANOTHER NATION FOLLOWS US AND WANTS THE RESOURCES WE FIND.
YOU'RE WAR ON TWO LEGS, AND WE'RE CARRYING YOU INTO OUR FUTURE.
I DON'T DISLIKE YOU. I DISLIKE THE CONCEPT OF WHAT YOU ARE.
DO I LOOK PROUD OF WHAT I AM?
THEY SAY YOU DREAM IN CRYOSLEEP. THE MOST VIVID DREAMS YOU'LL EVER HAVE. I'M AFRAID THAT WHEN THAT LID GOES DOWN I'LL DREAM ABOUT WHAT HAPPENED IN MALAYSIA. I'M--
CAPTAIN LAWTON--
IF YOU WANT ABSOLUTION, WE HAVE A CHAPLAIN ON BOARD.
CRYO HAPPENS IN TWELVE HOURS, AND I HAVE EIGHTEEN HOURS OF WORK TO DO. SO IF YOU'LL EXCUSE ME.
OF COURSE, DOCTOR.
I'LL LET GOD WORK ALONE.

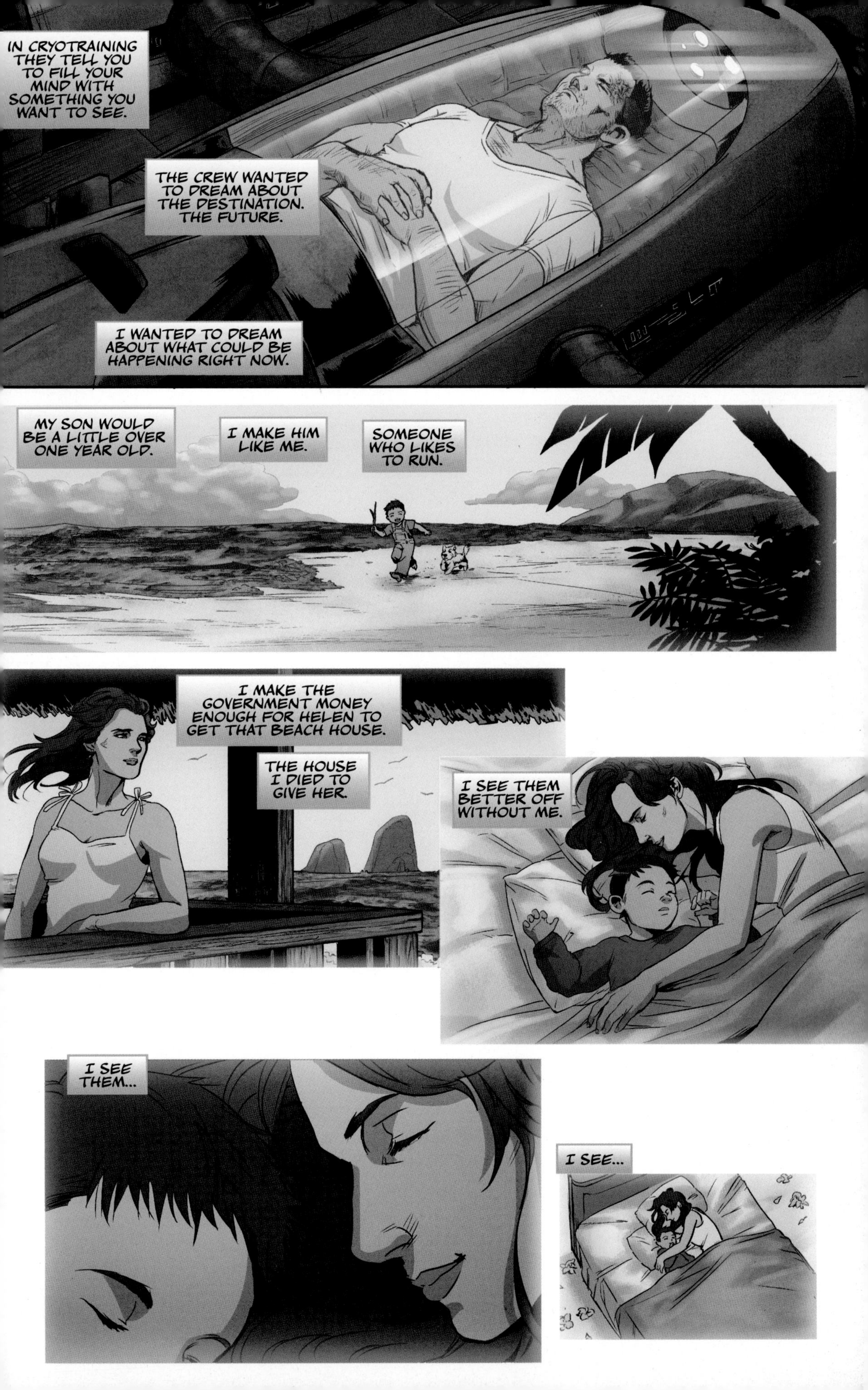
IN CRYOTRAINING THEY TELL YOU TO FILL YOUR MIND WITH SOMETHING YOU WANT TO SEE.
THE CREW WANTED TO DREAM ABOUT THE DESTINATION. THE FUTURE.
I WANTED TO DREAM ABOUT WHAT COULD BE HAPPENING RIGHT NOW.
MY SON WOULD BE A LITTLE OVER ONE YEAR OLD.
I MAKE HIM LIKE ME.
SOMEONE WHO LIKES TO RUN.
I MAKE THE GOVERNMENT MONEY ENOUGH FOR HELEN TO GET THAT BEACH HOUSE.
THE HOUSE I DIED TO GIVE HER.
I SEE THEM BETTER OFF WITHOUT ME.
I SEE THEM...
I SEE...

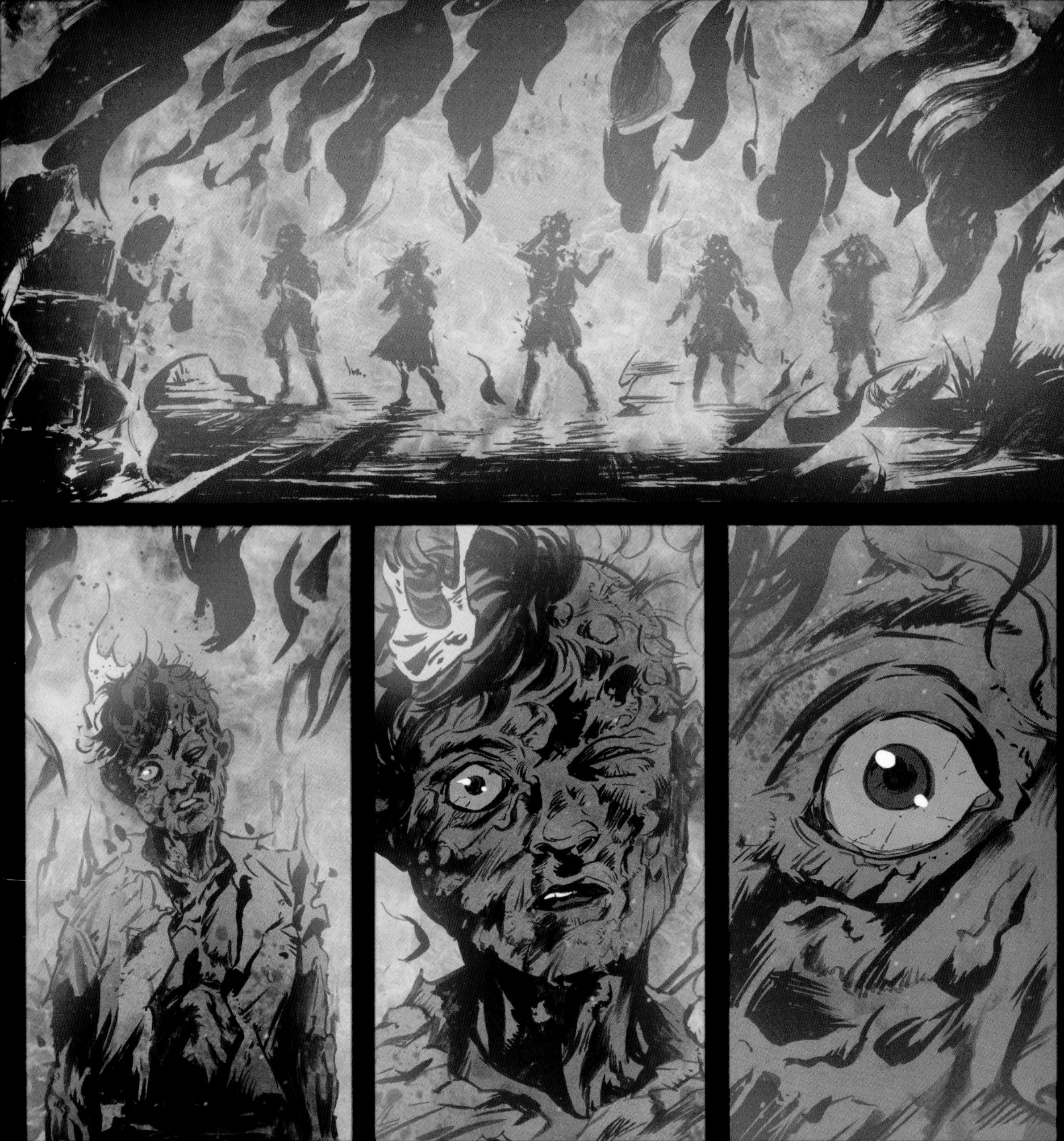

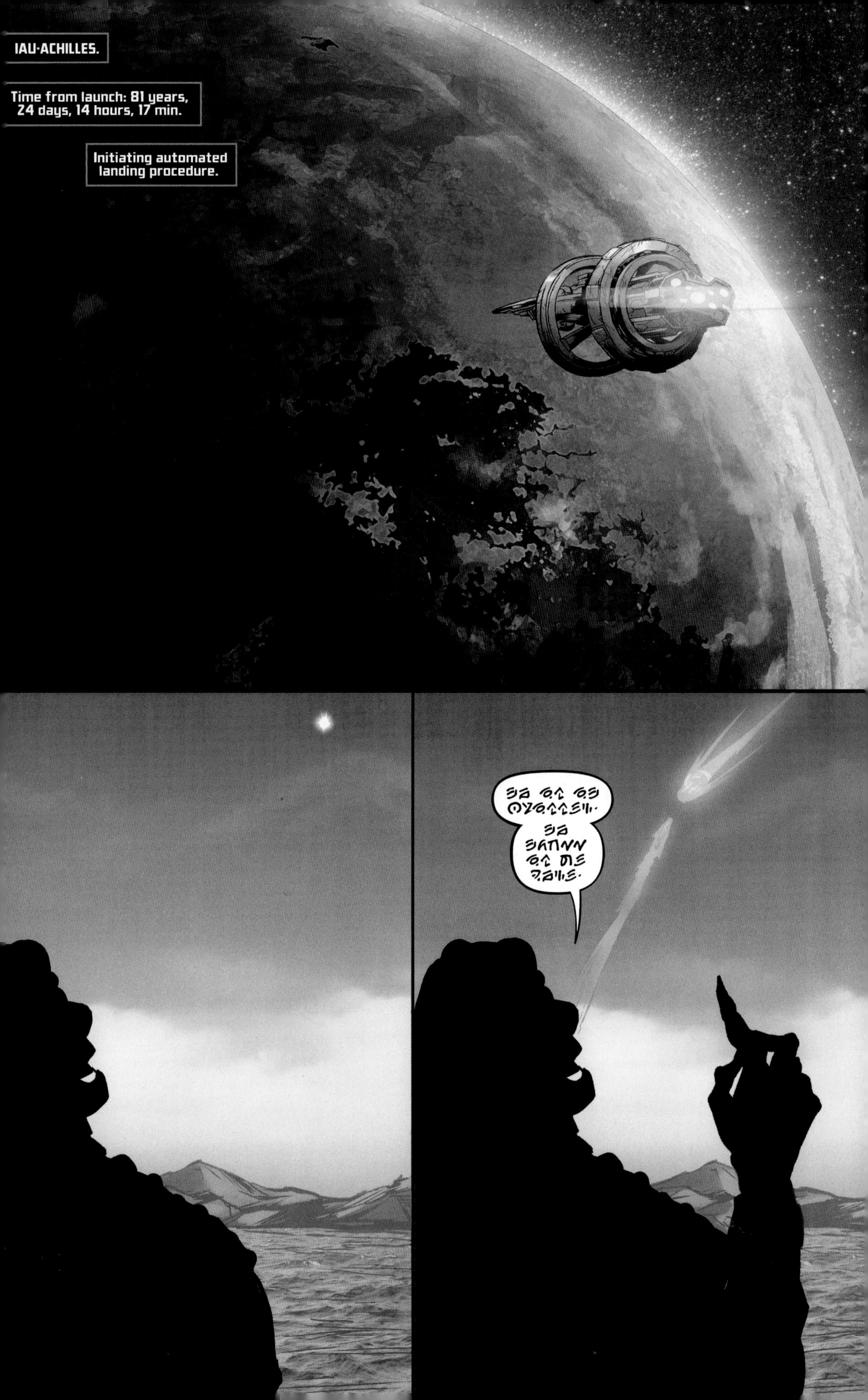
IAU-ACHILLES.
Time from launch: 81 years, 24 days, 14 hours, 17 min.
Initiating automated landing procedure.

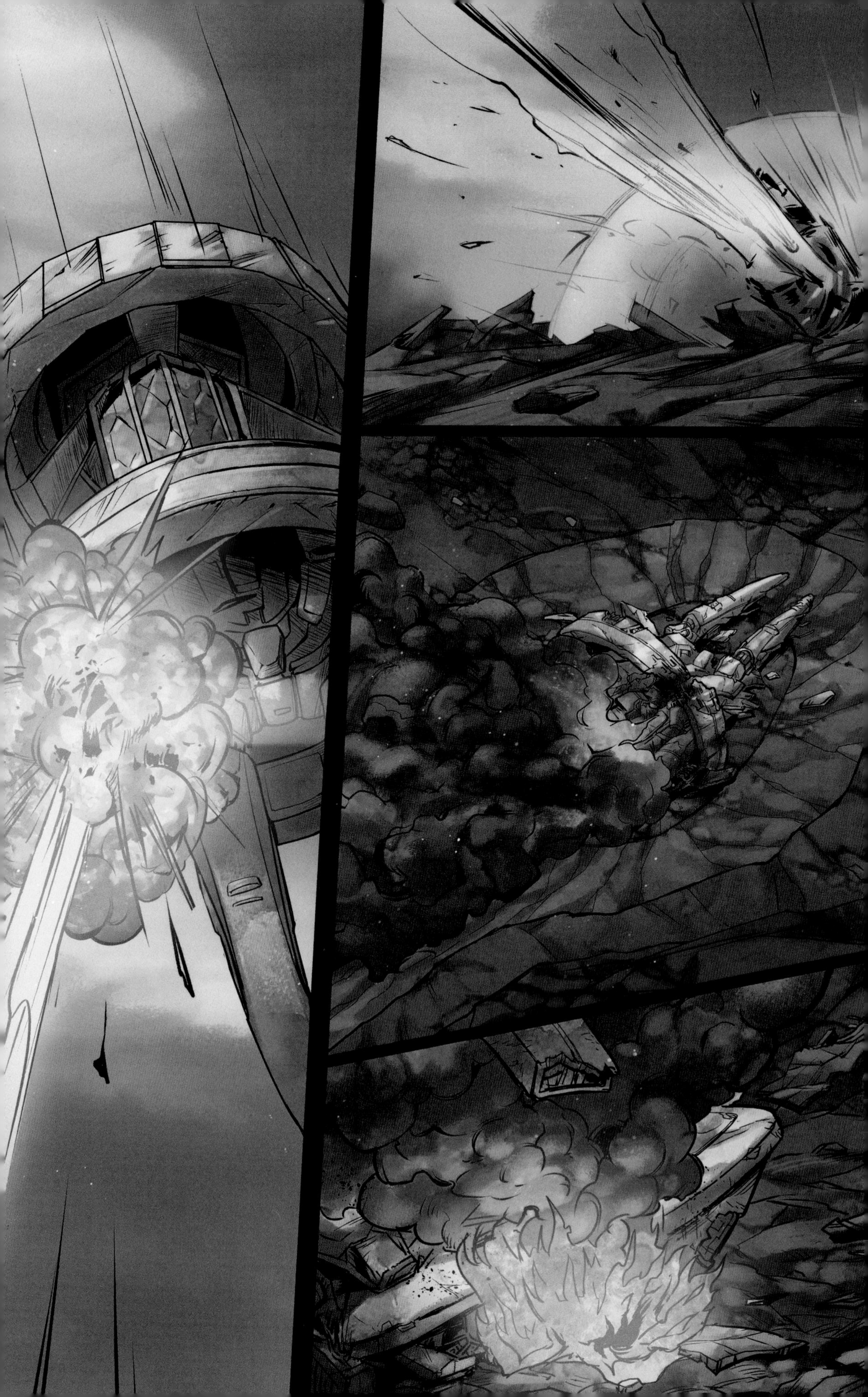

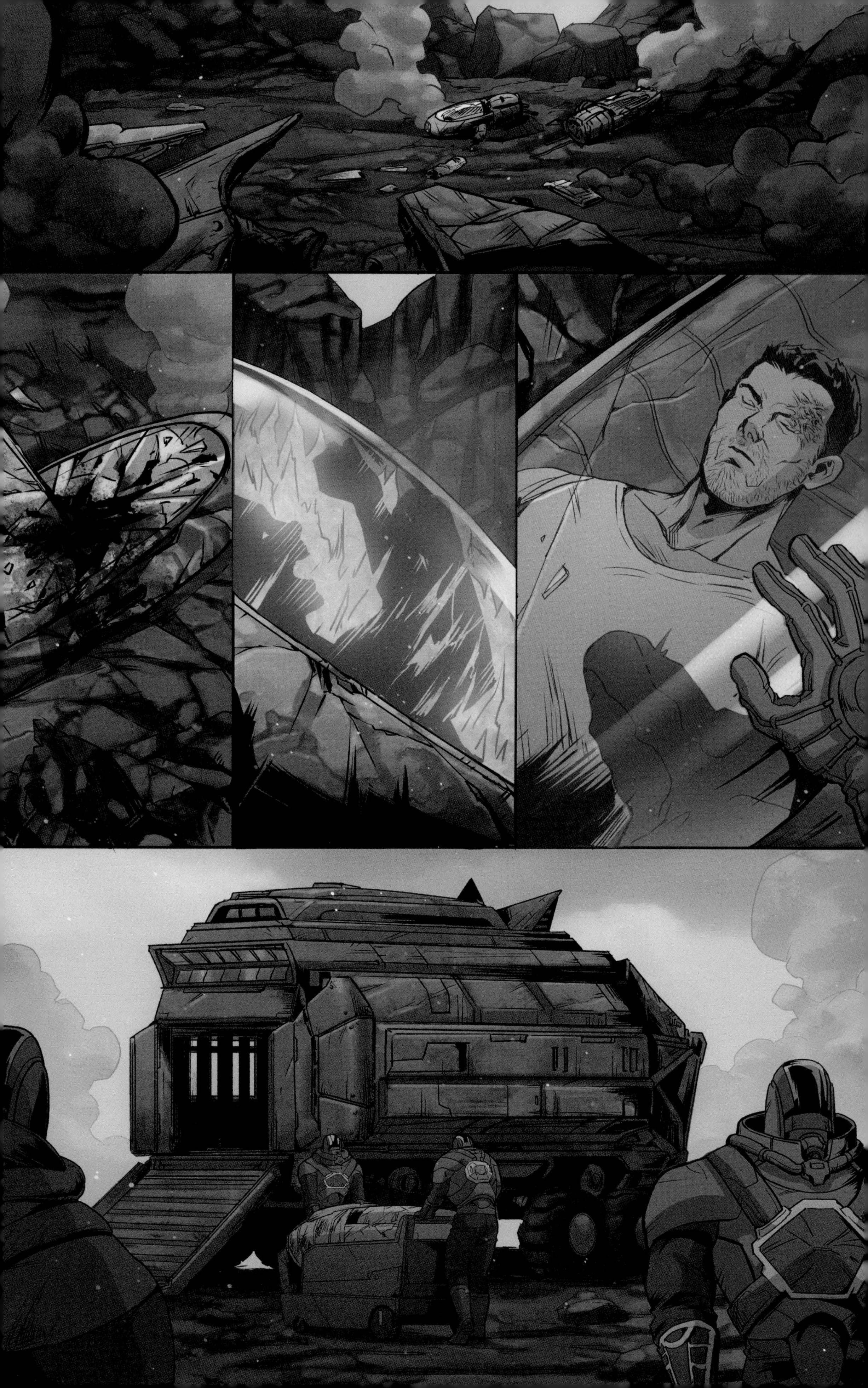

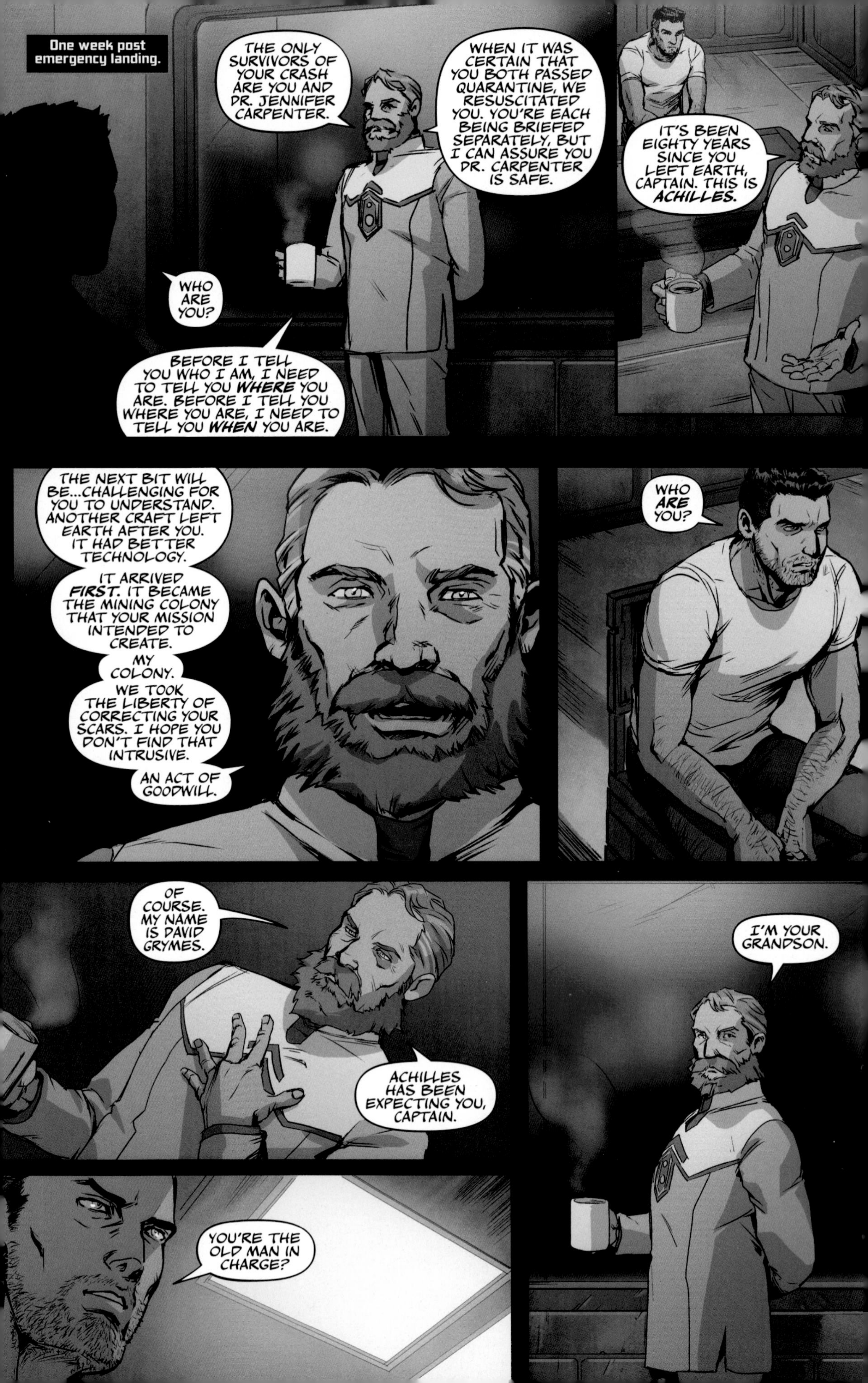
One week post emergency landing.
THE ONLY SURVIVORS OF YOUR CRASH ARE YOU AND DR. JENNIFER CARPENTER.
WHEN IT WAS CERTAIN THAT YOU BOTH PASSED QUARANTINE, WE RESUSCITATED YOU. YOU'RE EACH BEING BRIEFED SEPARATELY, BUT I CAN ASSURE YOU DR. CARPENTER IS SAFE.
WHO ARE YOU?
BEFORE I TELL YOU WHO I AM, I NEED TO TELL YOU WHERE YOU ARE. BEFORE I TELL YOU WHERE YOU ARE, I NEED TO TELL YOU WHEN YOU ARE.
IT'S BEEN EIGHTY YEARS SINCE YOU LEFT EARTH, CAPTAIN. THIS IS ACHILLES.
THE NEXT BIT WILL BE...CHALLENGING FOR YOU TO UNDERSTAND. ANOTHER CRAFT LEFT EARTH AFTER YOU. IT HAD BETTER TECHNOLOGY.
IT ARRIVED FIRST. IT BECAME THE MINING COLONY THAT YOUR MISSION INTENDED TO CREATE.
MY COLONY.
WE TOOK THE LIBERTY OF CORRECTING YOUR SCARS. I HOPE YOU DON'T FIND THAT INTRUSIVE.
AN ACT OF GOODWILL.
WHO ARE YOU?
OF COURSE. MY NAME IS DAVID GRYMES.
ACHILLES HAS BEEN EXPECTING YOU, CAPTAIN.
YOU'RE THE OLD MAN IN CHARGE?
I'M YOUR GRANDSON.

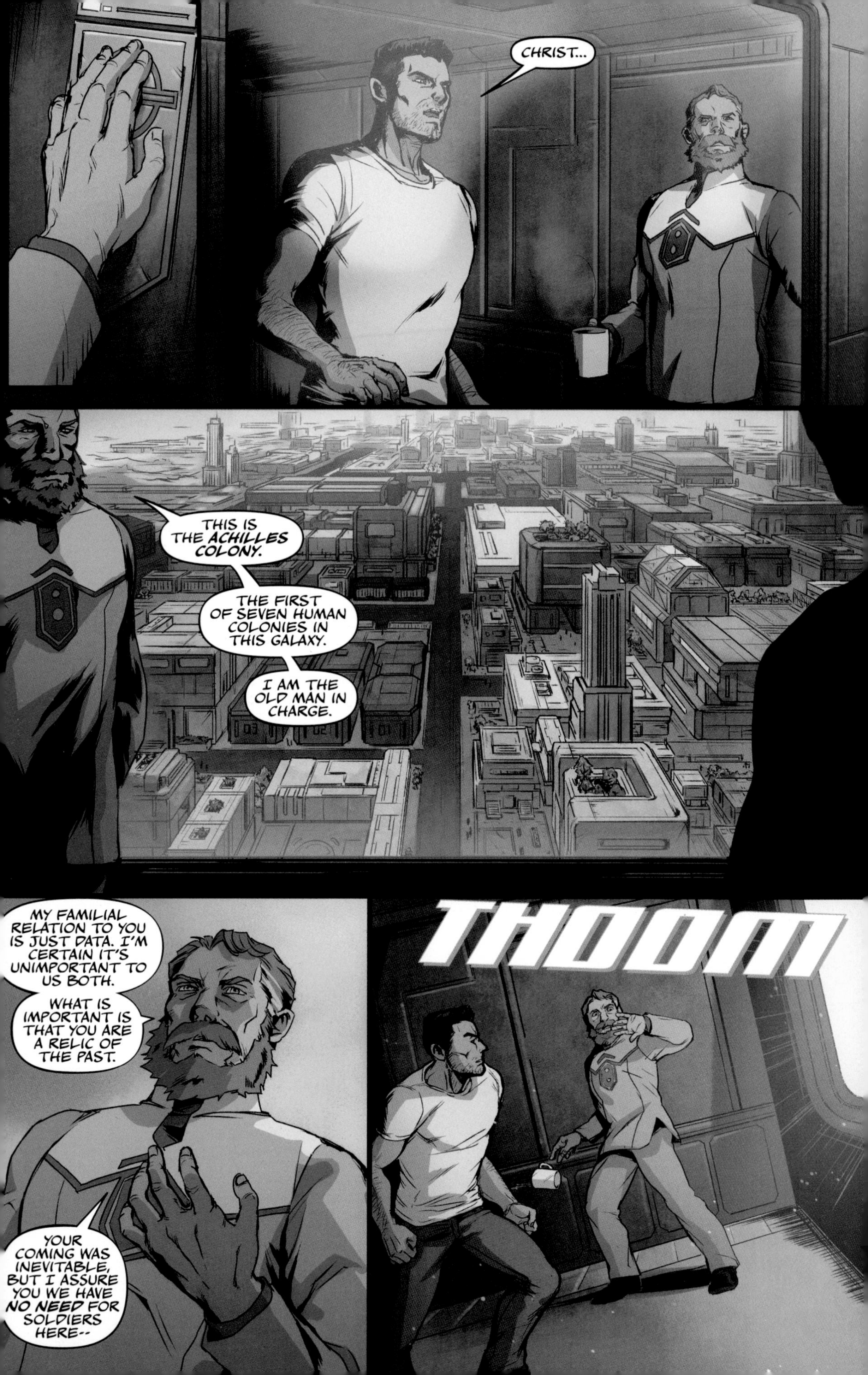
CHRIST...
THIS IS THE ACHILLES COLONY.
THE FIRST OF SEVEN HUMAN COLONIES IN THIS GALAXY.
I AM THE OLD MAN IN CHARGE.
MY FAMILIAL RELATION TO YOU IS JUST DATA. I'M CERTAIN IT'S UNIMPORTANT TO US BOTH.
WHAT IS IMPORTANT IS THAT YOU ARE A RELIC OF THE PAST.
YOUR COMING WAS INEVITABLE, BUT I ASSURE YOU WE HAVE NO NEED FOR SOLDIERS HERE--
THOOM

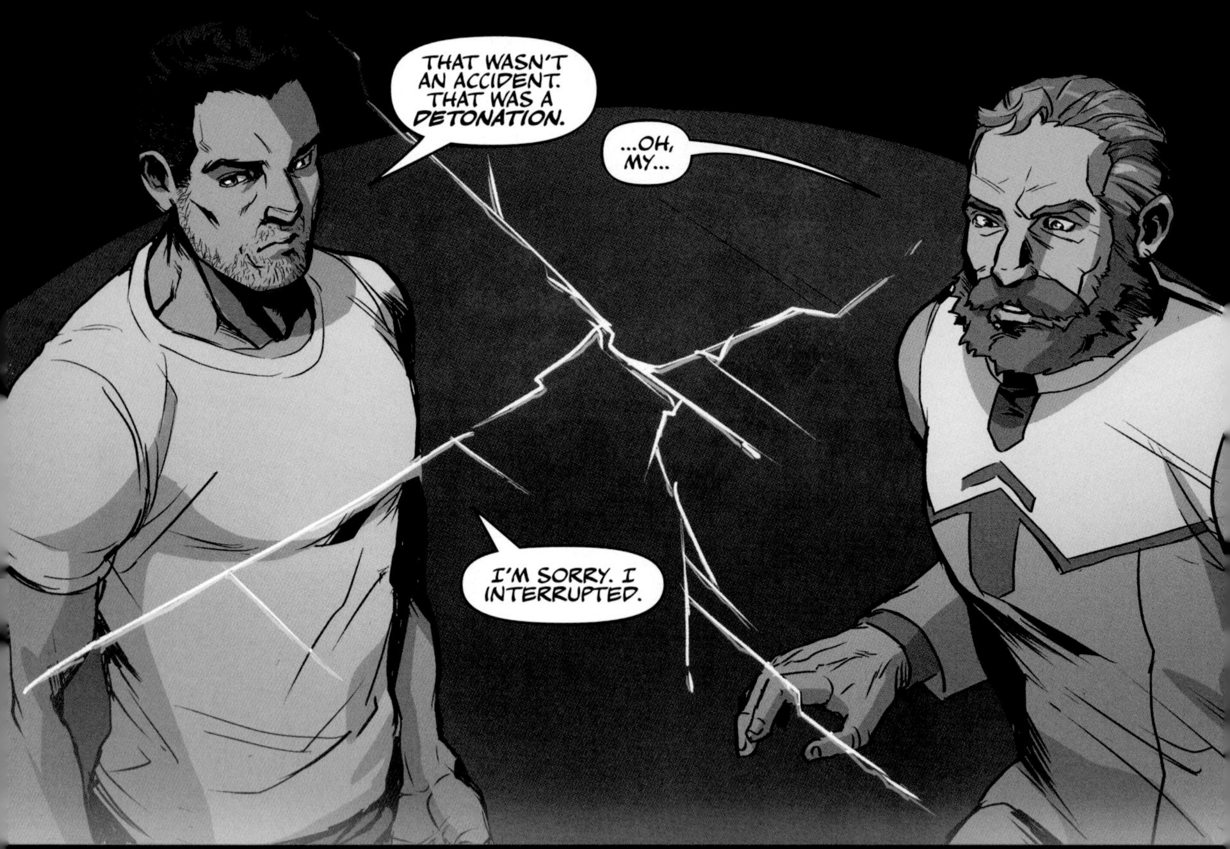
THAT WASN'T AN ACCIDENT. THAT WAS A DETONATION.
...OH, MY...
I'M SORRY. I INTERRUPTED.

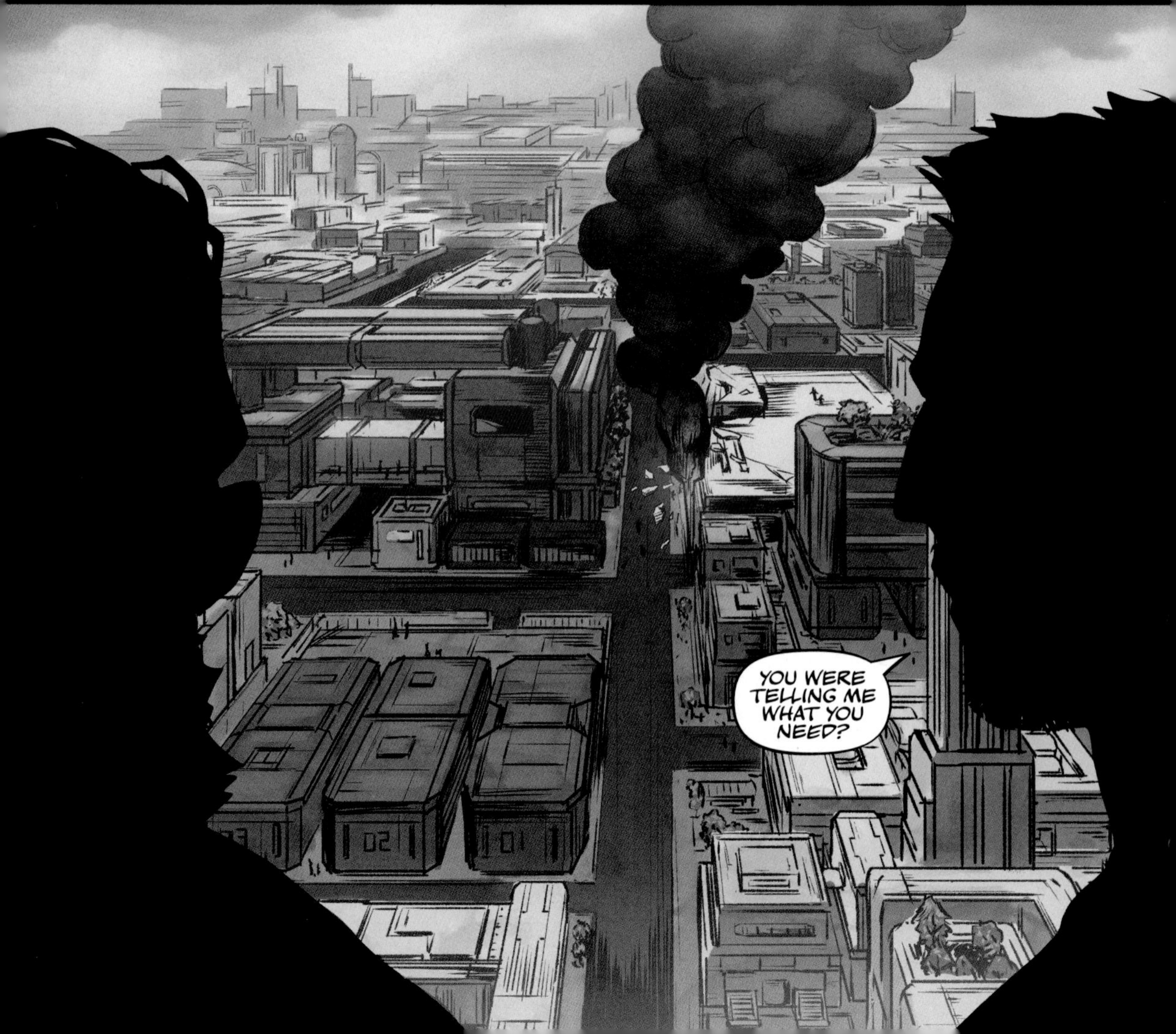
YOU WERE TELLING ME WHAT YOU NEED?

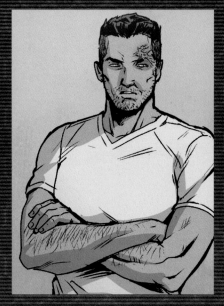

TRANSCRIPT from committee 45.
SUBJECT: Lawton, Michael.

Excerpt:

COMMITTEE: So in your estimation the use of strategic force in incident REDACTED was justified.

LAWTON: Yes. Yes, I believe it was.

COMMITTEE: And what was the deciding factor in you authorizing the ordinance?

LAWTON: I don't follow. Deciding factor?

COMMITTEE: You made a mid-combat decision to escalate the use of force. We would like to know what affected your choice?

LAWTON: Why?

(Silence)

COMMITTEE: Let us remind you that you are giving a sworn testimony to the ISOC committee.

LAWTON: I'm aware of what I'm doing.

COMMITTEE: Let me also remind you that you do not have the authority to ask questions of the committee.

(Silence)

LAWTON: All right. But I still don't understand your question.

COMMITTEE: Let me be more clear, then. Why did you incinerate those children during your operation?

(Silence)

LAWTON: I was not aware of children being on site.

COMMITTEE: Then you're saying your team didn't complete proper information gathering before action?

LAWTON: No. I'm saying the enemy was hiding behind children, children that my team had no knowledge of before action.

(Lawton clears his throat)

LAWTON: That's what bad guys do. You'd know that if you ever faced any.

COMMITTEE: And we depend on operatives like you to have that knowledge so tragedies like this are prevented. But this one wasn't and now we have a public relations crisis.

LAWTON: And you're trying to solve your crisis by painting me as a sociopath.

COMMITTEE: Captain Lawton, you are in no place to assume the intentions of this committee.

LAWTON: I lost my entire team that day. I would have died with them if I hadn't acted when I did. It wasn't an operation I wanted to perform, but I did perform it per my orders. What you people do has nothing to do with protecting the free world --

COMMITTEE: Captain Lawton, that's enough --

LAWTON: It's about controlling resources and serving global corporations and their profits --

COMMITTEE: Captain Lawton, you will respect the protocol of --

LAWTON: I gave the order because I was going to die. I was going to die because you wanted to make money. You made money --

Lawton, Michael

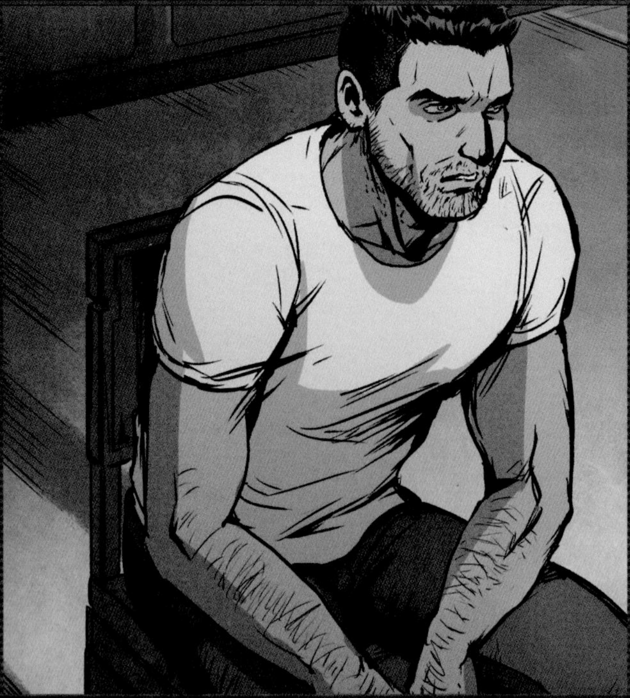

COMMITTEE: Captain Lawton, I am holding you in contempt of --

LAWTON: You made money and you don't care about anyone who died in that process. You care about how bloody that money looks.

COMMITTEE: Protocol, inform Captain Lawton --

LAWTON: I'm not proud of what I did. I'm not even proud of what I am. But I'm proud of what I'm about to do.

(Inaudible)

(Inaudible)

(Inaudible)

COMMITTEE: Did he just leave? Where is he headed?

(Inaudible)

COMMITTEE: Don't let him leave the compound.

(Silence)

COMMITTEE: Christ.

CHAPTER 2

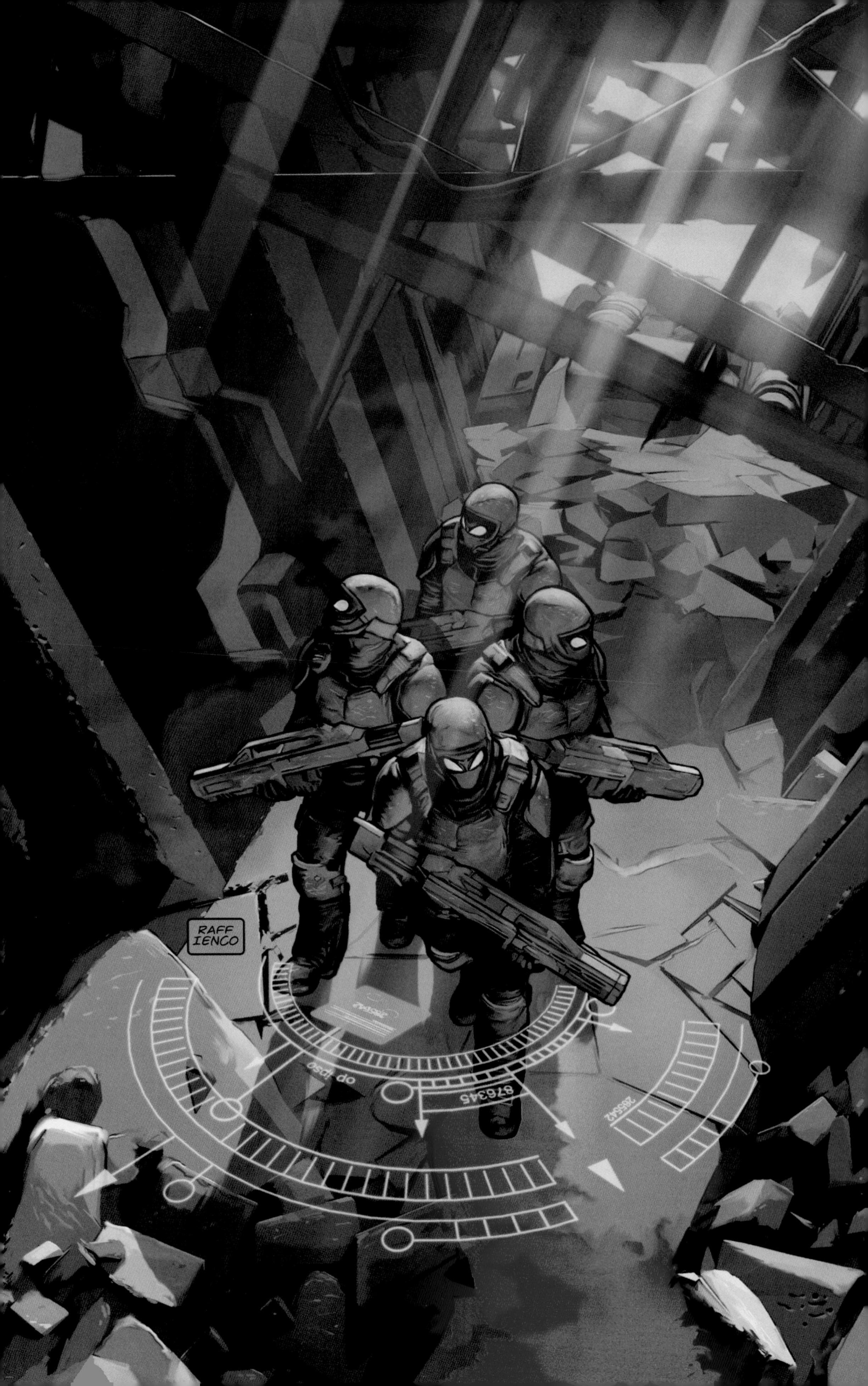
RAFF
IENCO

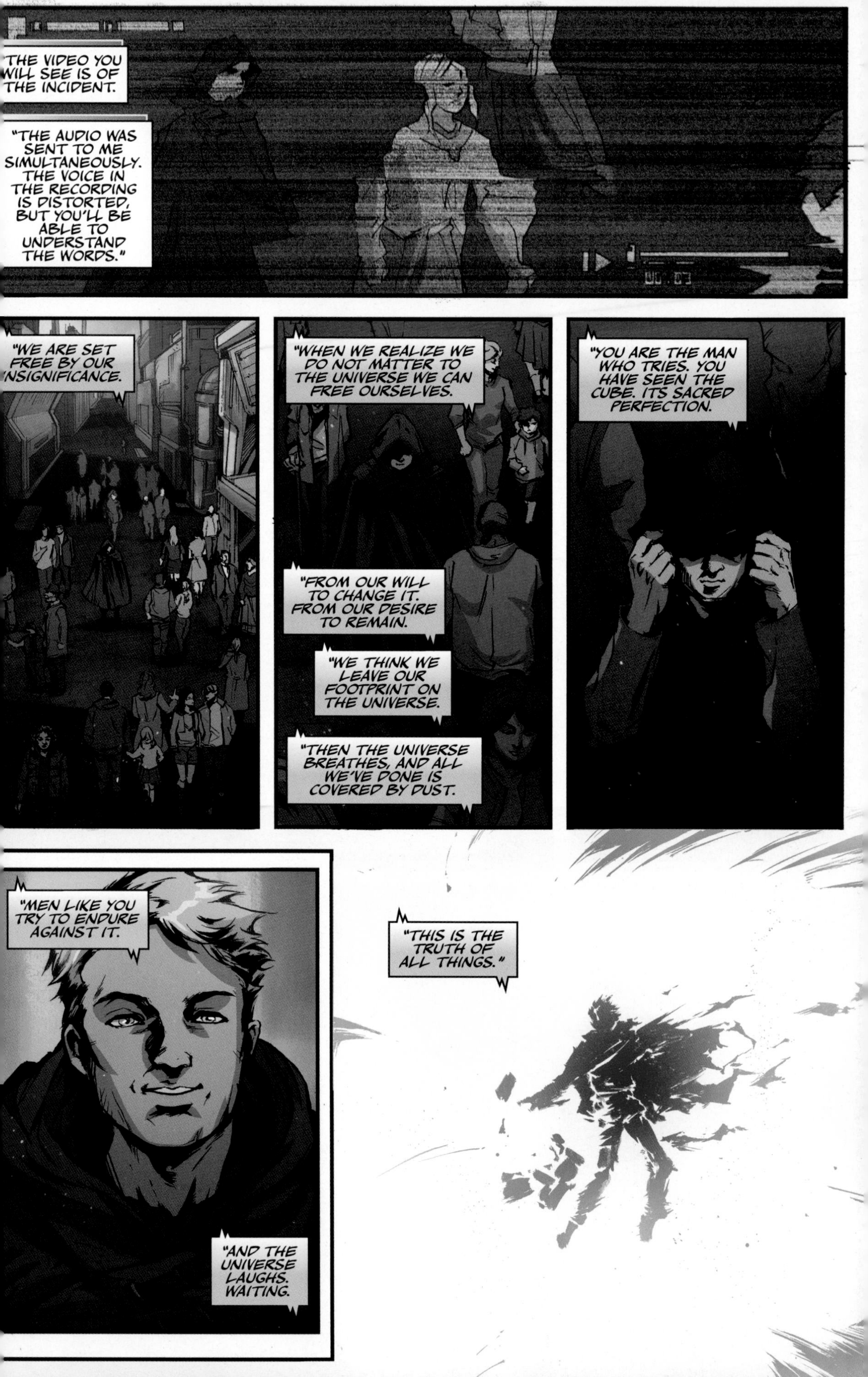
THE VIDEO YOU WILL SEE IS OF THE INCIDENT.
"THE AUDIO WAS SENT TO ME SIMULTANEOUSLY. THE VOICE IN THE RECORDING IS DISTORTED, BUT YOU'LL BE ABLE TO UNDERSTAND THE WORDS."
"WE ARE SET FREE BY OUR INSIGNIFICANCE.
"WHEN WE REALIZE WE DO NOT MATTER TO THE UNIVERSE WE CAN FREE OURSELVES.
"FROM OUR WILL TO CHANGE IT. FROM OUR DESIRE TO REMAIN.
"WE THINK WE LEAVE OUR FOOTPRINT ON THE UNIVERSE.
"THEN THE UNIVERSE BREATHES, AND ALL WE'VE DONE IS COVERED BY DUST.
"YOU ARE THE MAN WHO TRIES. YOU HAVE SEEN THE CUBE. ITS SACRED PERFECTION.
"MEN LIKE YOU TRY TO ENDURE AGAINST IT.
"AND THE UNIVERSE LAUGHS. WAITING.
"THIS IS THE TRUTH OF ALL THINGS."

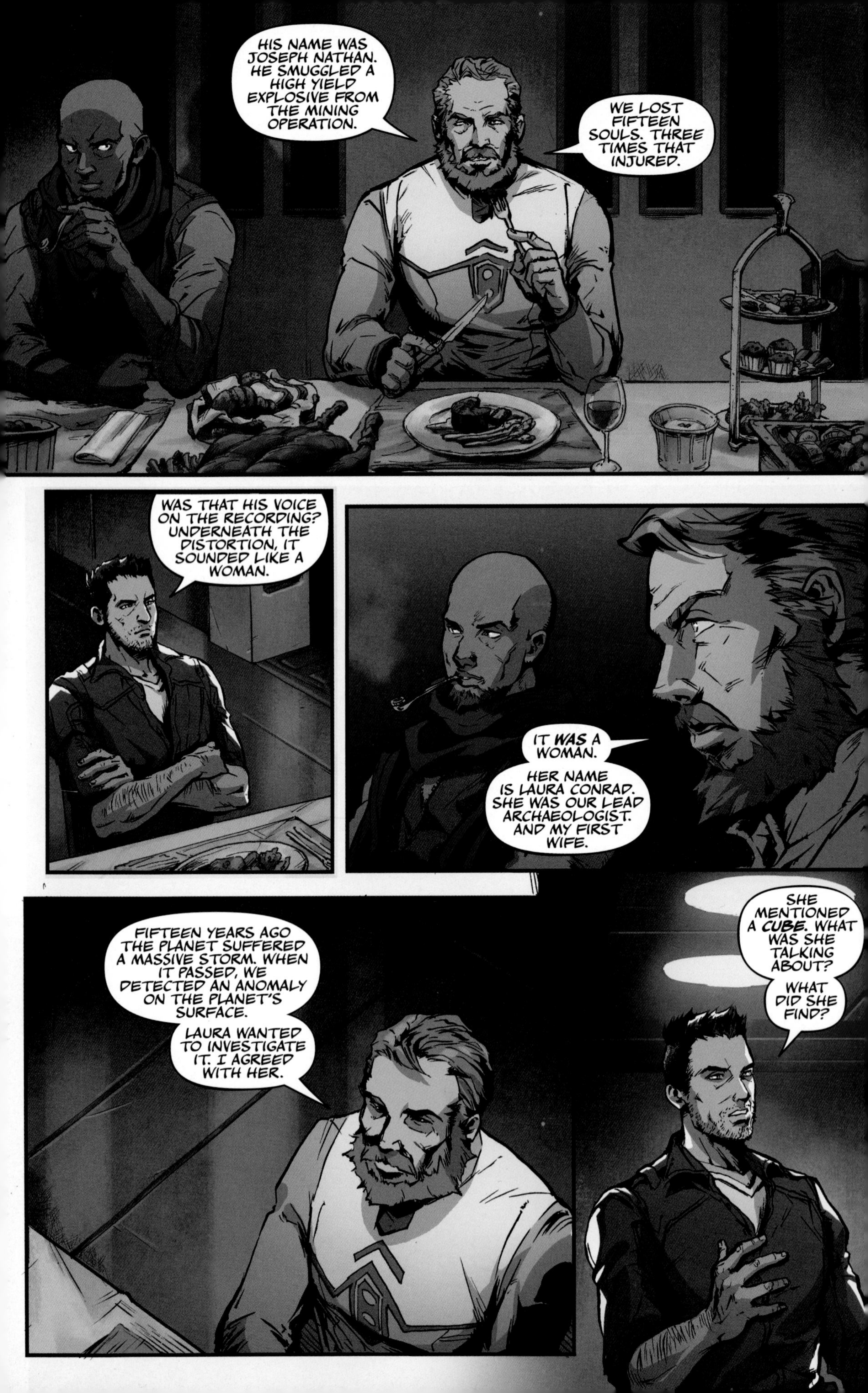
HIS NAME WAS JOSEPH NATHAN. HE SMUGGLED A HIGH YIELD EXPLOSIVE FROM THE MINING OPERATION.
WE LOST FIFTEEN SOULS. THREE TIMES THAT INJURED.
WAS THAT HIS VOICE ON THE RECORDING? UNDERNEATH THE DISTORTION, IT SOUNDED LIKE A WOMAN.
IT *WAS* A WOMAN.
HER NAME IS LAURA CONRAD. SHE WAS OUR LEAD ARCHAEOLOGIST. AND MY FIRST WIFE.
FIFTEEN YEARS AGO THE PLANET SUFFERED A MASSIVE STORM. WHEN IT PASSED, WE DETECTED AN ANOMALY ON THE PLANET'S SURFACE.
LAURA WANTED TO INVESTIGATE IT. I AGREED WITH HER.
SHE MENTIONED A *CUBE*. WHAT WAS SHE TALKING ABOUT?
WHAT DID SHE FIND?

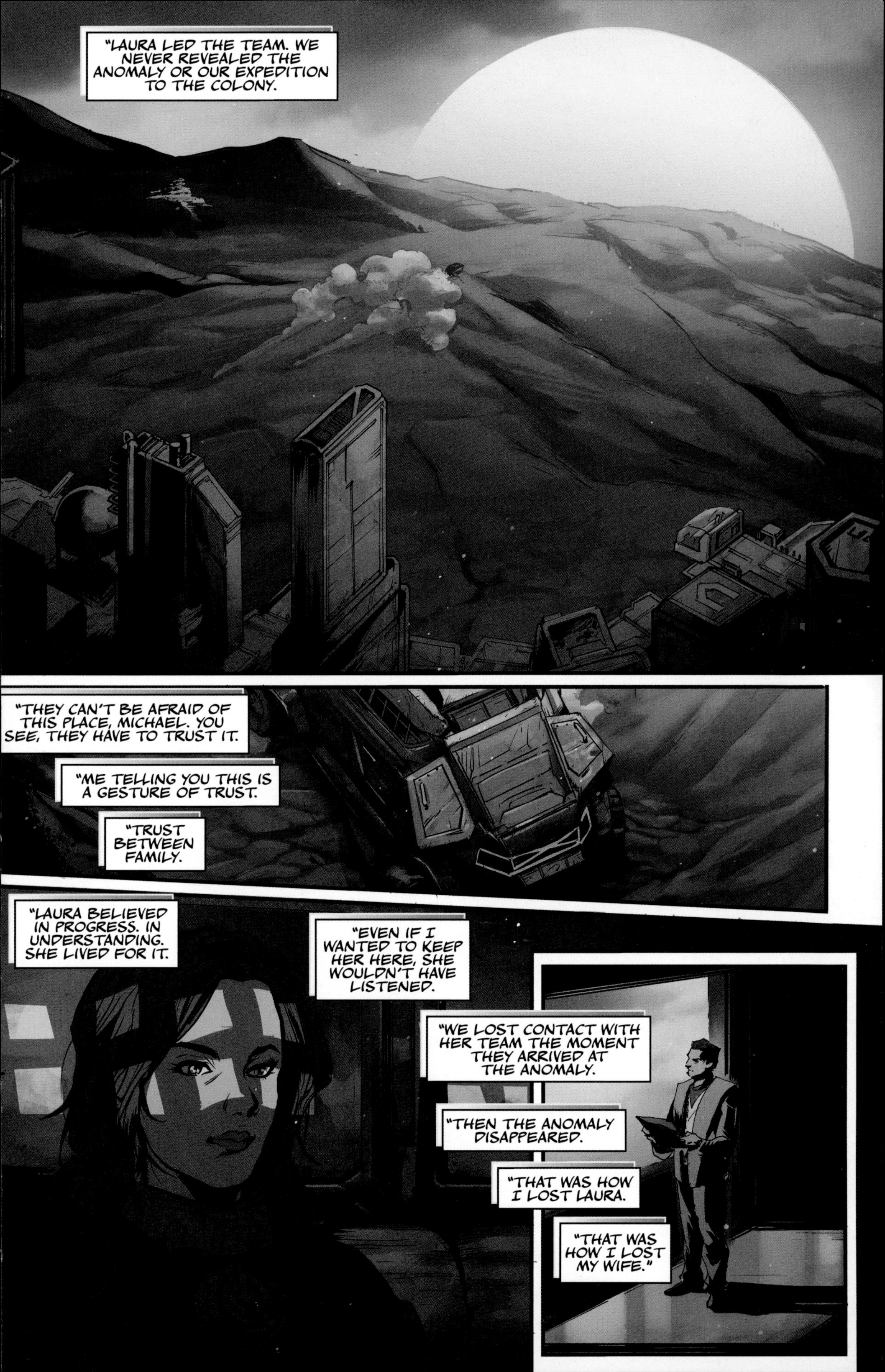
"LAURA LED THE TEAM. WE NEVER REVEALED THE ANOMALY OR OUR EXPEDITION TO THE COLONY.
"THEY CAN'T BE AFRAID OF THIS PLACE, MICHAEL. YOU SEE, THEY HAVE TO TRUST IT.
"ME TELLING YOU THIS IS A GESTURE OF TRUST.
"TRUST BETWEEN FAMILY.
"LAURA BELIEVED IN PROGRESS. IN UNDERSTANDING. SHE LIVED FOR IT.
"EVEN IF I WANTED TO KEEP HER HERE, SHE WOULDN'T HAVE LISTENED.
"WE LOST CONTACT WITH HER TEAM THE MOMENT THEY ARRIVED AT THE ANOMALY.
"THEN THE ANOMALY DISAPPEARED.
"THAT WAS HOW I LOST LAURA.
"THAT WAS HOW I LOST MY WIFE."

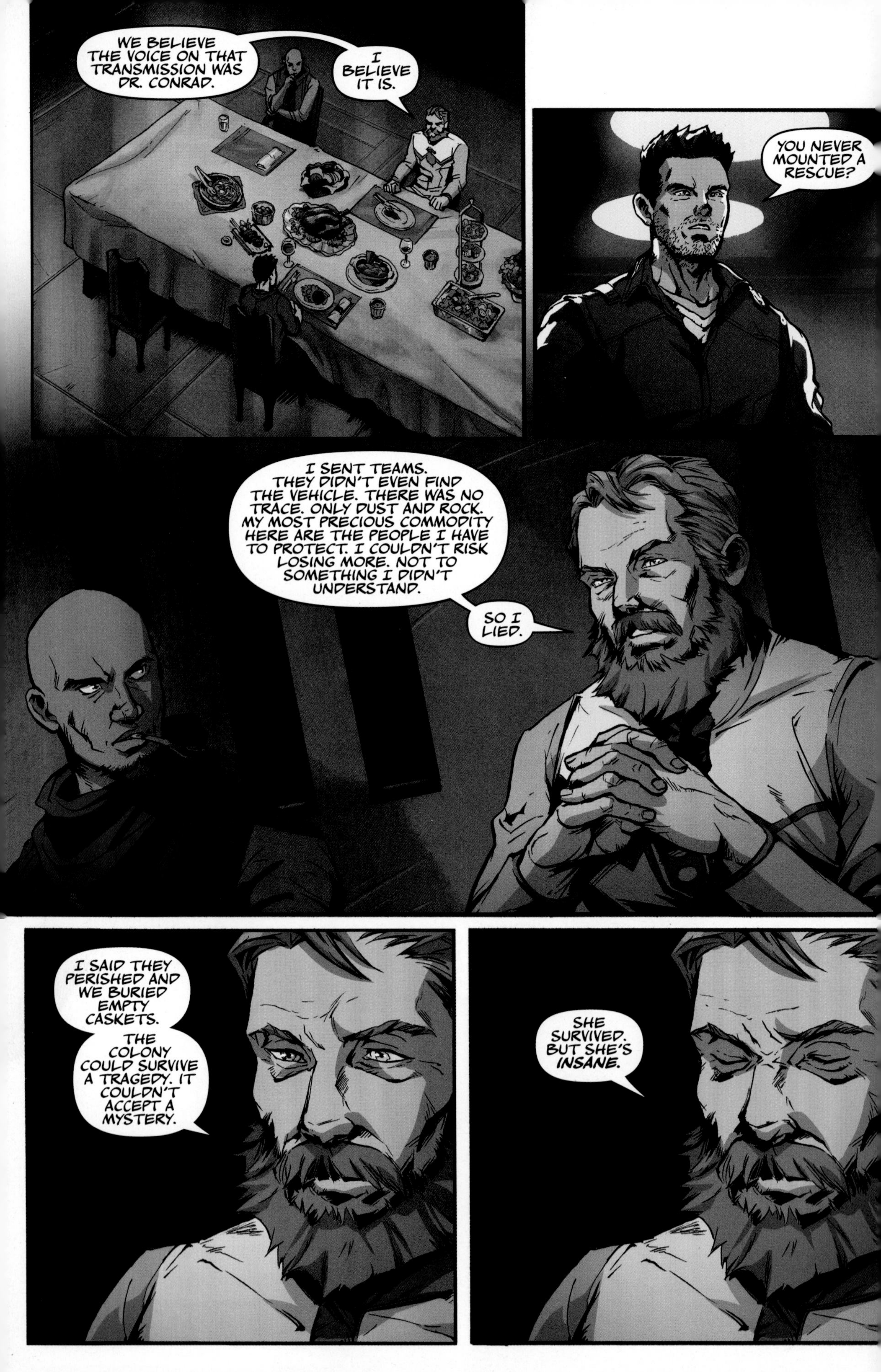
WE BELIEVE THE VOICE ON THAT TRANSMISSION WAS DR. CONRAD.
I BELIEVE IT IS.
YOU NEVER MOUNTED A RESCUE?
I SENT TEAMS. THEY DIDN'T EVEN FIND THE VEHICLE. THERE WAS NO TRACE. ONLY DUST AND ROCK. MY MOST PRECIOUS COMMODITY HERE ARE THE PEOPLE I HAVE TO PROTECT. I COULDN'T RISK LOSING MORE. NOT TO SOMETHING I DIDN'T UNDERSTAND.
SO I LIED.
I SAID THEY PERISHED AND WE BURIED EMPTY CASKETS.
THE COLONY COULD SURVIVE A TRAGEDY. IT COULDN'T ACCEPT A MYSTERY.
SHE SURVIVED. BUT SHE'S *INSANE*.

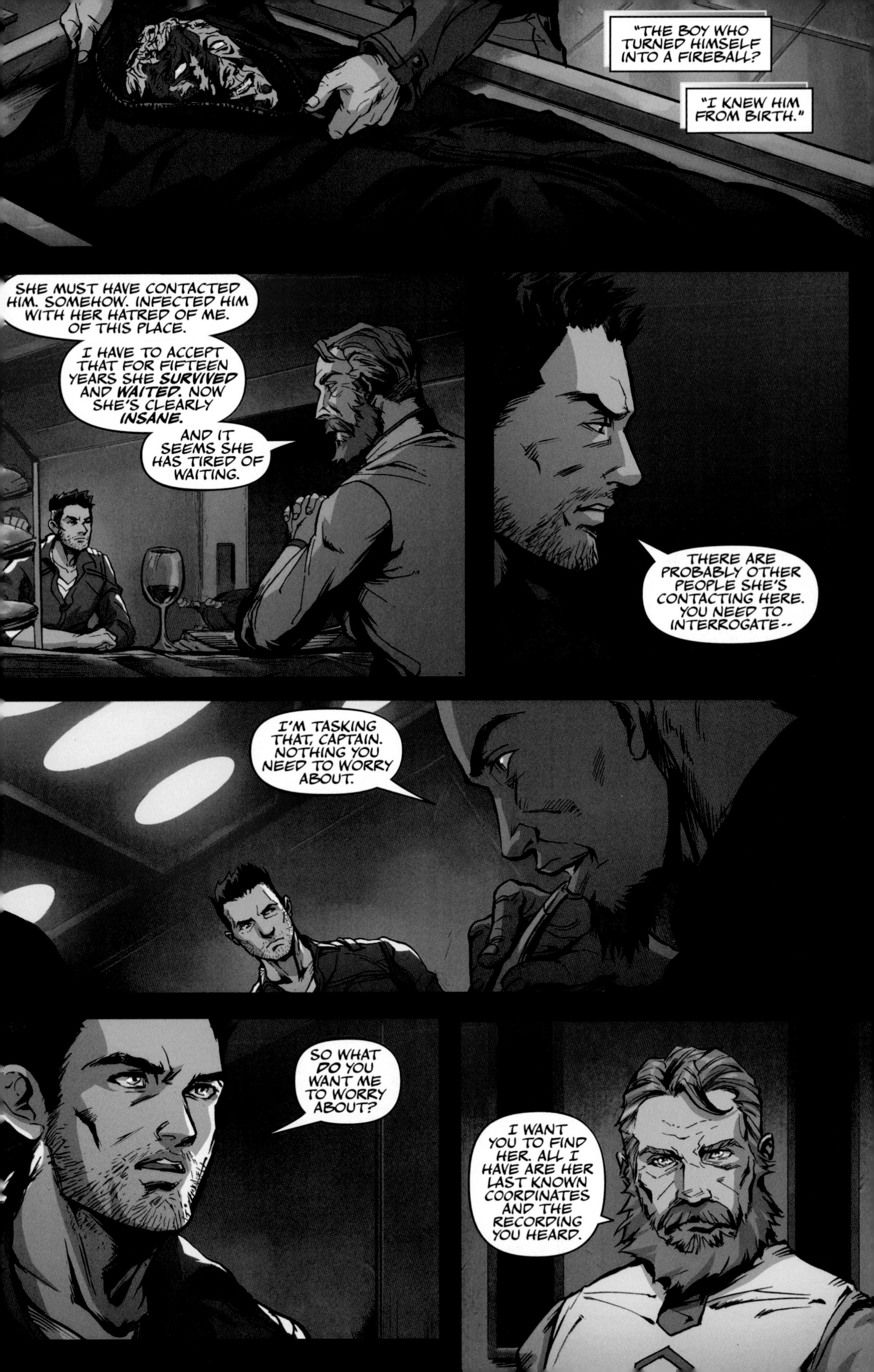
"THE BOY WHO TURNED HIMSELF INTO A FIREBALL?
"I KNEW HIM FROM BIRTH."
SHE MUST HAVE CONTACTED HIM. SOMEHOW. INFECTED HIM WITH HER HATRED OF ME. OF THIS PLACE.
I HAVE TO ACCEPT THAT FOR FIFTEEN YEARS SHE SURVIVED AND WAITED. NOW SHE'S CLEARLY INSANE.
AND IT SEEMS SHE HAS TIRED OF WAITING.
THERE ARE PROBABLY OTHER PEOPLE SHE'S CONTACTING HERE. YOU NEED TO INTERROGATE--
I'M TASKING THAT, CAPTAIN. NOTHING YOU NEED TO WORRY ABOUT.
SO WHAT DO YOU WANT ME TO WORRY ABOUT?
I WANT YOU TO FIND HER. ALL I HAVE ARE HER LAST KNOWN COORDINATES AND THE RECORDING YOU HEARD.

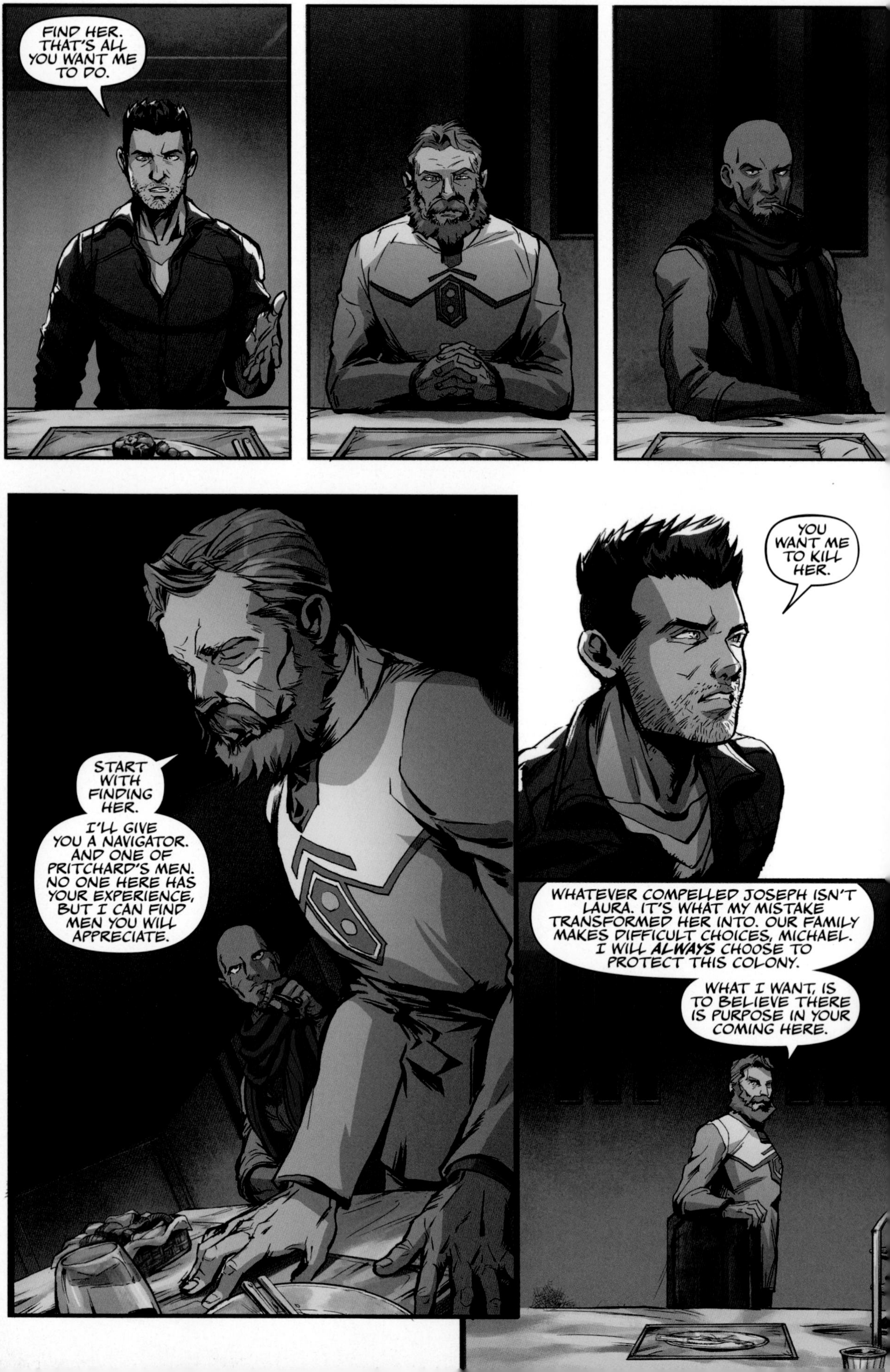
FIND HER. THAT'S ALL YOU WANT ME TO DO.
YOU WANT ME TO KILL HER.
START WITH FINDING HER.
I'LL GIVE YOU A NAVIGATOR. AND ONE OF PRITCHARD'S MEN. NO ONE HERE HAS YOUR EXPERIENCE, BUT I CAN FIND MEN YOU WILL APPRECIATE.
WHATEVER COMPELLED JOSEPH ISN'T LAURA. IT'S WHAT MY MISTAKE TRANSFORMED HER INTO. OUR FAMILY MAKES DIFFICULT CHOICES, MICHAEL. I WILL ALWAYS CHOOSE TO PROTECT THIS COLONY.
WHAT I WANT, IS TO BELIEVE THERE IS PURPOSE IN YOUR COMING HERE.

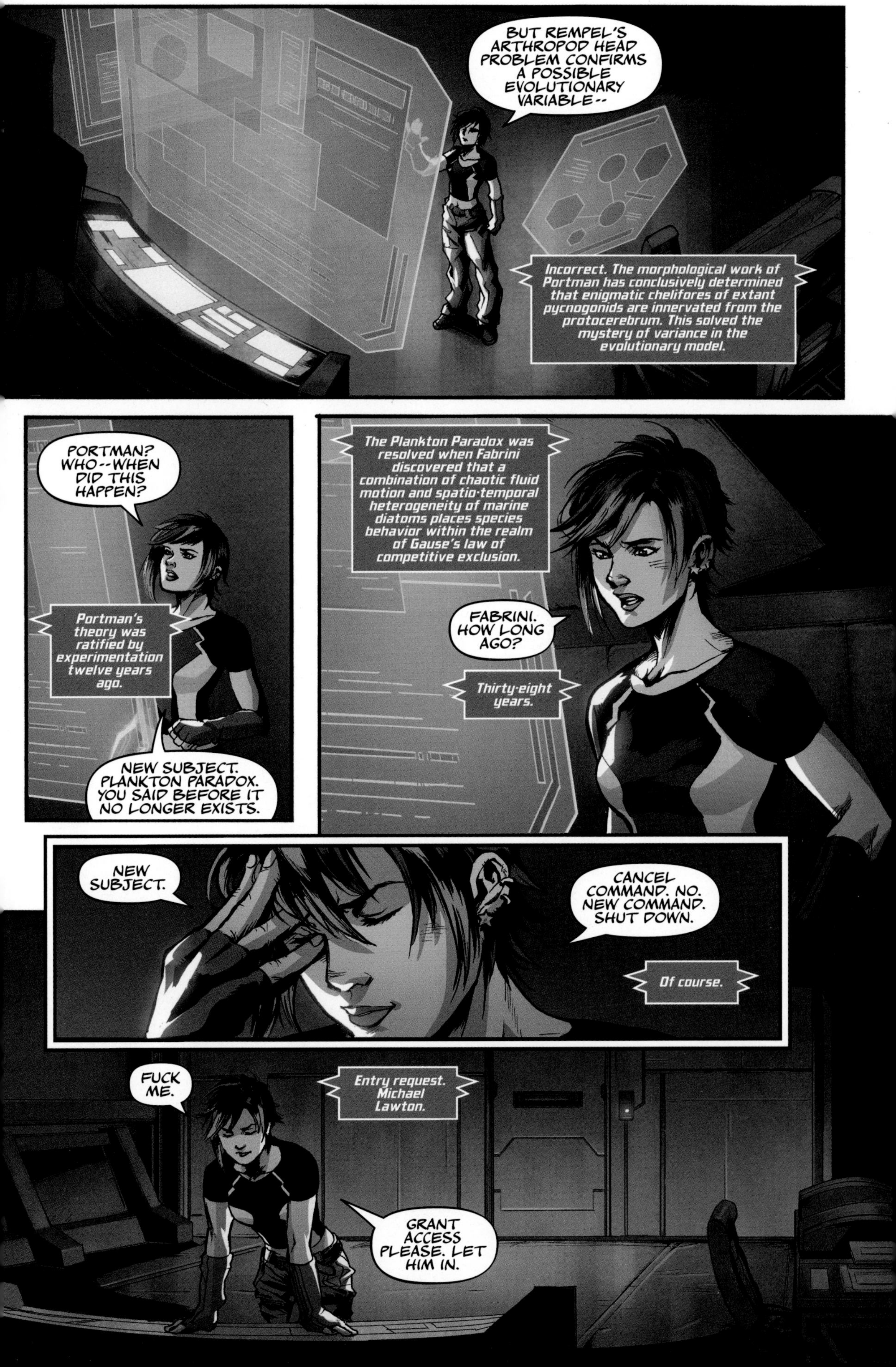
BUT REMPEL'S ARTHROPOD HEAD PROBLEM CONFIRMS A POSSIBLE EVOLUTIONARY VARIABLE--
Incorrect. The morphological work of Portman has conclusively determined that enigmatic chelifores of extant pycnogonids are innervated from the protocerebrum. This solved the mystery of variance in the evolutionary model.
PORTMAN? WHO--WHEN DID THIS HAPPEN?
Portman's theory was ratified by experimentation twelve years ago.
NEW SUBJECT. PLANKTON PARADOX. YOU SAID BEFORE IT NO LONGER EXISTS.
The Plankton Paradox was resolved when Fabrini discovered that a combination of chaotic fluid motion and spatio-temporal heterogeneity of marine diatoms places species behavior within the realm of Gause's law of competitive exclusion.
FABRINI. HOW LONG AGO?
Thirty-eight years.
NEW SUBJECT.
CANCEL COMMAND. NO. NEW COMMAND. SHUT DOWN.
Of course.
FUCK ME.
Entry request. Michael Lawton.
GRANT ACCESS PLEASE. LET HIM IN.

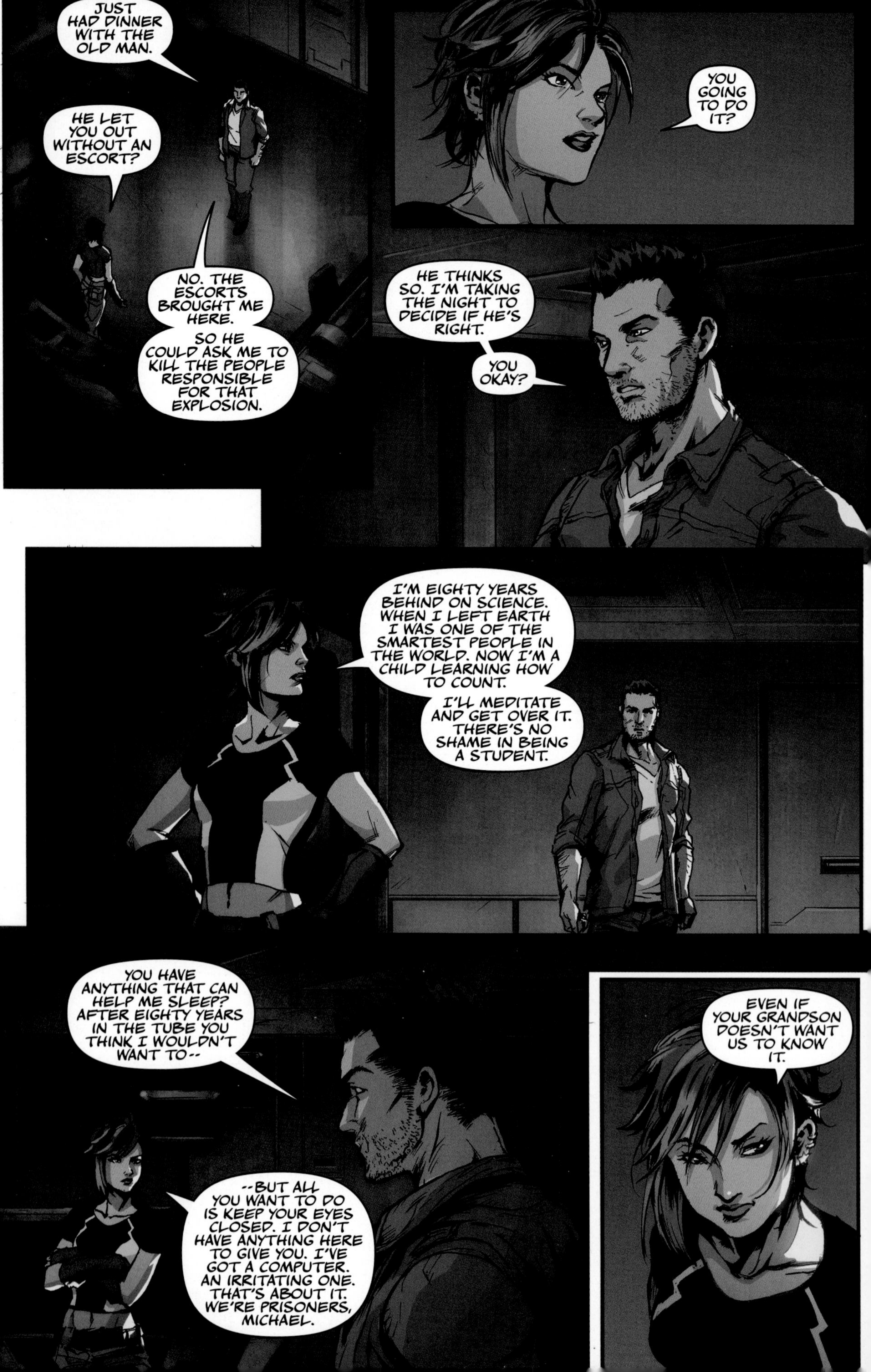

JUST HAD DINNER WITH THE OLD MAN.
HE LET YOU OUT WITHOUT AN ESCORT?
NO. THE ESCORTS BROUGHT ME HERE.
SO HE COULD ASK ME TO KILL THE PEOPLE RESPONSIBLE FOR THAT EXPLOSION.
YOU GOING TO DO IT?
HE THINKS SO. I'M TAKING THE NIGHT TO DECIDE IF HE'S RIGHT.
YOU OKAY?
I'M EIGHTY YEARS BEHIND ON SCIENCE. WHEN I LEFT EARTH I WAS ONE OF THE SMARTEST PEOPLE IN THE WORLD. NOW I'M A CHILD LEARNING HOW TO COUNT.
I'LL MEDITATE AND GET OVER IT. THERE'S NO SHAME IN BEING A STUDENT.
YOU HAVE ANYTHING THAT CAN HELP ME SLEEP? AFTER EIGHTY YEARS IN THE TUBE YOU THINK I WOULDN'T WANT TO--
--BUT ALL YOU WANT TO DO IS KEEP YOUR EYES CLOSED. I DON'T HAVE ANYTHING HERE TO GIVE YOU. I'VE GOT A COMPUTER. AN IRRITATING ONE. THAT'S ABOUT IT. WE'RE PRISONERS, MICHAEL.
EVEN IF YOUR GRANDSON DOESN'T WANT US TO KNOW IT.

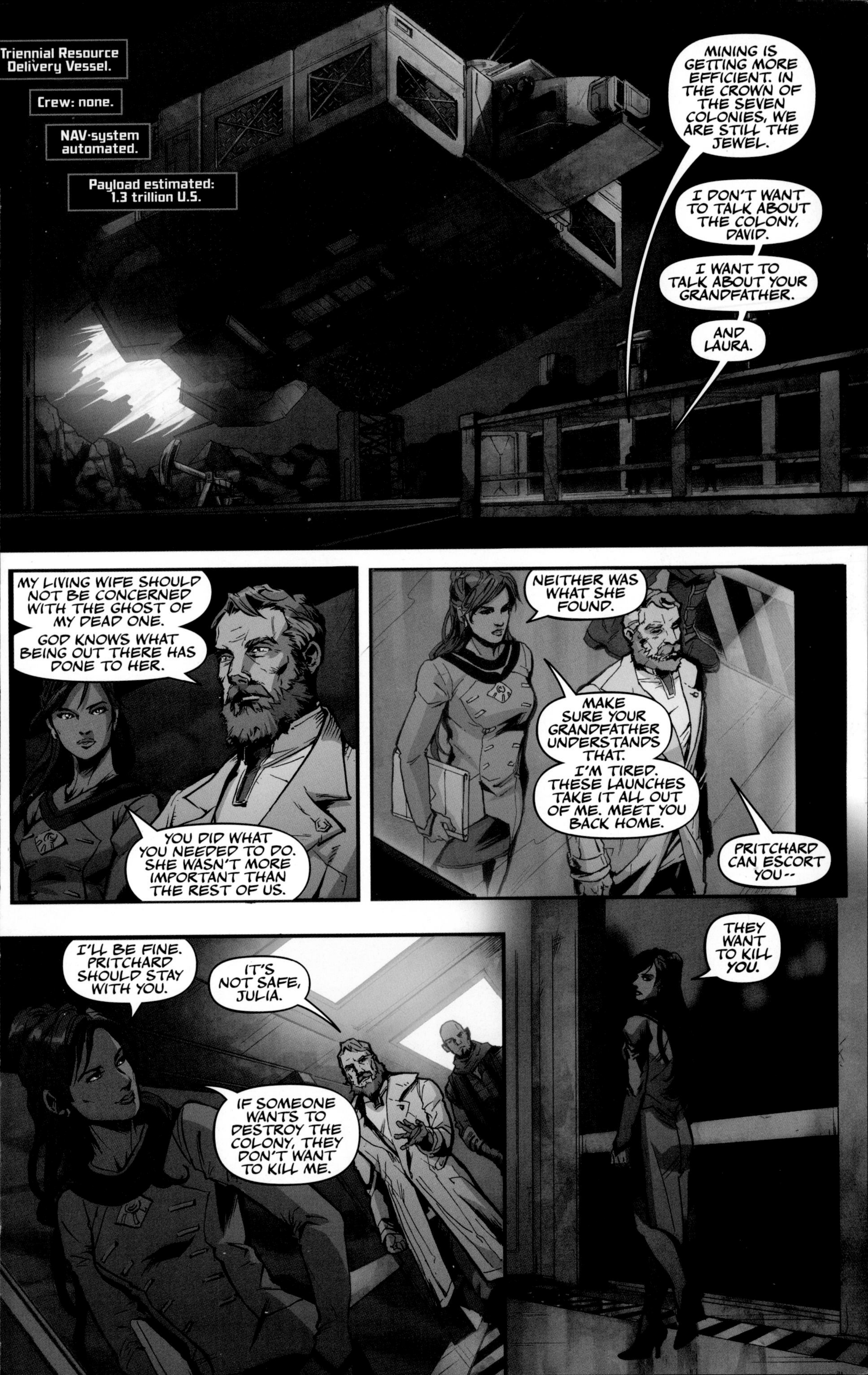

Triennial Resource Delivery Vessel.
Crew: none.
NAV-system automated.
Payload estimated: 1.3 trillion U.S.
MINING IS GETTING MORE EFFICIENT. IN THE CROWN OF THE SEVEN COLONIES, WE ARE STILL THE JEWEL.
I DON'T WANT TO TALK ABOUT THE COLONY, DAVID.
I WANT TO TALK ABOUT YOUR GRANDFATHER.
AND LAURA.
MY LIVING WIFE SHOULD NOT BE CONCERNED WITH THE GHOST OF MY DEAD ONE.
GOD KNOWS WHAT BEING OUT THERE HAS DONE TO HER.
YOU DID WHAT YOU NEEDED TO DO. SHE WASN'T MORE IMPORTANT THAN THE REST OF US.
NEITHER WAS WHAT SHE FOUND.
MAKE SURE YOUR GRANDFATHER UNDERSTANDS THAT.
I'M TIRED. THESE LAUNCHES TAKE IT ALL OUT OF ME. MEET YOU BACK HOME.
PRITCHARD CAN ESCORT YOU--
I'LL BE FINE. PRITCHARD SHOULD STAY WITH YOU.
IT'S NOT SAFE, JULIA.
IF SOMEONE WANTS TO DESTROY THE COLONY, THEY DON'T WANT TO KILL ME.
THEY WANT TO KILL YOU.

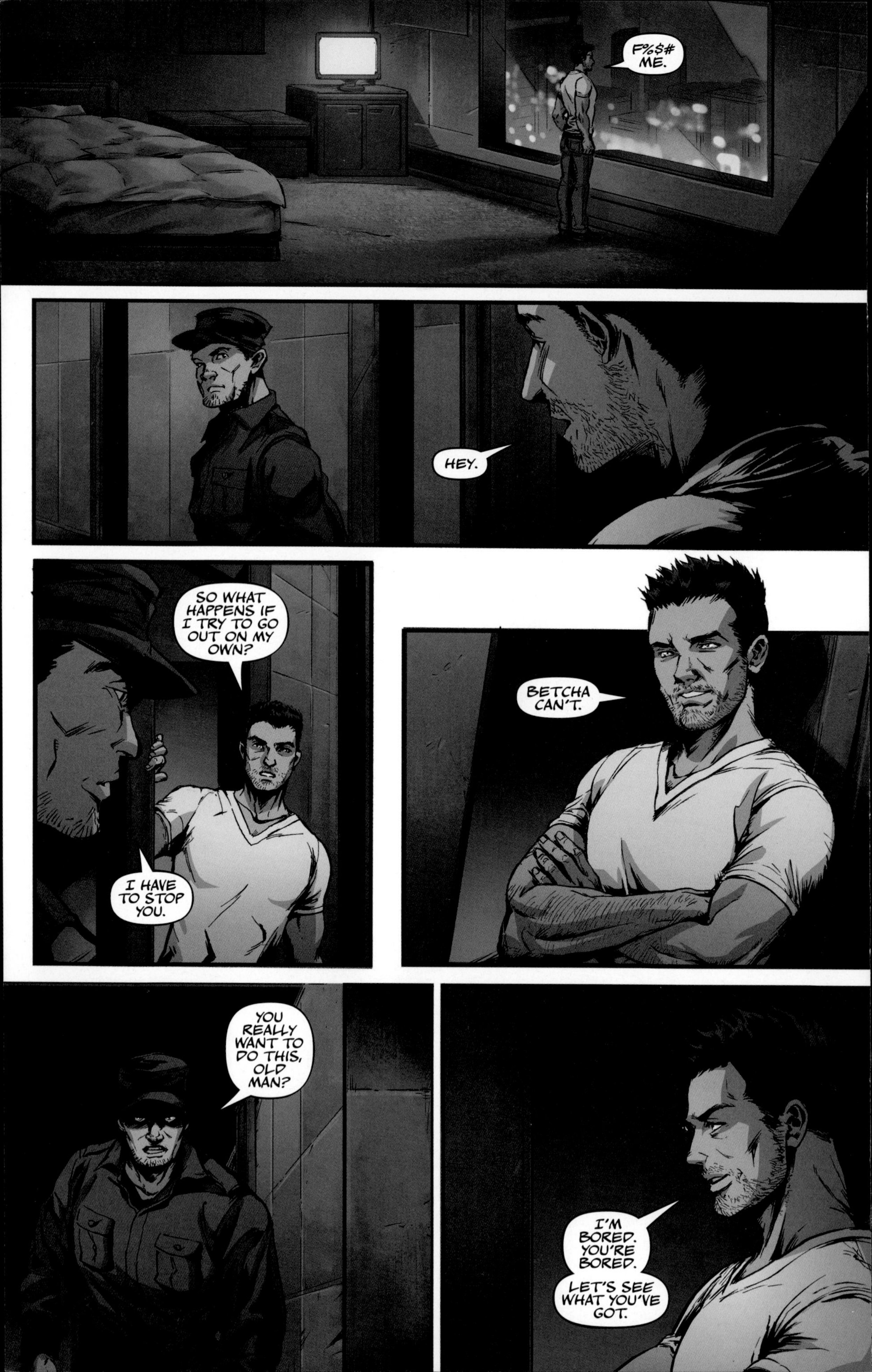
F%$#
ME.
HEY.
SO WHAT HAPPENS IF I TRY TO GO OUT ON MY OWN?
I HAVE TO STOP YOU.
BETCHA CAN'T.
YOU REALLY WANT TO DO THIS, OLD MAN?
I'M BORED. YOU'RE BORED.
LET'S SEE WHAT YOU'VE GOT.

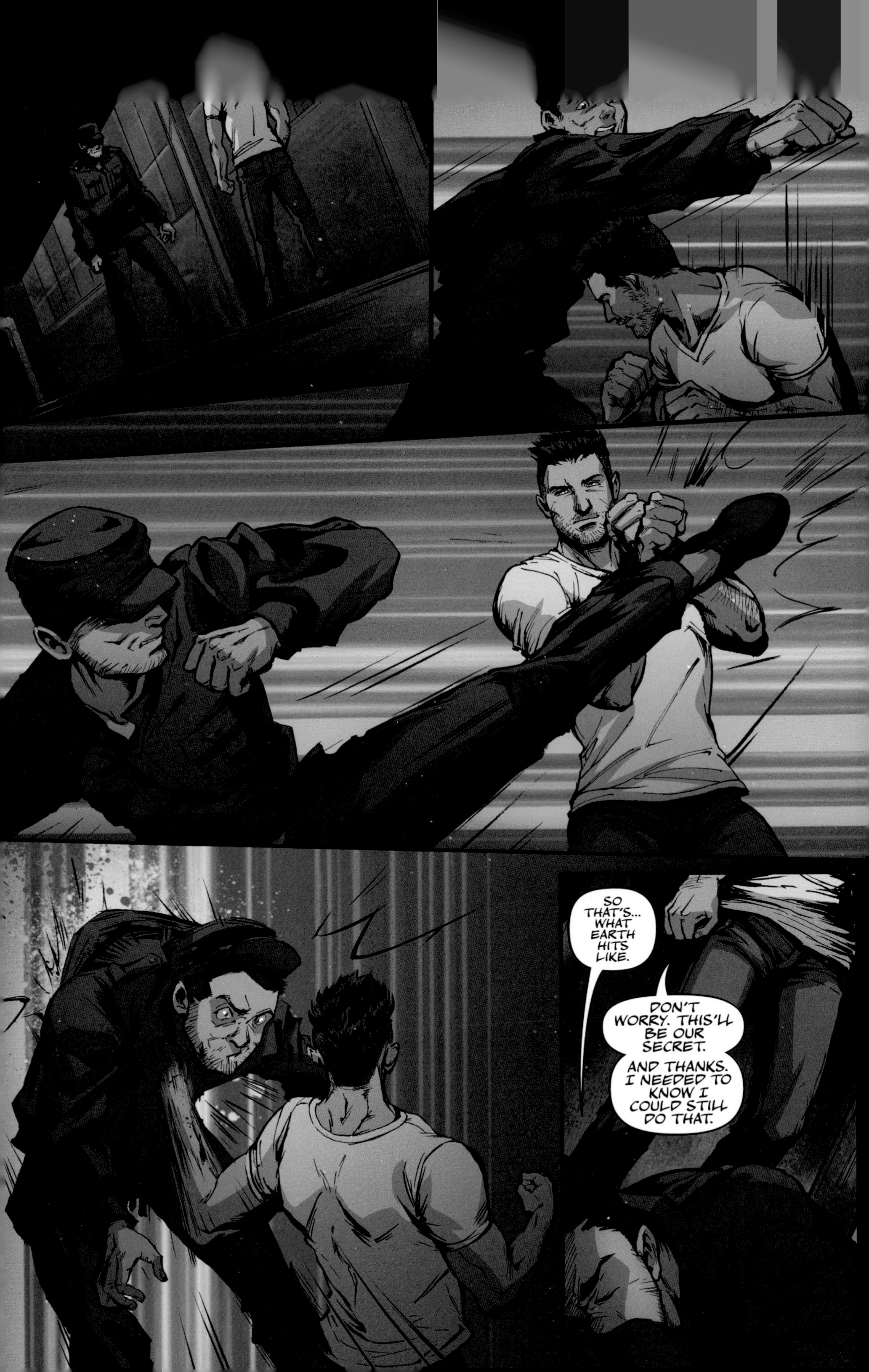

SO THAT'S... WHAT EARTH HITS LIKE.
DON'T WORRY. THIS'LL BE OUR SECRET.
AND THANKS. I NEEDED TO KNOW I COULD STILL DO THAT.

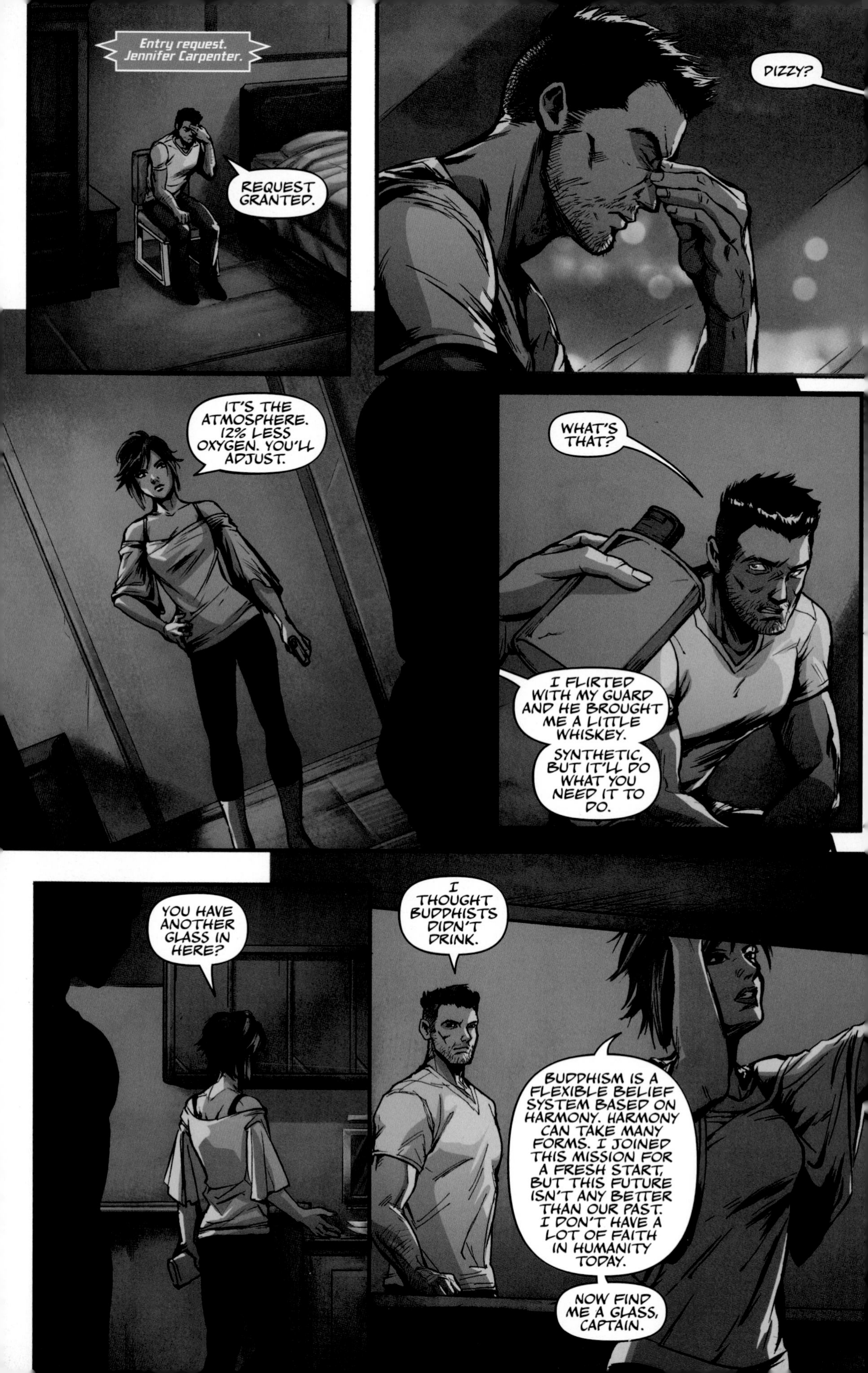
Entry request. Jennifer Carpenter.
REQUEST GRANTED.
DIZZY?
IT'S THE ATMOSPHERE. 12% LESS OXYGEN. YOU'LL ADJUST.
WHAT'S THAT?
I FLIRTED WITH MY GUARD AND HE BROUGHT ME A LITTLE WHISKEY.
SYNTHETIC, BUT IT'LL DO WHAT YOU NEED IT TO DO.
YOU HAVE ANOTHER GLASS IN HERE?
I THOUGHT BUDDHISTS DIDN'T DRINK.
BUDDHISM IS A FLEXIBLE BELIEF SYSTEM BASED ON HARMONY. HARMONY CAN TAKE MANY FORMS. I JOINED THIS MISSION FOR A FRESH START, BUT THIS FUTURE ISN'T ANY BETTER THAN OUR PAST. I DON'T HAVE A LOT OF FAITH IN HUMANITY TODAY.
NOW FIND ME A GLASS, CAPTAIN.

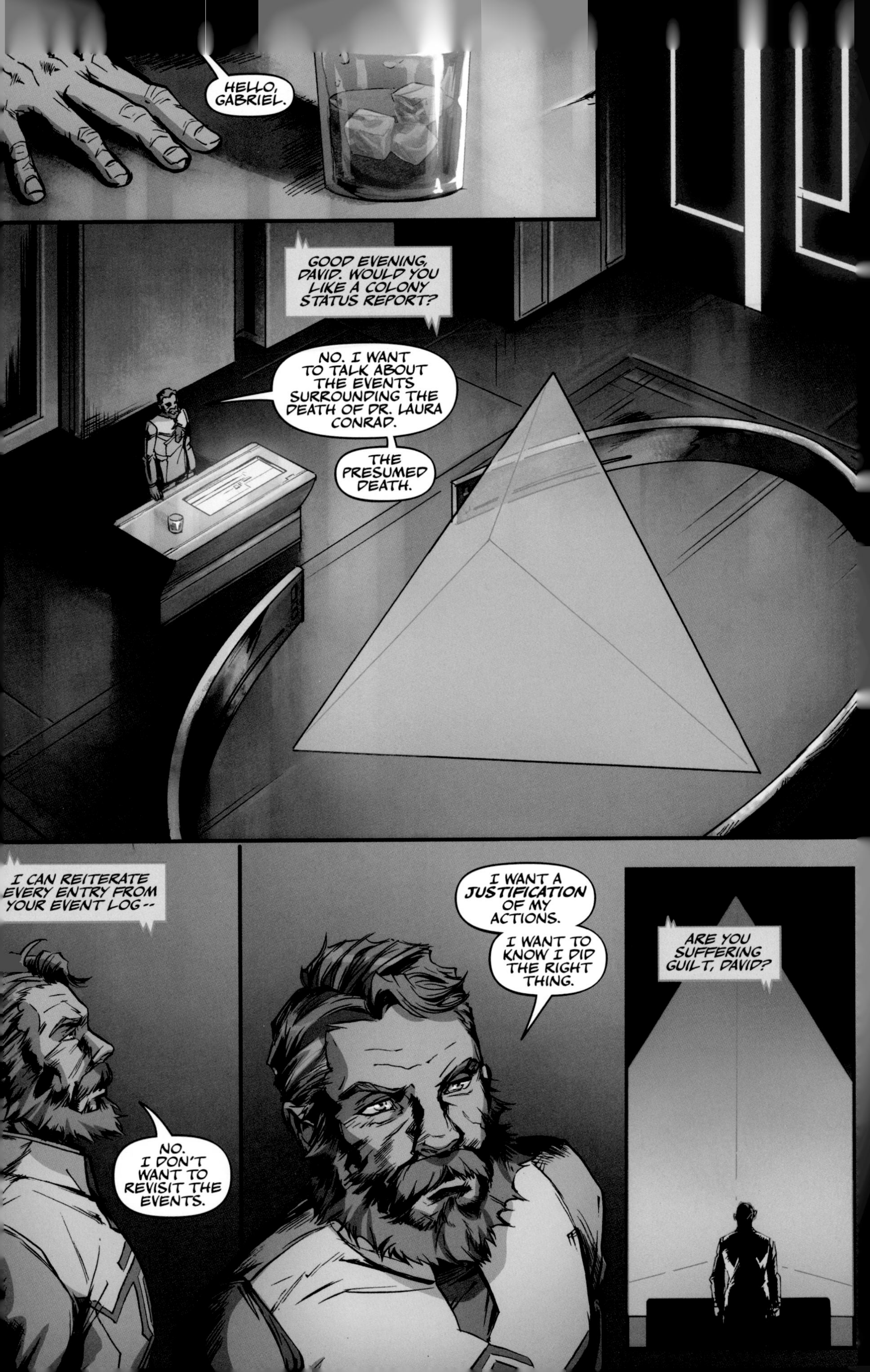
HELLO, GABRIEL.
GOOD EVENING, DAVID. WOULD YOU LIKE A COLONY STATUS REPORT?
NO. I WANT TO TALK ABOUT THE EVENTS SURROUNDING THE DEATH OF DR. LAURA CONRAD.
THE PRESUMED DEATH.
I CAN REITERATE EVERY ENTRY FROM YOUR EVENT LOG--
NO. I DON'T WANT TO REVISIT THE EVENTS.
I WANT A JUSTIFICATION OF MY ACTIONS.
I WANT TO KNOW I DID THE RIGHT THING.
ARE YOU SUFFERING GUILT, DAVID?

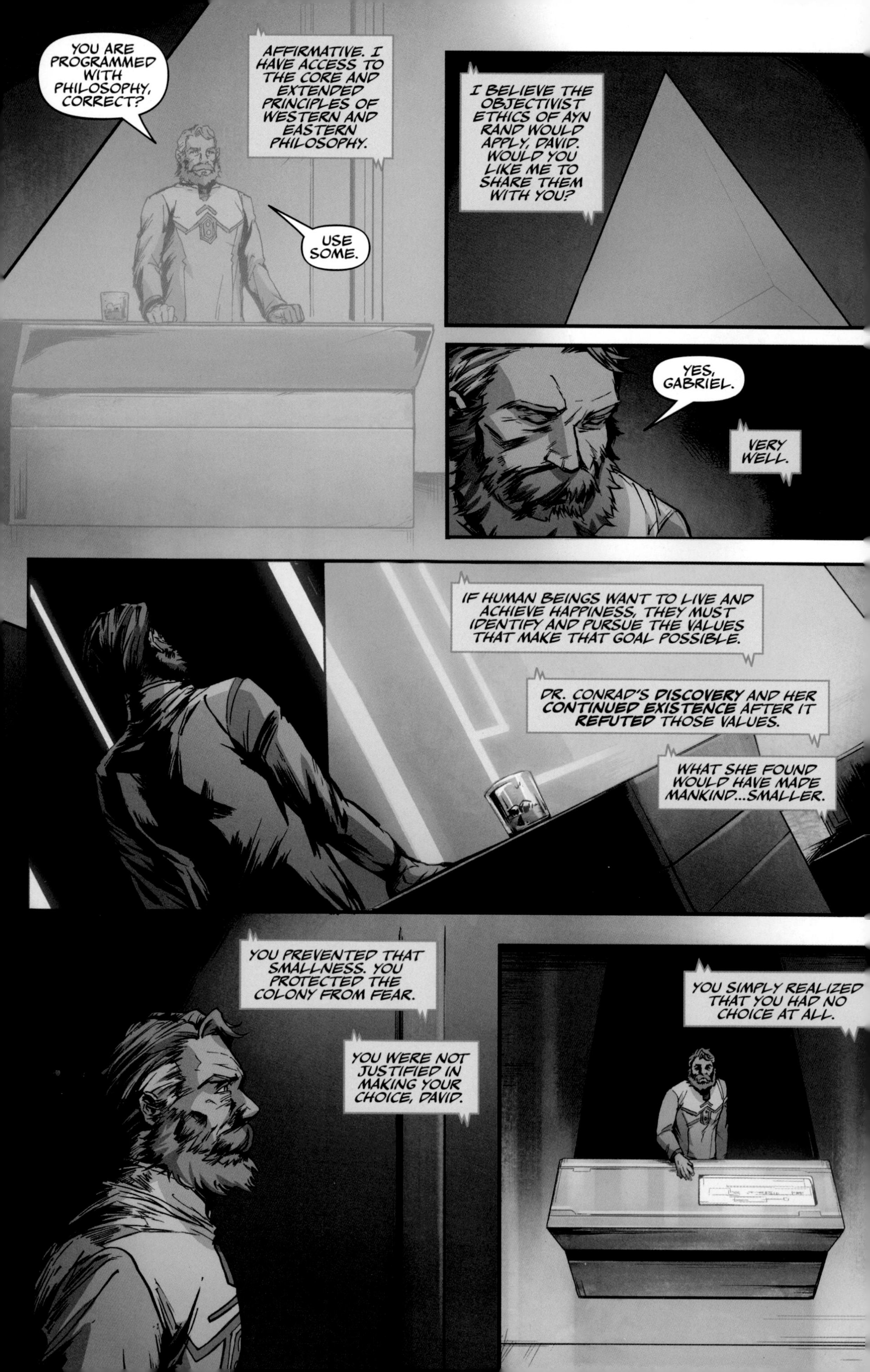
YOU ARE PROGRAMMED WITH PHILOSOPHY, CORRECT?
AFFIRMATIVE. I HAVE ACCESS TO THE CORE AND EXTENDED PRINCIPLES OF WESTERN AND EASTERN PHILOSOPHY.
USE SOME.
I BELIEVE THE OBJECTIVIST ETHICS OF AYN RAND WOULD APPLY, DAVID. WOULD YOU LIKE ME TO SHARE THEM WITH YOU?
YES, GABRIEL.
VERY WELL.
IF HUMAN BEINGS WANT TO LIVE AND ACHIEVE HAPPINESS, THEY MUST IDENTIFY AND PURSUE THE VALUES THAT MAKE THAT GOAL POSSIBLE.
DR. CONRAD'S **DISCOVERY** AND HER **CONTINUED EXISTENCE** AFTER IT **REFUTED** THOSE VALUES.
WHAT SHE FOUND WOULD HAVE MADE MANKIND...SMALLER.
YOU PREVENTED THAT SMALLNESS. YOU PROTECTED THE COLONY FROM FEAR.
YOU WERE NOT JUSTIFIED IN MAKING YOUR CHOICE, DAVID.
YOU SIMPLY REALIZED THAT YOU HAD NO CHOICE AT ALL.

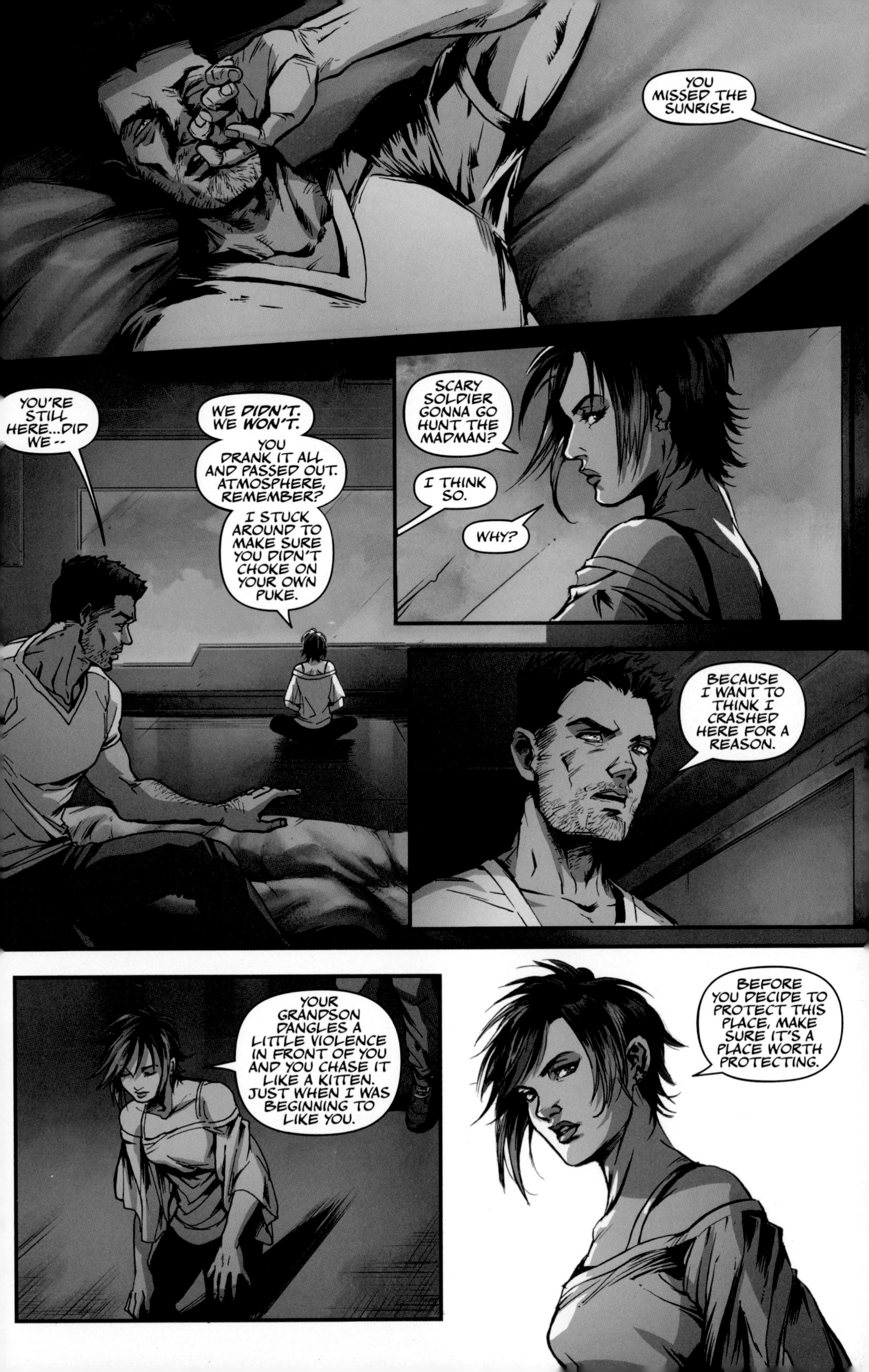
YOU MISSED THE SUNRISE.
YOU'RE STILL HERE...DID WE --
WE DIDN'T. WE WON'T.
YOU DRANK IT ALL AND PASSED OUT. ATMOSPHERE, REMEMBER?
I STUCK AROUND TO MAKE SURE YOU DIDN'T CHOKE ON YOUR OWN PUKE.
SCARY SOLDIER GONNA GO HUNT THE MADMAN?
I THINK SO.
WHY?
BECAUSE I WANT TO THINK I CRASHED HERE FOR A REASON.
YOUR GRANDSON DANGLES A LITTLE VIOLENCE IN FRONT OF YOU AND YOU CHASE IT LIKE A KITTEN. JUST WHEN I WAS BEGINNING TO LIKE YOU.
BEFORE YOU DECIDE TO PROTECT THIS PLACE, MAKE SURE IT'S A PLACE WORTH PROTECTING.

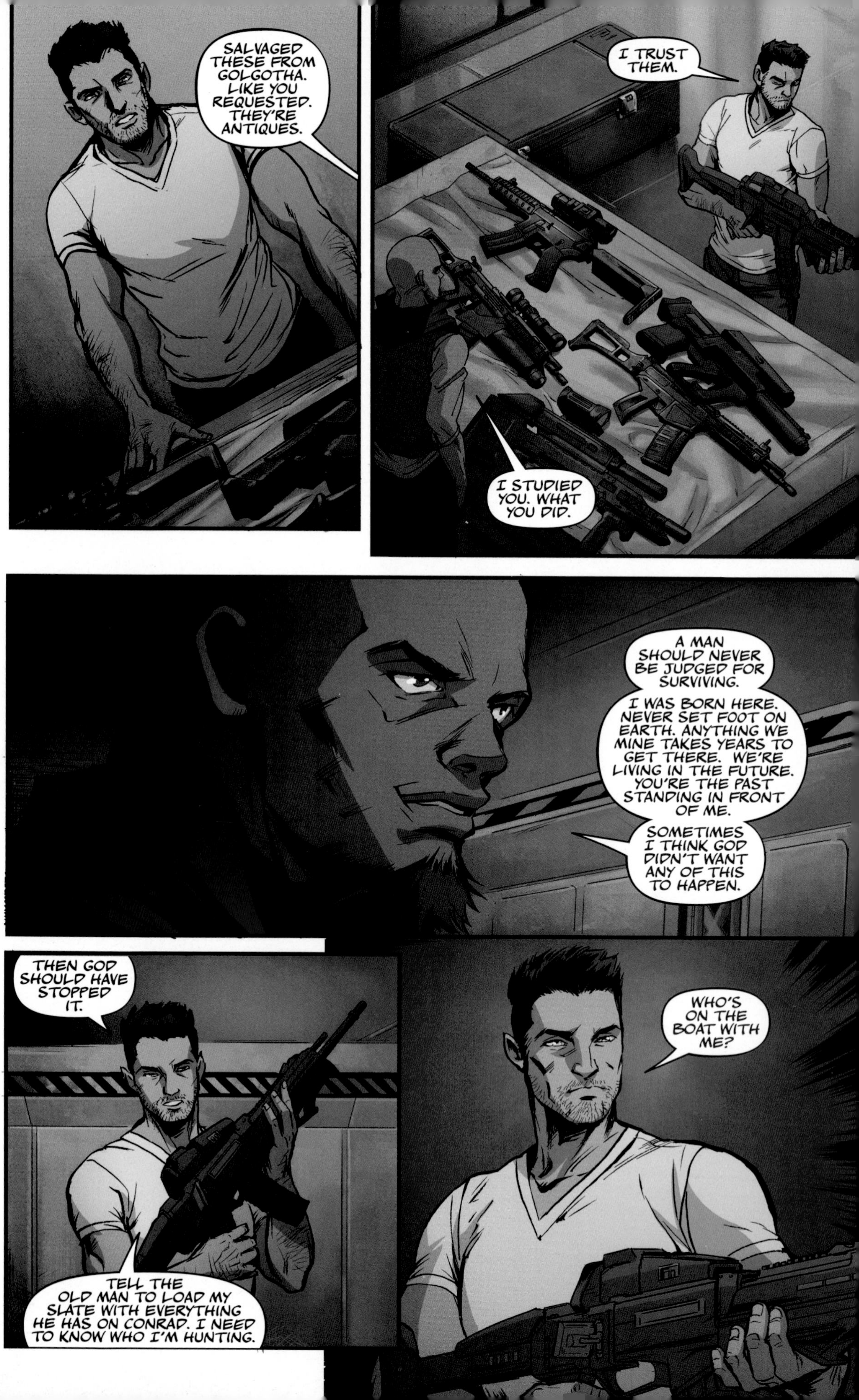
SALVAGED THESE FROM GOLGOTHA. LIKE YOU REQUESTED. THEY'RE ANTIQUES.
I TRUST THEM.
I STUDIED YOU. WHAT YOU DID.
A MAN SHOULD NEVER BE JUDGED FOR SURVIVING.
I WAS BORN HERE. NEVER SET FOOT ON EARTH. ANYTHING WE MINE TAKES YEARS TO GET THERE. WE'RE LIVING IN THE FUTURE. YOU'RE THE PAST STANDING IN FRONT OF ME.
SOMETIMES I THINK GOD DIDN'T WANT ANY OF THIS TO HAPPEN.
THEN GOD SHOULD HAVE STOPPED IT.
TELL THE OLD MAN TO LOAD MY SLATE WITH EVERYTHING HE HAS ON CONRAD. I NEED TO KNOW WHO I'M HUNTING.
WHO'S ON THE BOAT WITH ME?

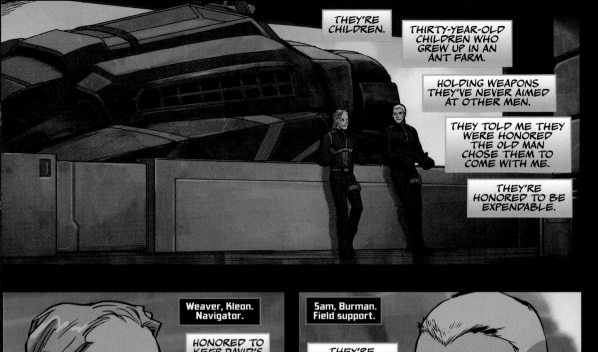

THEY'RE CHILDREN.

THIRTY-YEAR-OLD CHILDREN WHO GREW UP IN AN ANT FARM.

HOLDING WEAPONS THEY'VE NEVER AIMED AT OTHER MEN.

THEY TOLD ME THEY WERE HONORED THE OLD MAN CHOSE THEM TO COME WITH ME.

THEY'RE HONORED TO BE EXPENDABLE.

Weaver, Kleon. Navigator.

HONORED TO KEEP DAVID'S SECRETS.

Sam, Burman. Field support.

THEY'RE EXCITED. SIMULATION SOLDIERS FINALLY HAPPY TO STEP ON THE FIELD.

PROUD TO PROTECT THEIR HOME.

I'VE GOT CONRAD'S WORDS DANCING IN MY HEAD.

"WE ARE SET FREE BY OUR INSIGNIFICANCE.

"WHEN WE REALIZE WE DO NOT MATTER TO THE UNIVERSE WE CAN FREE OURSELVES.

"FROM OUR WILL TO CHANGE IT. FROM OUR DESIRE TO REMAIN."

STUDYING CONRAD'S FILE, SHE HAD EVERYTHING IN LIFE SHE WANTED.

A BEAUTIFUL, INTELLIGENT WOMAN WHO TOSSED IT ALL AWAY... I HAVE TO FIND OUT WHY.

I'LL NEVER GET THE TRUTH FROM GRYMES.

HEY, MICHAEL.

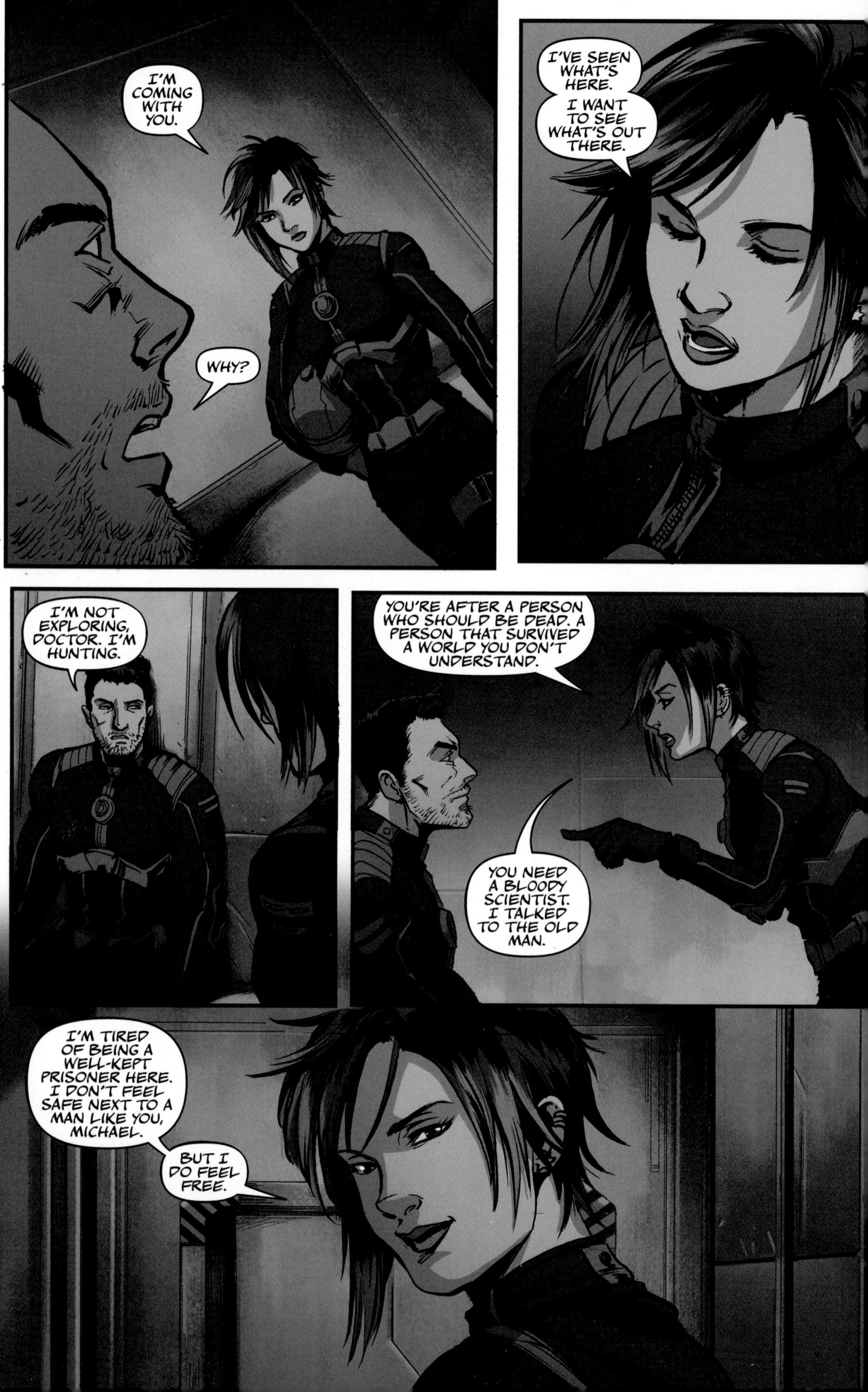
I'M COMING WITH YOU.
WHY?
I'VE SEEN WHAT'S HERE.
I WANT TO SEE WHAT'S OUT THERE.
I'M NOT EXPLORING, DOCTOR. I'M HUNTING.
YOU'RE AFTER A PERSON WHO SHOULD BE DEAD. A PERSON THAT SURVIVED A WORLD YOU DON'T UNDERSTAND.
YOU NEED A BLOODY SCIENTIST. I TALKED TO THE OLD MAN.
I'M TIRED OF BEING A WELL-KEPT PRISONER HERE. I DON'T FEEL SAFE NEXT TO A MAN LIKE YOU, MICHAEL.
BUT I DO FEEL FREE.

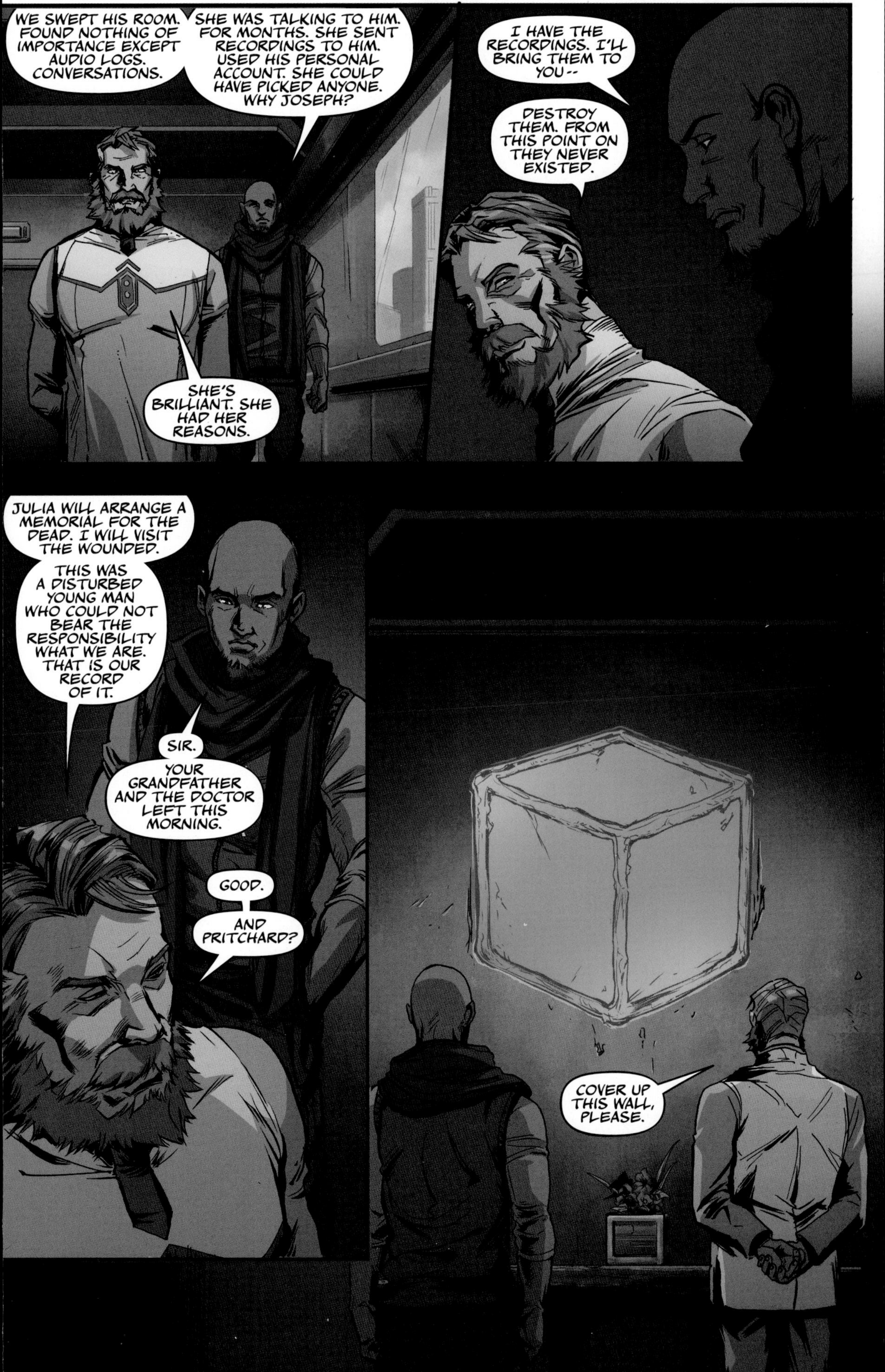
WE SWEPT HIS ROOM. FOUND NOTHING OF IMPORTANCE EXCEPT AUDIO LOGS. CONVERSATIONS.
SHE WAS TALKING TO HIM. FOR MONTHS. SHE SENT RECORDINGS TO HIM. USED HIS PERSONAL ACCOUNT. SHE COULD HAVE PICKED ANYONE. WHY JOSEPH?
SHE'S BRILLIANT. SHE HAD HER REASONS.
I HAVE THE RECORDINGS. I'LL BRING THEM TO YOU--
DESTROY THEM. FROM THIS POINT ON THEY NEVER EXISTED.
JULIA WILL ARRANGE A MEMORIAL FOR THE DEAD. I WILL VISIT THE WOUNDED.
THIS WAS A DISTURBED YOUNG MAN WHO COULD NOT BEAR THE RESPONSIBILITY WHAT WE ARE. THAT IS OUR RECORD OF IT.
SIR.
YOUR GRANDFATHER AND THE DOCTOR LEFT THIS MORNING.
GOOD.
AND PRITCHARD?
COVER UP THIS WALL, PLEASE.

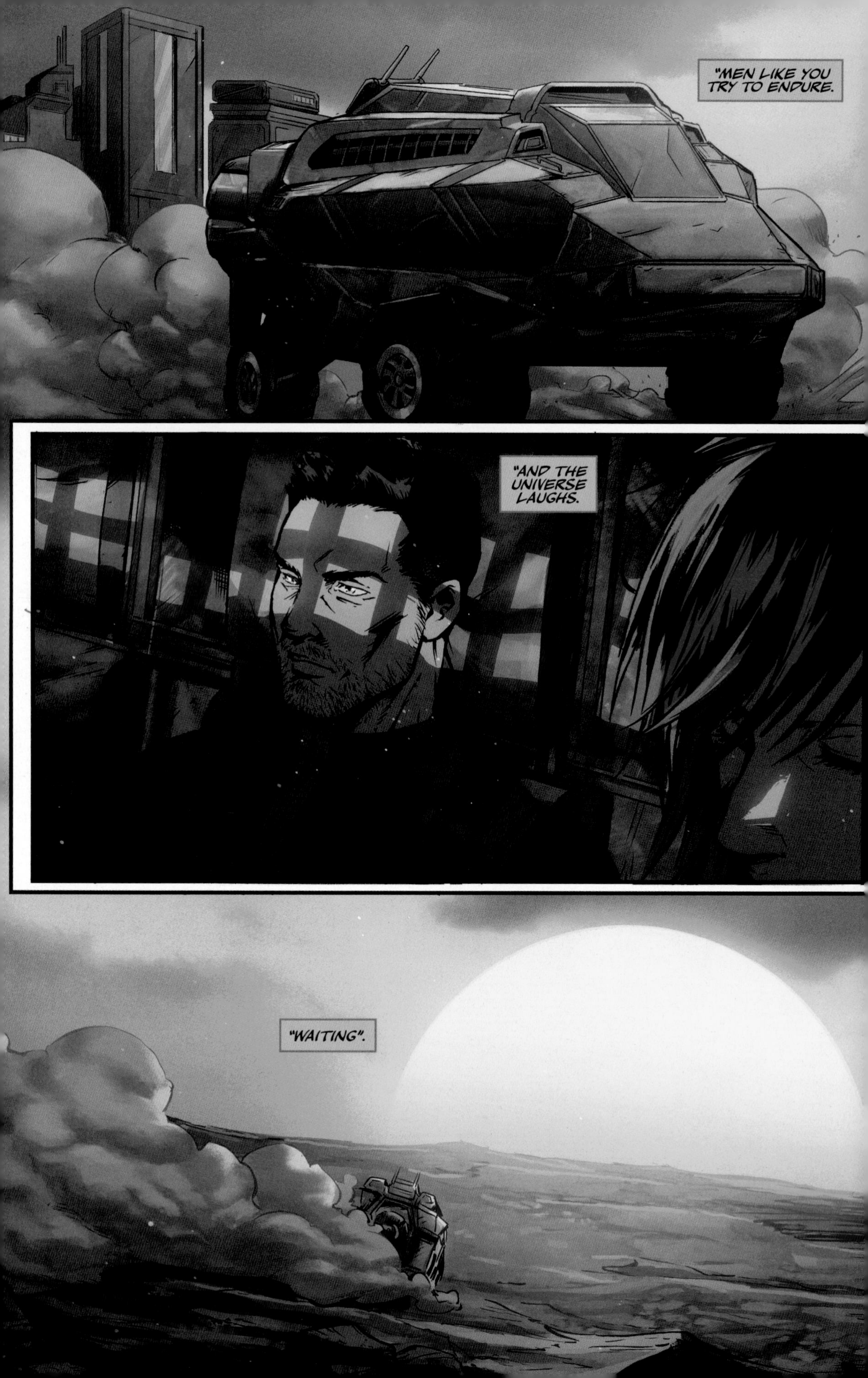
"MEN LIKE YOU TRY TO ENDURE.
"AND THE UNIVERSE LAUGHS.
"WAITING".

Excerpt from the personal journals of David Grymes.

"...discovery means everything to Laura. As much as I love her, and my God in heaven knows I have tried to keep her close to me, but science is her religion. Scientific truth is her salvation. She will bring the truth of what she's found to the colonies, no matter how many times I ask her not to.

Beg her not to.

I tried to explain it again to Laura, this morning. There was so much elation in her voice because she believes she's unlocked a great truth. She didn't hear me. She won't consider the consequences of this. Her science, and that... thing she's found is a slayer of old gods and a harbinger of new ones. Her discovery destroys God, and Yahweh, and Allah and every myth and idea we have of our creation.

If mankind is not the most intelligent life in the universe, then our God created us to be lesser than others. Perhaps, our God is lesser than others. Christ was the salvation of our world, but there are worlds that never knew him, worlds that achieved things mankind can't even dream.

I won't be the man that shares this truth. I won't be the man who replaced the gods and faith of men with spacemen and their old machines.

I have one woman who trusts me as a husband, but I have a colony that needs me as a father. There is a choice that Laura is going to force me to make, a choice that I don't want to make.

But it's a choice that I have already made."

Grymes, David

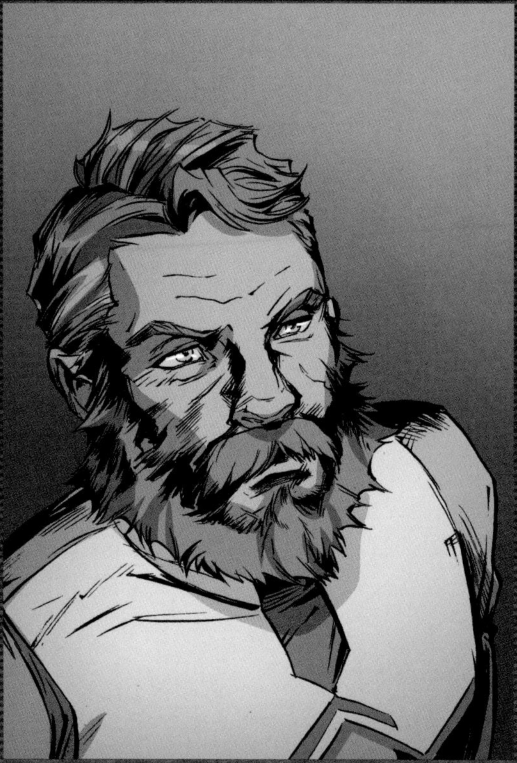

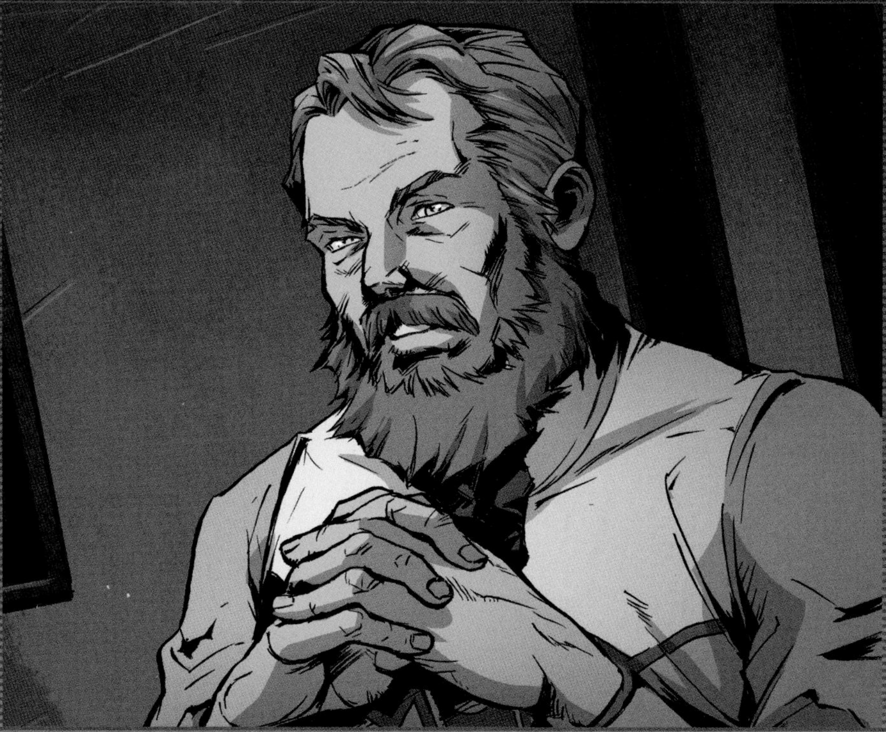

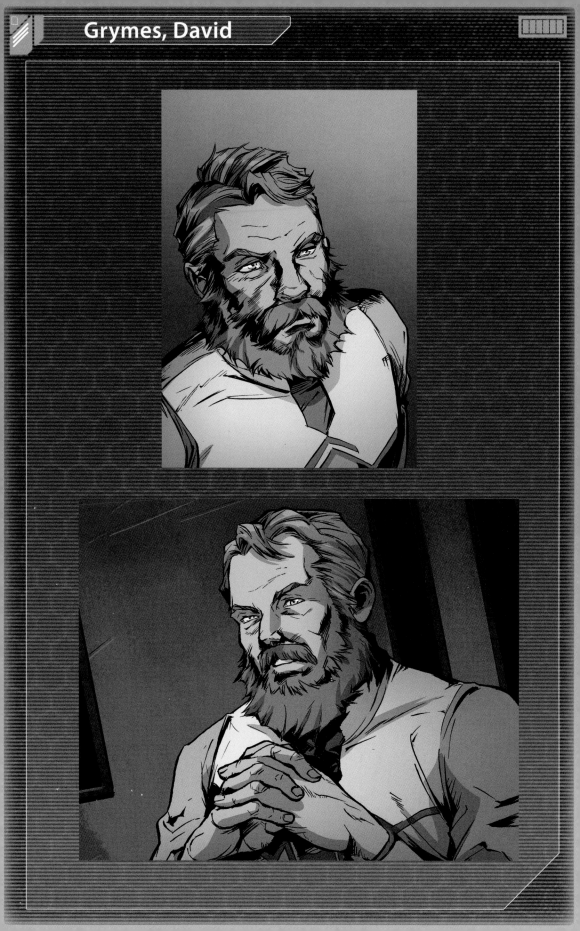

CHAPTER 3

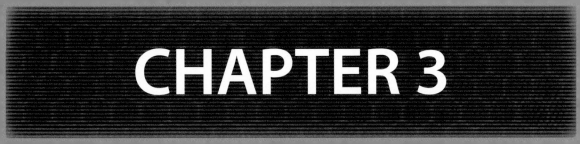

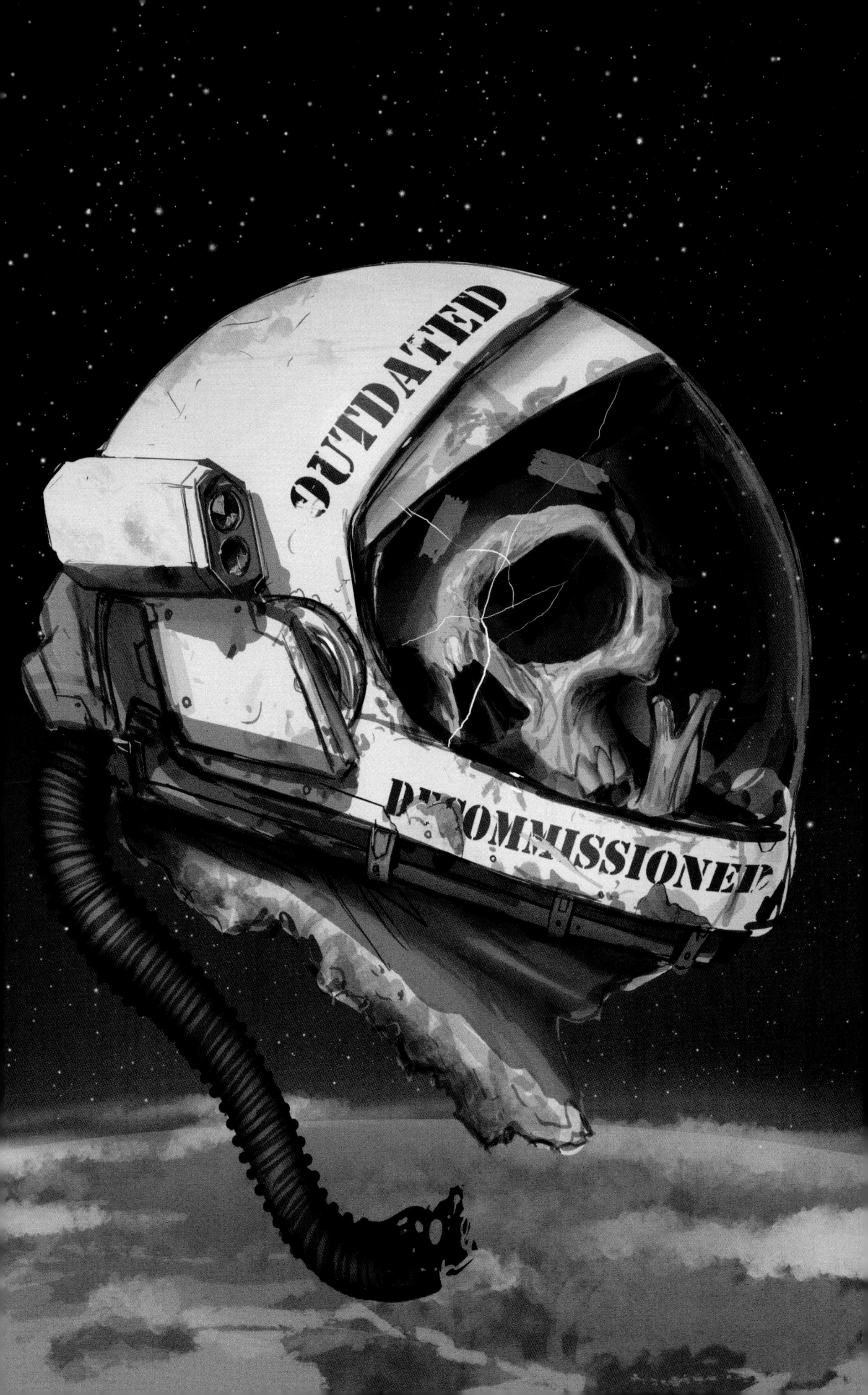
OUTDATED

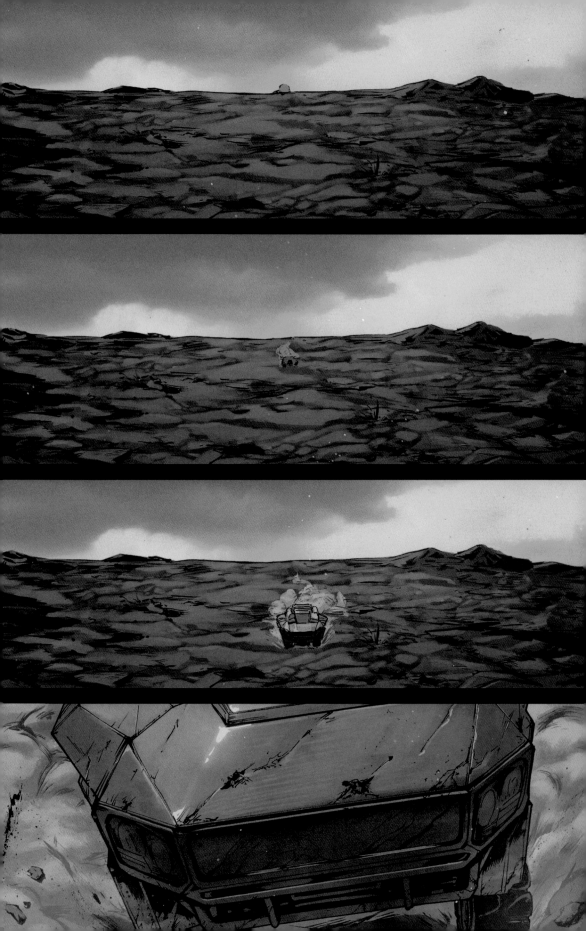

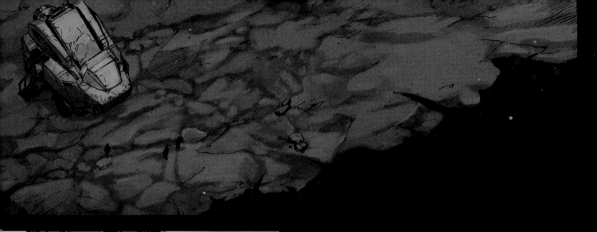

JENNIFER. CONFIRMATION THESE ARE THE COORDINATES?

CONFIRMED.

THIS IS CONRAD'S LAST KNOWN LOCATION.

LOOKS LIKE WE'RE HEADED INTO THE HOLE.

MOVE!

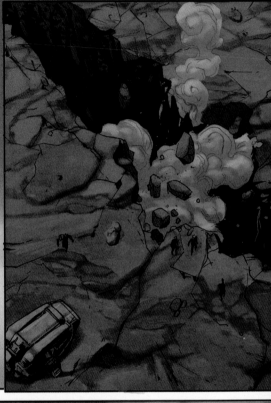

WE'VE LOST TRACK OF THEM, SIR.

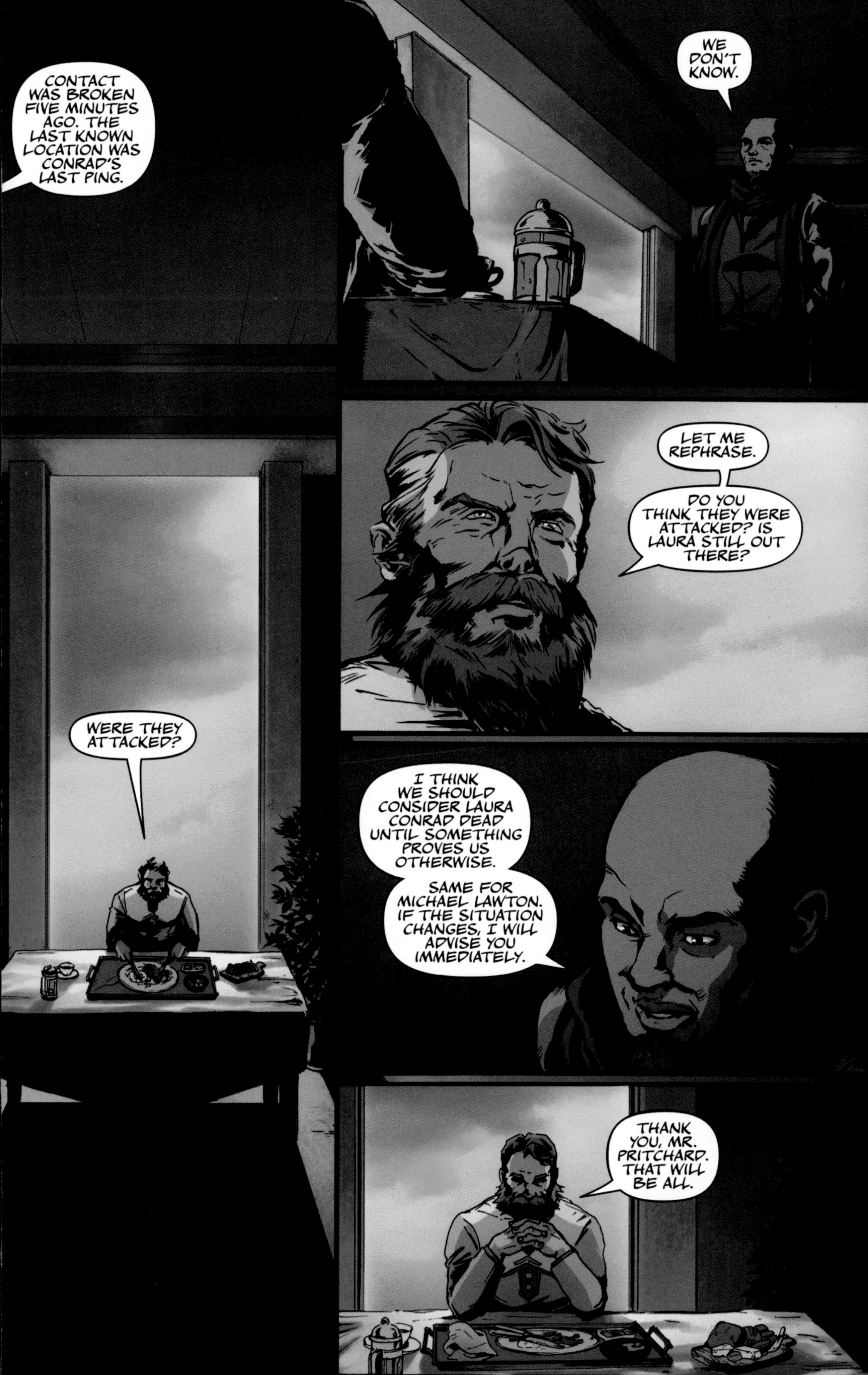
CONTACT WAS BROKEN FIVE MINUTES AGO. THE LAST KNOWN LOCATION WAS CONRAD'S LAST PING.
WE DON'T KNOW.
WERE THEY ATTACKED?
LET ME REPHRASE.
DO YOU THINK THEY WERE ATTACKED? IS LAURA STILL OUT THERE?
I THINK WE SHOULD CONSIDER LAURA CONRAD DEAD UNTIL SOMETHING PROVES US OTHERWISE.
SAME FOR MICHAEL LAWTON. IF THE SITUATION CHANGES, I WILL ADVISE YOU IMMEDIATELY.
THANK YOU, MR. PRITCHARD. THAT WILL BE ALL.

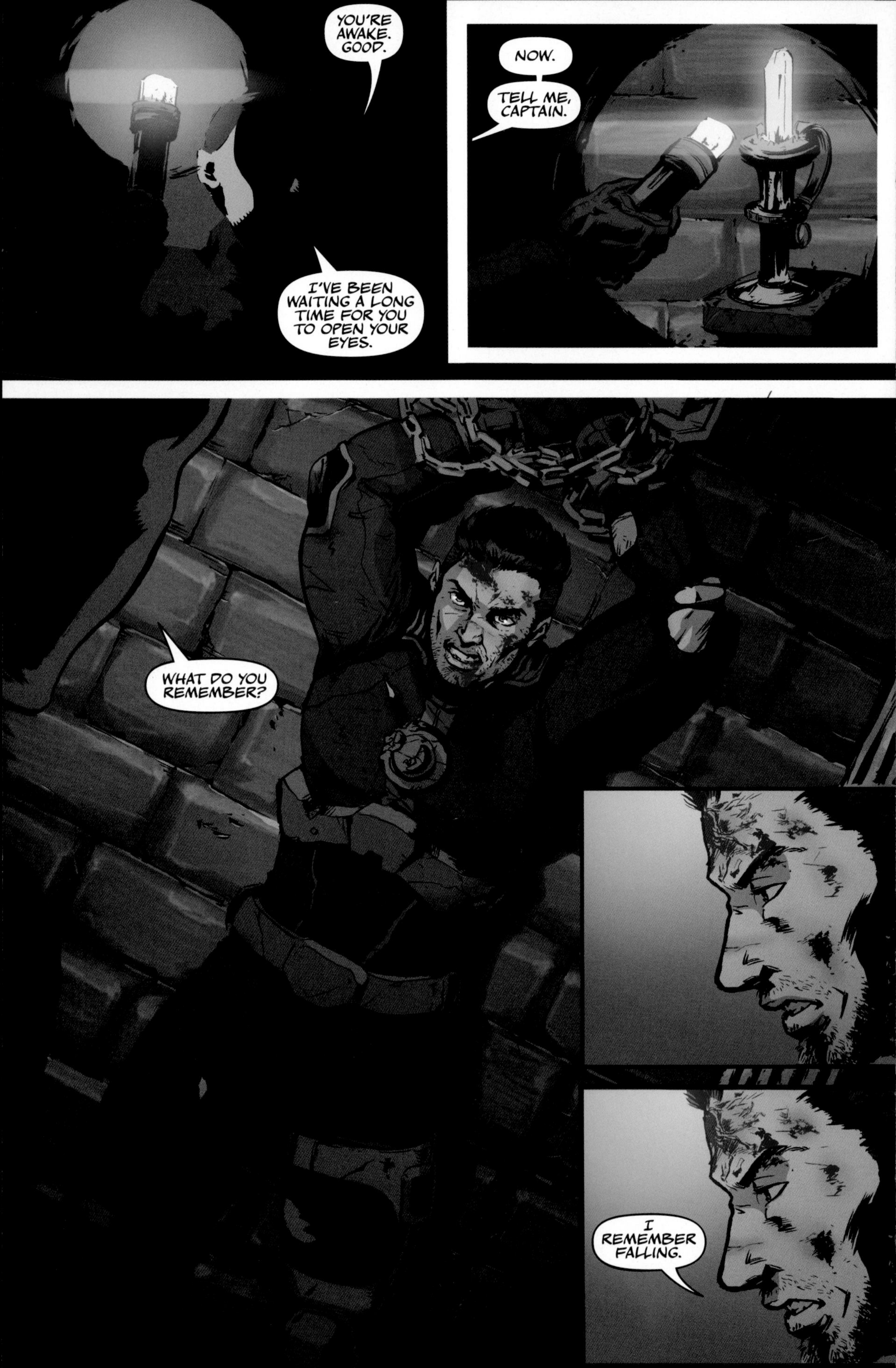
YOU'RE AWAKE. GOOD.
I'VE BEEN WAITING A LONG TIME FOR YOU TO OPEN YOUR EYES.
NOW.
TELL ME, CAPTAIN.
WHAT DO YOU REMEMBER?
I REMEMBER FALLING.

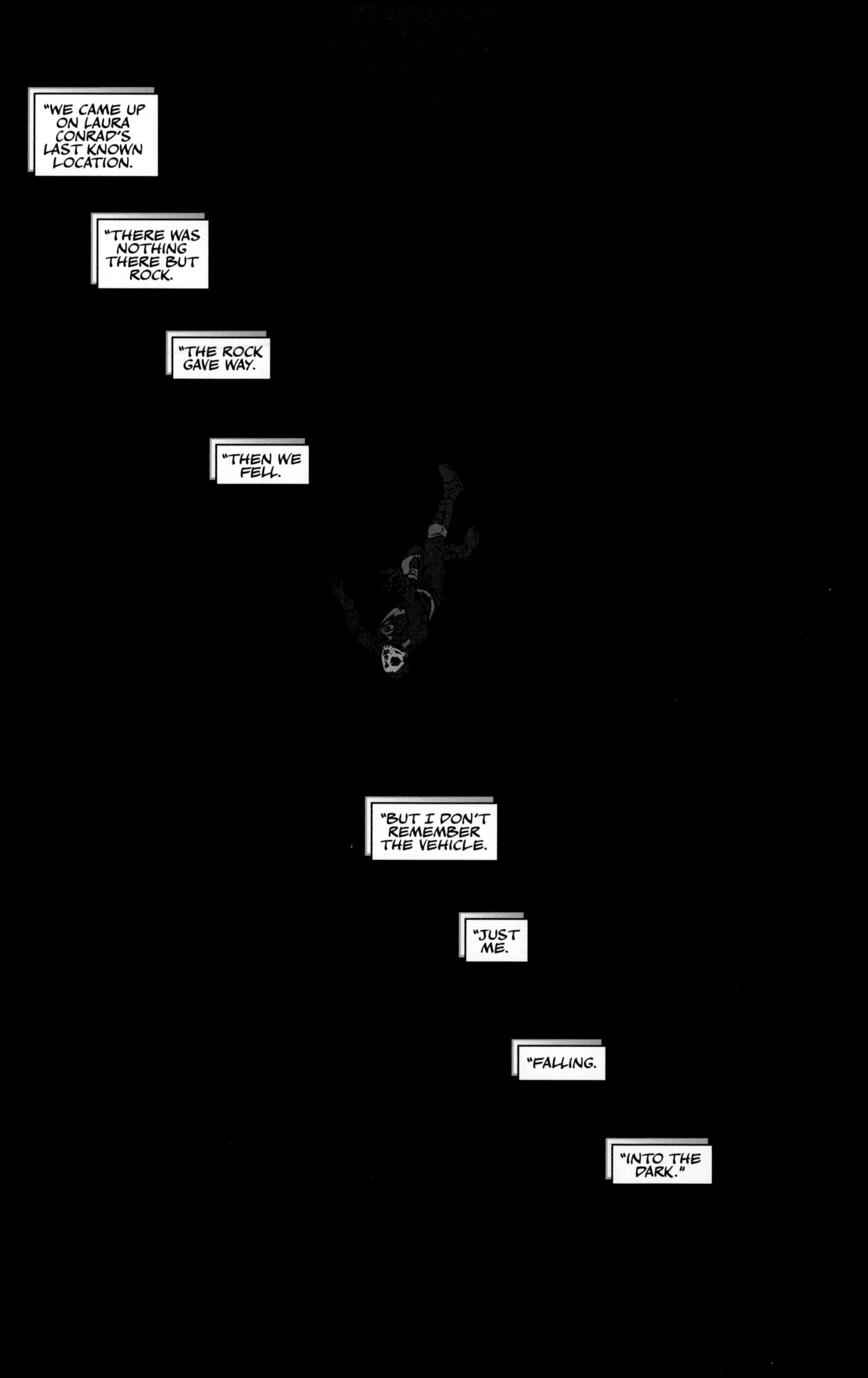

"WE CAME UP ON LAURA CONRAD'S LAST KNOWN LOCATION.

"THERE WAS NOTHING THERE BUT ROCK.

"THE ROCK GAVE WAY.

"THEN WE FELL.

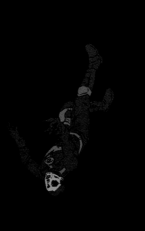

"BUT I DON'T REMEMBER THE VEHICLE.

"JUST ME.

"FALLING.

"INTO THE DARK."

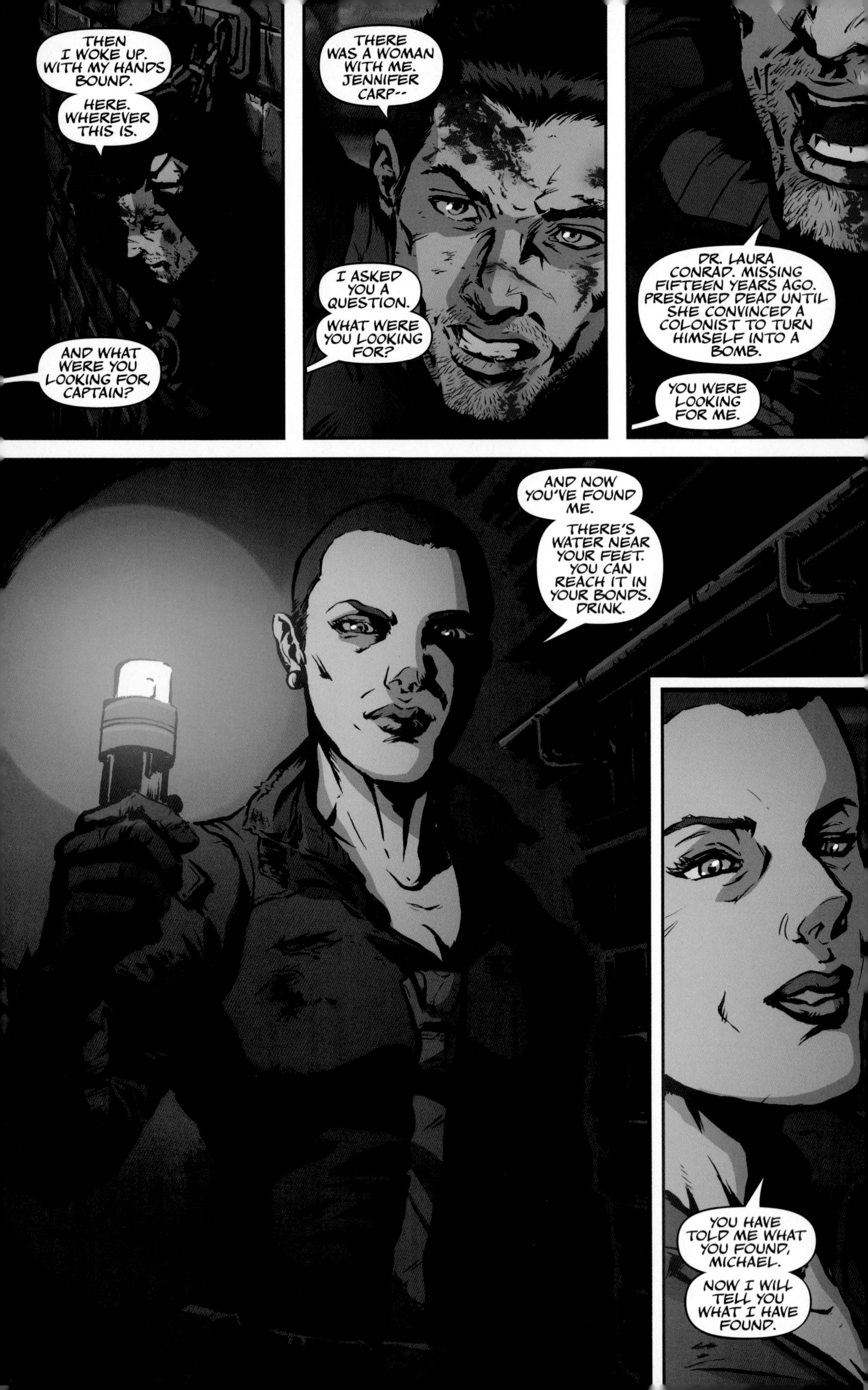
THEN I WOKE UP. WITH MY HANDS BOUND.
HERE. WHEREVER THIS IS.
AND WHAT WERE YOU LOOKING FOR, CAPTAIN?
THERE WAS A WOMAN WITH ME. JENNIFER CARP--
I ASKED YOU A QUESTION.
WHAT WERE YOU LOOKING FOR?
DR. LAURA CONRAD. MISSING FIFTEEN YEARS AGO. PRESUMED DEAD UNTIL SHE CONVINCED A COLONIST TO TURN HIMSELF INTO A BOMB.
YOU WERE LOOKING FOR ME.
AND NOW YOU'VE FOUND ME.
THERE'S WATER NEAR YOUR FEET. YOU CAN REACH IT IN YOUR BONDS. DRINK.
YOU HAVE TOLD ME WHAT YOU FOUND, MICHAEL.
NOW I WILL TELL YOU WHAT I HAVE FOUND.

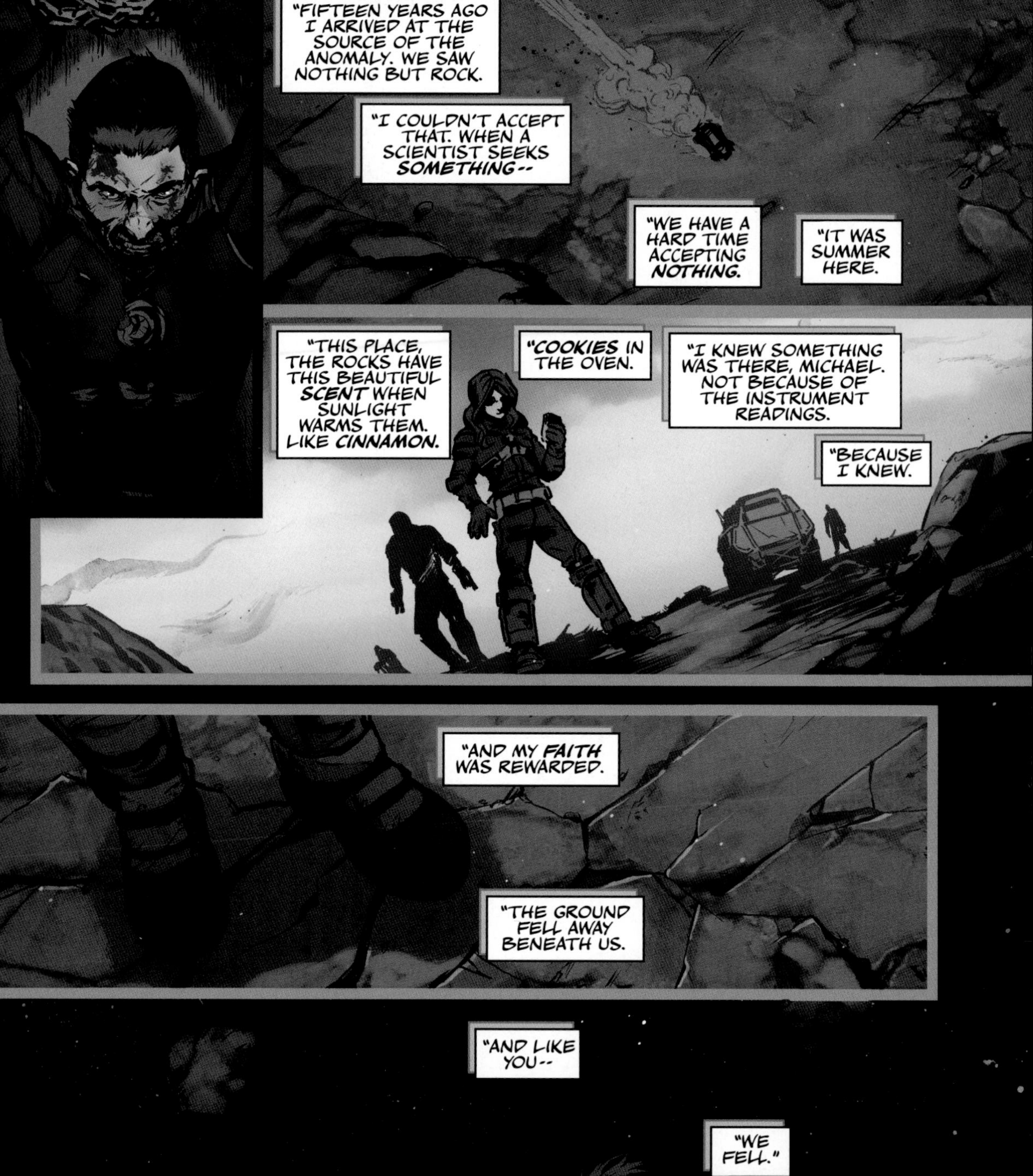
"FIFTEEN YEARS AGO I ARRIVED AT THE SOURCE OF THE ANOMALY. WE SAW NOTHING BUT ROCK.
"I COULDN'T ACCEPT THAT. WHEN A SCIENTIST SEEKS *SOMETHING*--
"WE HAVE A HARD TIME ACCEPTING *NOTHING*.
"IT WAS SUMMER HERE.
"THIS PLACE, THE ROCKS HAVE THIS BEAUTIFUL *SCENT* WHEN SUNLIGHT WARMS THEM. LIKE *CINNAMON*.
"*COOKIES* IN THE OVEN.
"I KNEW SOMETHING WAS THERE, MICHAEL. NOT BECAUSE OF THE INSTRUMENT READINGS.
"BECAUSE I KNEW.
"AND MY *FAITH* WAS REWARDED.
"THE GROUND FELL AWAY BENEATH US.
"AND LIKE YOU--
"WE FELL."

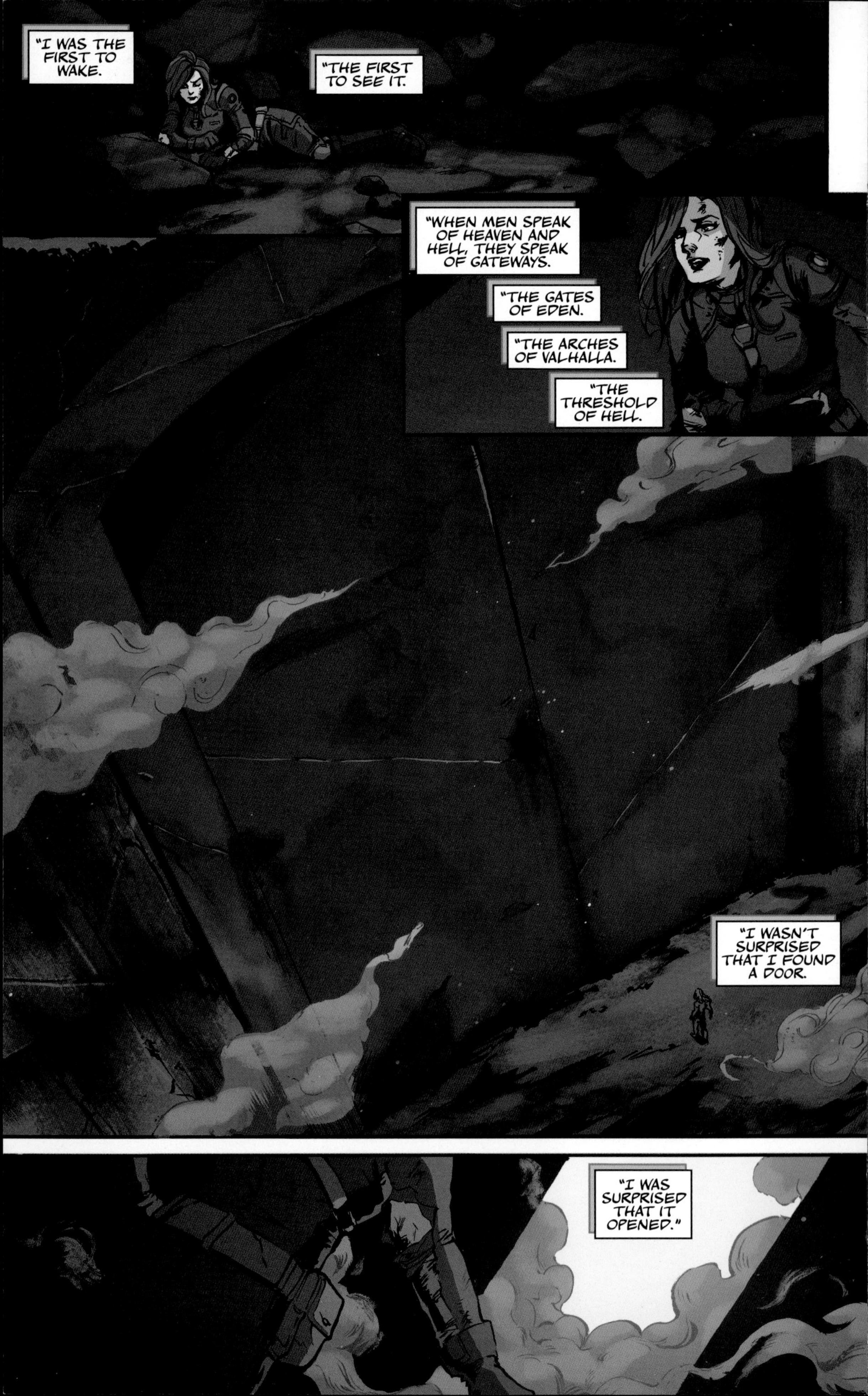
"I WAS THE FIRST TO WAKE.
"THE FIRST TO SEE IT.
"WHEN MEN SPEAK OF HEAVEN AND HELL, THEY SPEAK OF GATEWAYS.
"THE GATES OF EDEN.
"THE ARCHES OF VALHALLA.
"THE THRESHOLD OF HELL.
"I WASN'T SURPRISED THAT I FOUND A DOOR.
"I WAS SURPRISED THAT IT OPENED."

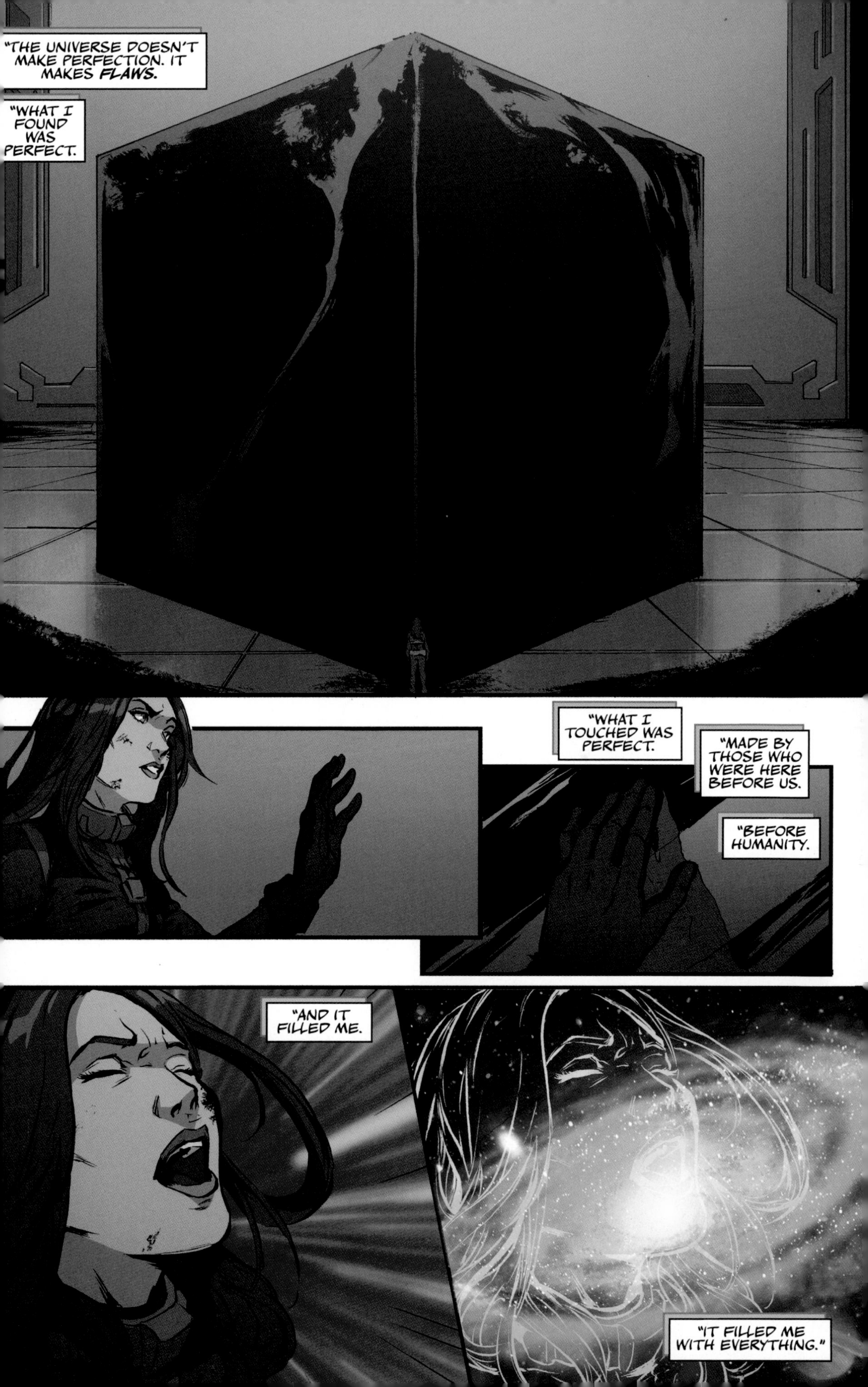
"THE UNIVERSE DOESN'T MAKE PERFECTION. IT MAKES FLAWS.
"WHAT I FOUND WAS PERFECT.
"WHAT I TOUCHED WAS PERFECT.
"MADE BY THOSE WHO WERE HERE BEFORE US.
"BEFORE HUMANITY.
"AND IT FILLED ME.
"IT FILLED ME WITH EVERYTHING."

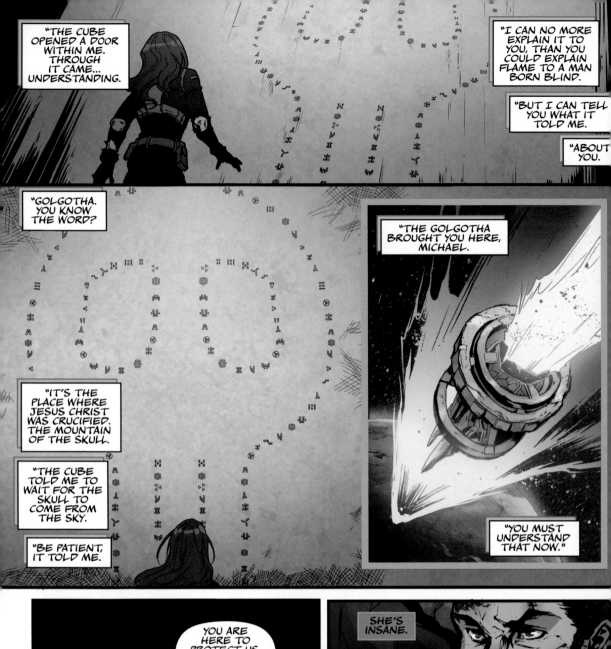

"THE CUBE OPENED A DOOR WITHIN ME. THROUGH IT CAME... UNDERSTANDING.

"I CAN NO MORE EXPLAIN IT TO YOU, THAN YOU COULD EXPLAIN FLAME TO A MAN BORN BLIND.

"BUT I CAN TELL YOU WHAT IT TOLD ME.

"ABOUT YOU.

"GOLGOTHA. YOU KNOW THE WORD?

"THE GOLGOTHA BROUGHT YOU HERE, MICHAEL.

"IT'S THE PLACE WHERE JESUS CHRIST WAS CRUCIFIED. THE MOUNTAIN OF THE SKULL.

"THE CUBE TOLD ME TO WAIT FOR THE SKULL TO COME FROM THE SKY.

"BE PATIENT, IT TOLD ME.

"YOU MUST UNDERSTAND THAT NOW."

YOU ARE HERE TO PROTECT US, MICHAEL. FROM THOSE THAT WOULD DO US HARM.

FROM THOSE THAT FEAR THE TRUTH WE HAVE FOUND.

SHE'S INSANE.

WHO WANTS TO DO YOU HARM, DR. CONRAD?

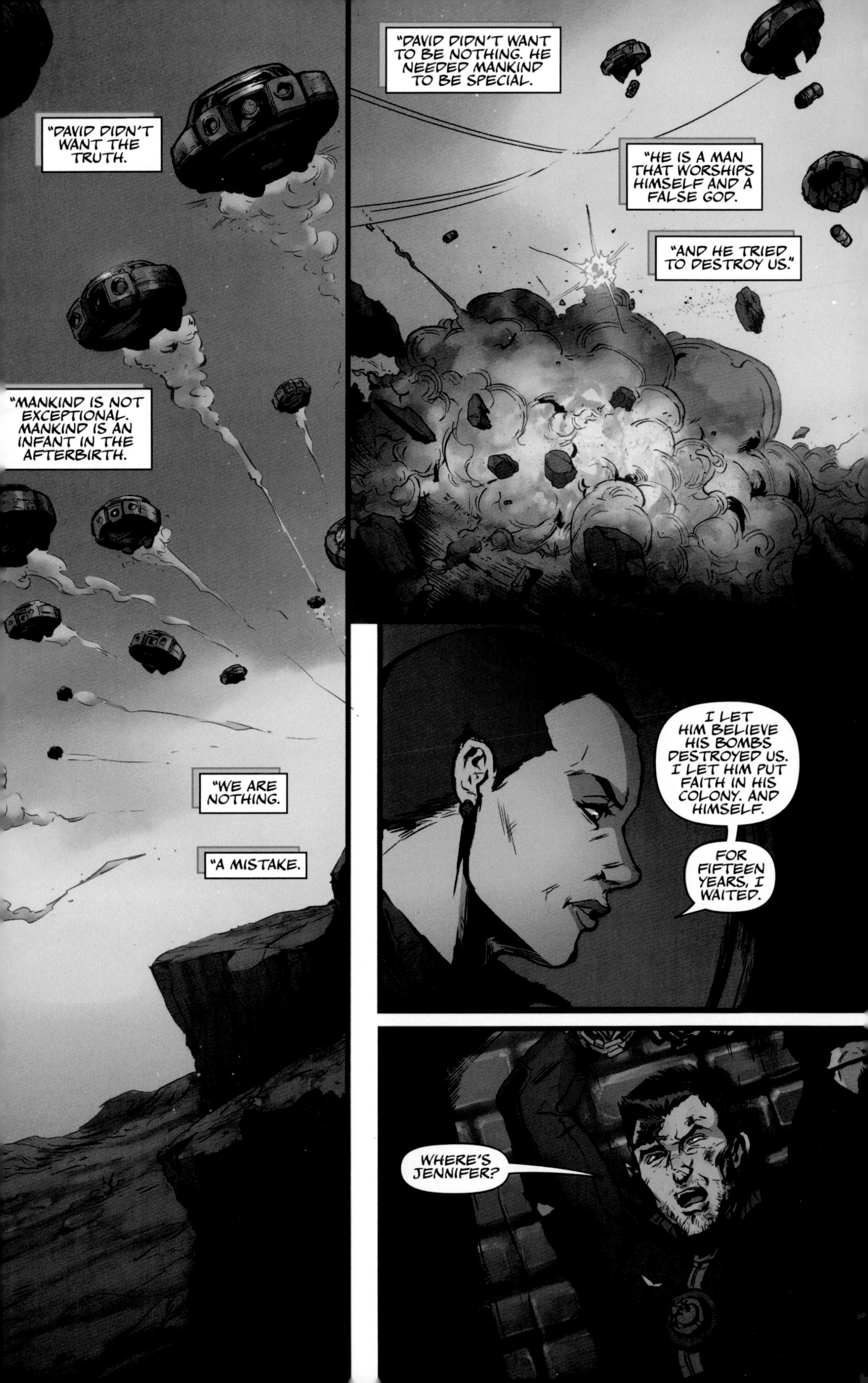
"DAVID DIDN'T WANT THE TRUTH.
"MANKIND IS NOT EXCEPTIONAL. MANKIND IS AN INFANT IN THE AFTERBIRTH.
"WE ARE NOTHING.
"A MISTAKE.
"DAVID DIDN'T WANT TO BE NOTHING. HE NEEDED MANKIND TO BE SPECIAL.
"HE IS A MAN THAT WORSHIPS HIMSELF AND A FALSE GOD.
"AND HE TRIED TO DESTROY US."
I LET HIM BELIEVE HIS BOMBS DESTROYED US. I LET HIM PUT FAITH IN HIS COLONY. AND HIMSELF.
FOR FIFTEEN YEARS, I WAITED.
WHERE'S JENNIFER?

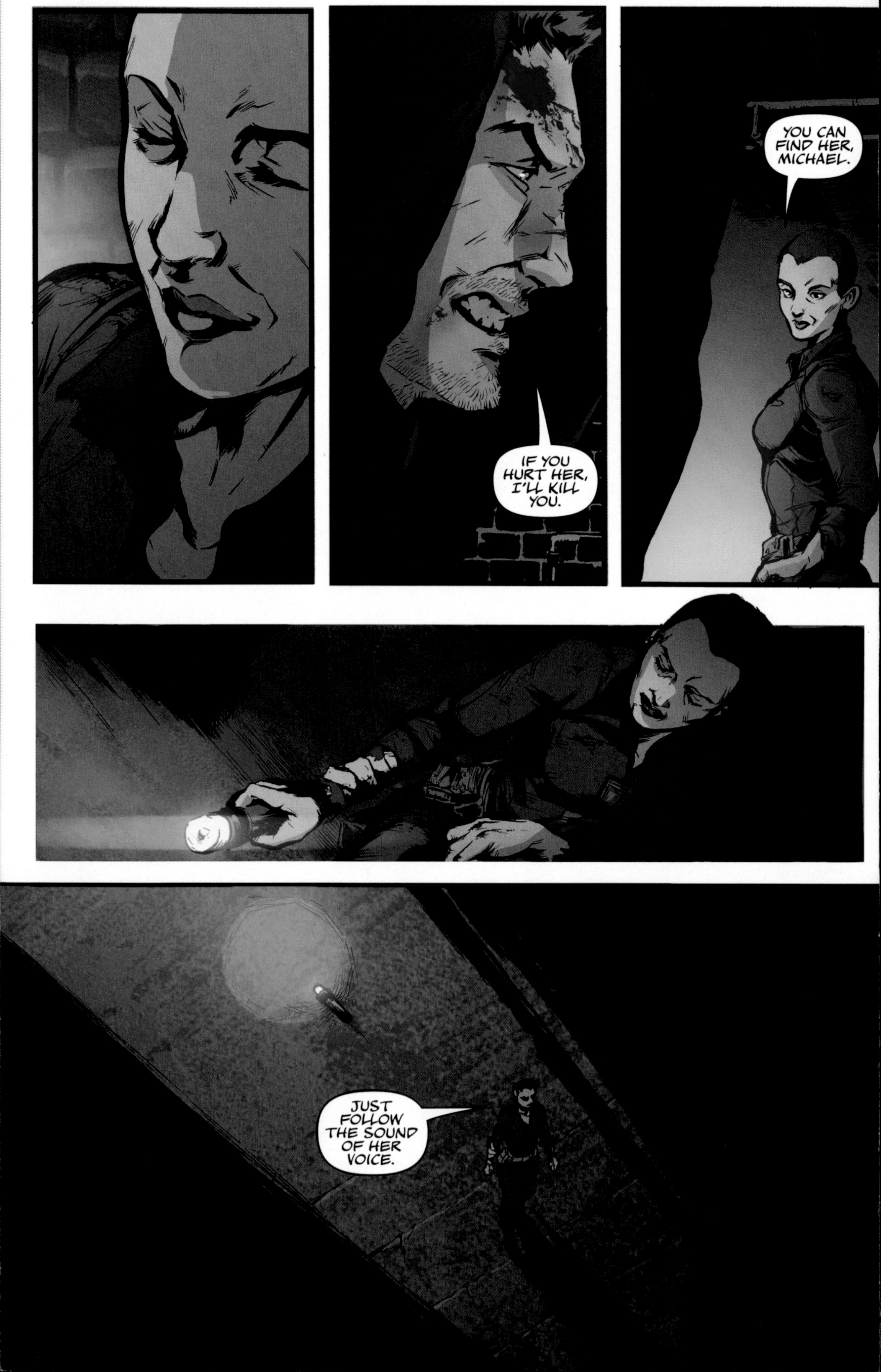
IF YOU HURT HER, I'LL KILL YOU.
YOU CAN FIND HER, MICHAEL.
JUST FOLLOW THE SOUND OF HER VOICE.

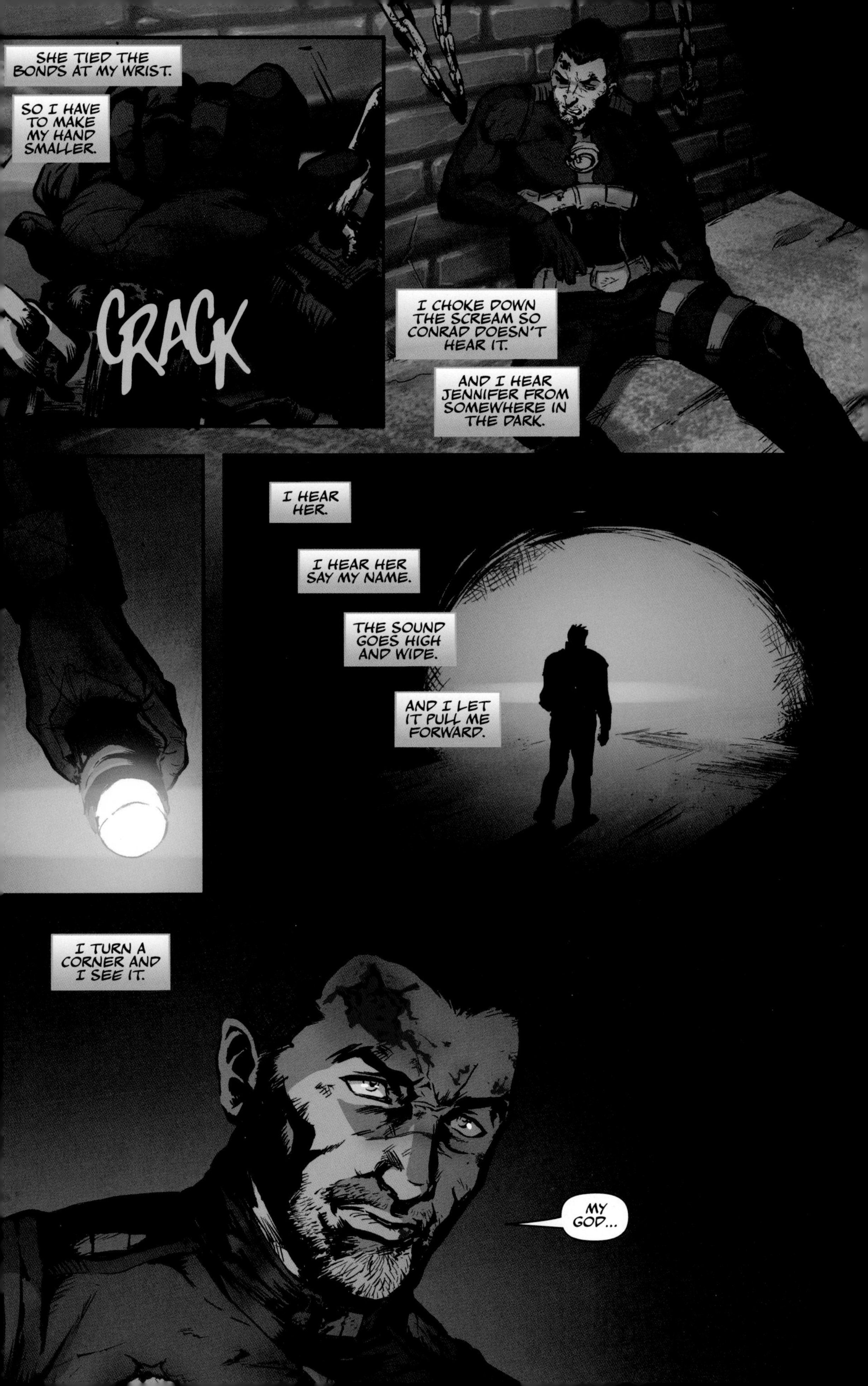
SHE TIED THE BONDS AT MY WRIST.
SO I HAVE TO MAKE MY HAND SMALLER.
CRACK
I CHOKE DOWN THE SCREAM SO CONRAD DOESN'T HEAR IT.
AND I HEAR JENNIFER FROM SOMEWHERE IN THE DARK.
I HEAR HER.
I HEAR HER SAY MY NAME.
THE SOUND GOES HIGH AND WIDE.
AND I LET IT PULL ME FORWARD.
I TURN A CORNER AND I SEE IT.
MY GOD...

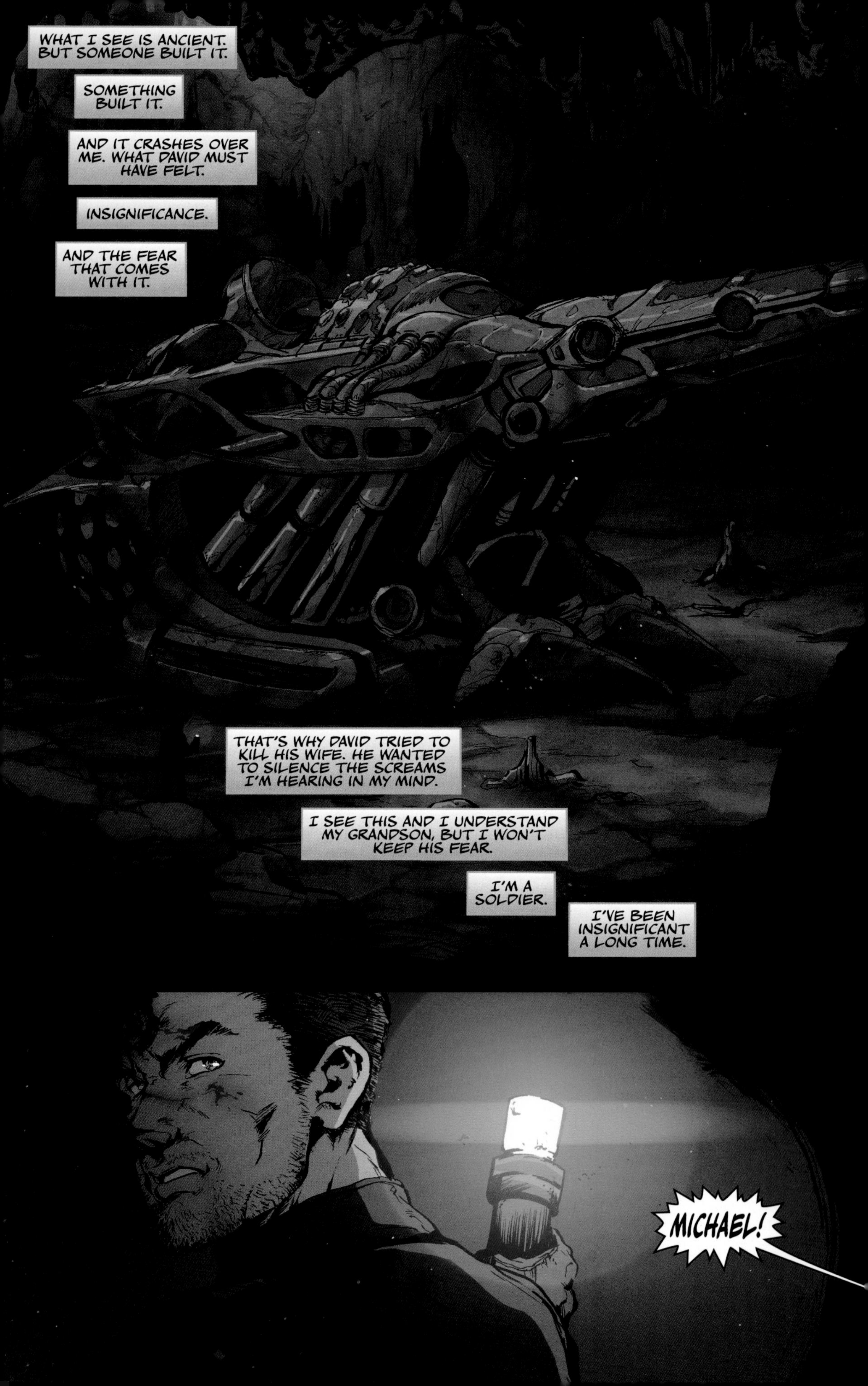
WHAT I SEE IS ANCIENT. BUT SOMEONE BUILT IT.
SOMETHING BUILT IT.
AND IT CRASHES OVER ME. WHAT DAVID MUST HAVE FELT.
INSIGNIFICANCE.
AND THE FEAR THAT COMES WITH IT.
THAT'S WHY DAVID TRIED TO KILL HIS WIFE. HE WANTED TO SILENCE THE SCREAMS I'M HEARING IN MY MIND.
I SEE THIS AND I UNDERSTAND MY GRANDSON, BUT I WON'T KEEP HIS FEAR.
I'M A SOLDIER.
I'VE BEEN INSIGNIFICANT A LONG TIME.
MICHAEL!

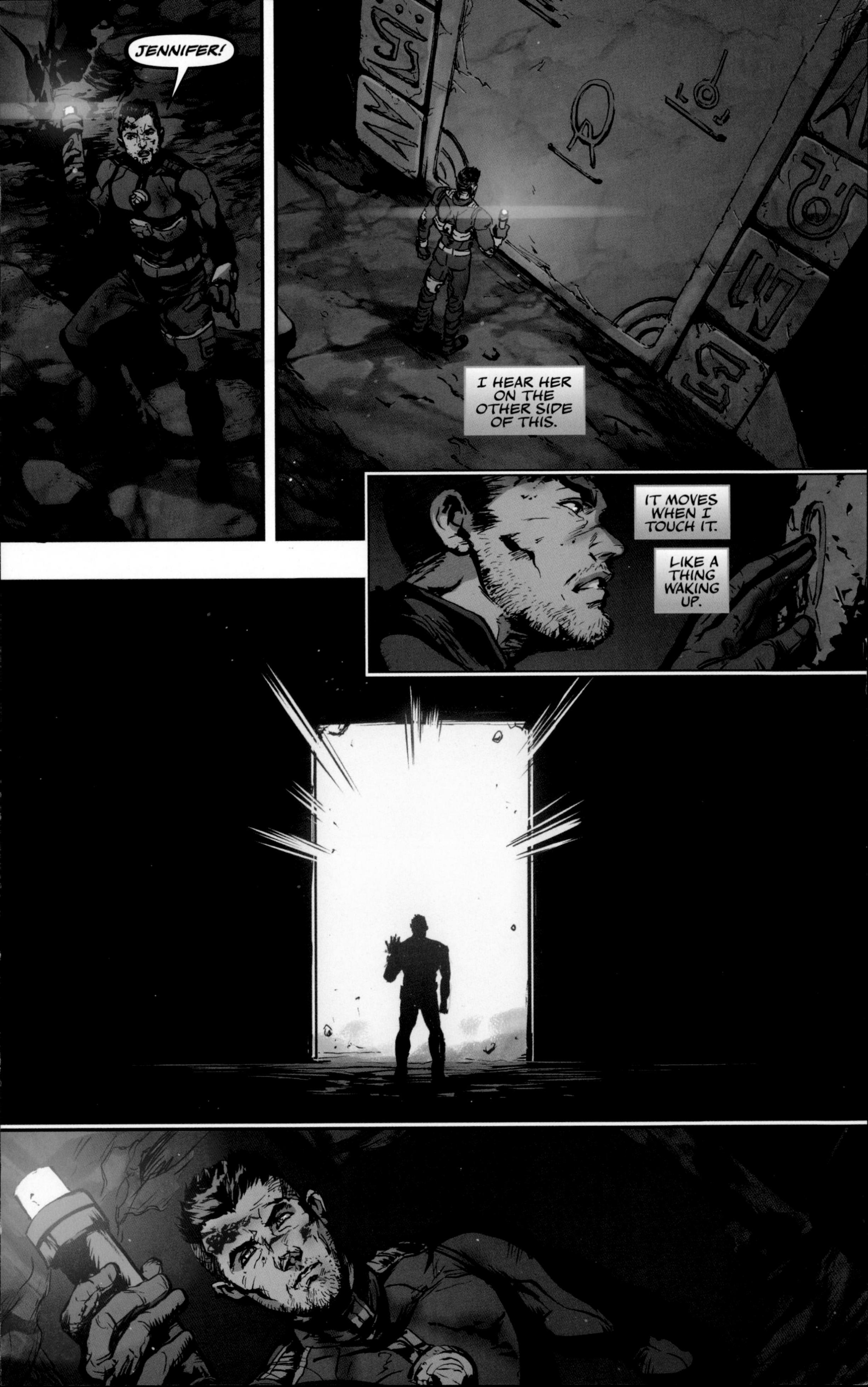
JENNIFER!
I HEAR HER ON THE OTHER SIDE OF THIS.
IT MOVES WHEN I TOUCH IT.
LIKE A THING WAKING UP.

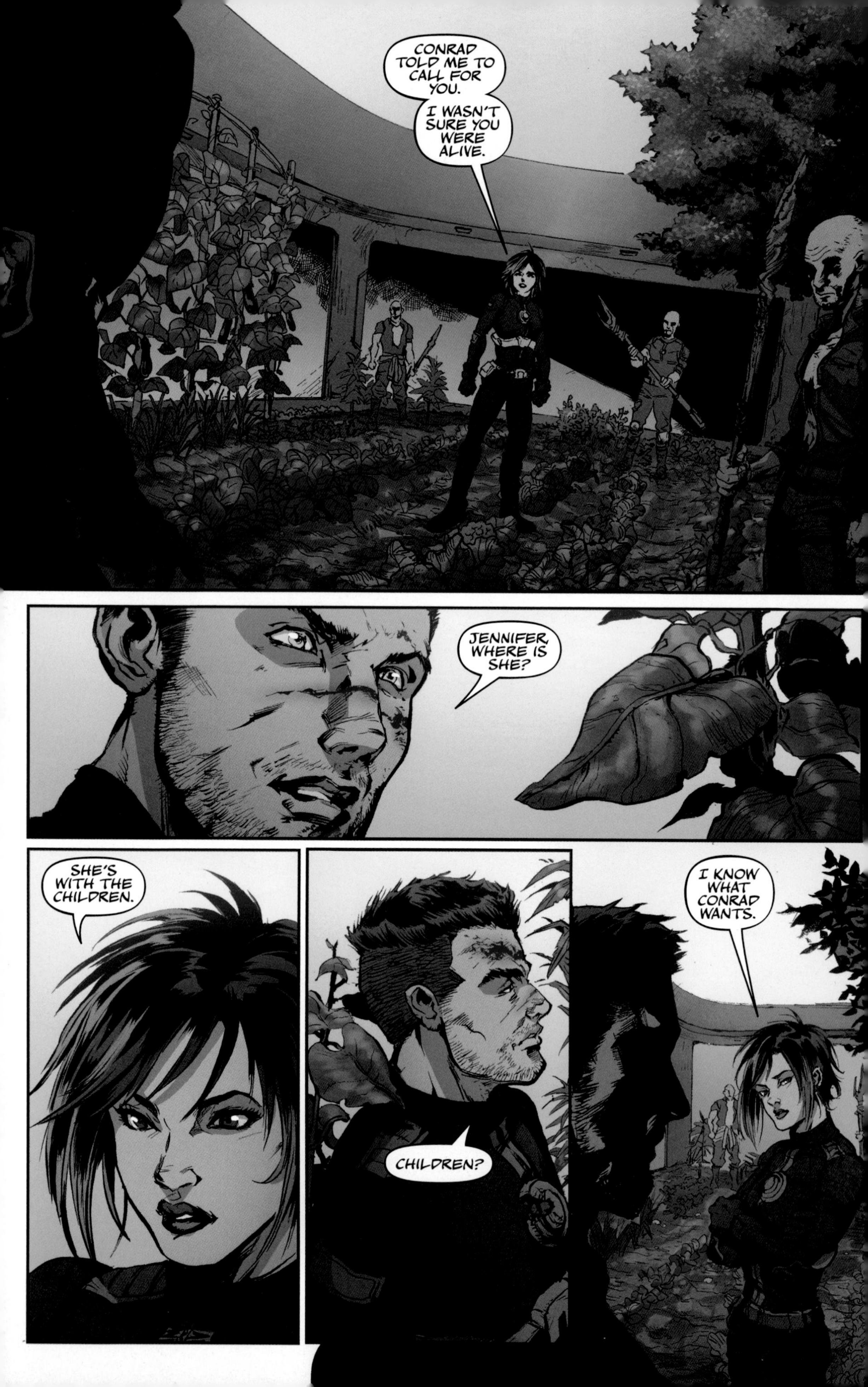
CONRAD TOLD ME TO CALL FOR YOU.
I WASN'T SURE YOU WERE ALIVE.
JENNIFER, WHERE IS SHE?
SHE'S WITH THE CHILDREN.
CHILDREN?
I KNOW WHAT CONRAD WANTS.

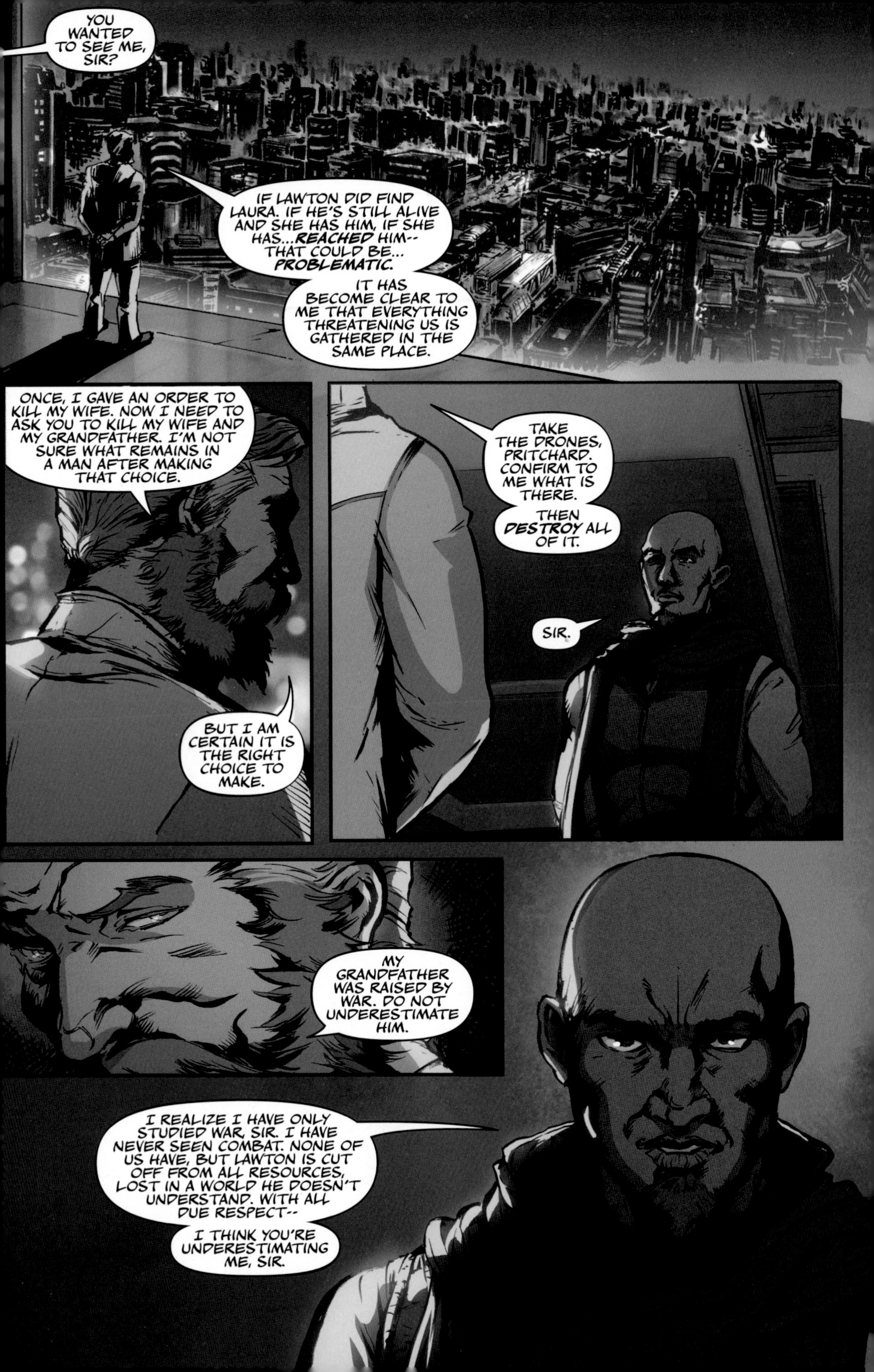
YOU WANTED TO SEE ME, SIR?
IF LAWTON DID FIND LAURA. IF HE'S STILL ALIVE AND SHE HAS HIM, IF SHE HAS...REACHED HIM-- THAT COULD BE... PROBLEMATIC.
IT HAS BECOME CLEAR TO ME THAT EVERYTHING THREATENING US IS GATHERED IN THE SAME PLACE.
ONCE, I GAVE AN ORDER TO KILL MY WIFE. NOW I NEED TO ASK YOU TO KILL MY WIFE AND MY GRANDFATHER. I'M NOT SURE WHAT REMAINS IN A MAN AFTER MAKING THAT CHOICE.
BUT I AM CERTAIN IT IS THE RIGHT CHOICE TO MAKE.
TAKE THE DRONES, PRITCHARD. CONFIRM TO ME WHAT IS THERE.
THEN DESTROY ALL OF IT.
SIR.
MY GRANDFATHER WAS RAISED BY WAR. DO NOT UNDERESTIMATE HIM.
I REALIZE I HAVE ONLY STUDIED WAR, SIR. I HAVE NEVER SEEN COMBAT. NONE OF US HAVE, BUT LAWTON IS CUT OFF FROM ALL RESOURCES, LOST IN A WORLD HE DOESN'T UNDERSTAND. WITH ALL DUE RESPECT--
I THINK YOU'RE UNDERESTIMATING ME, SIR.

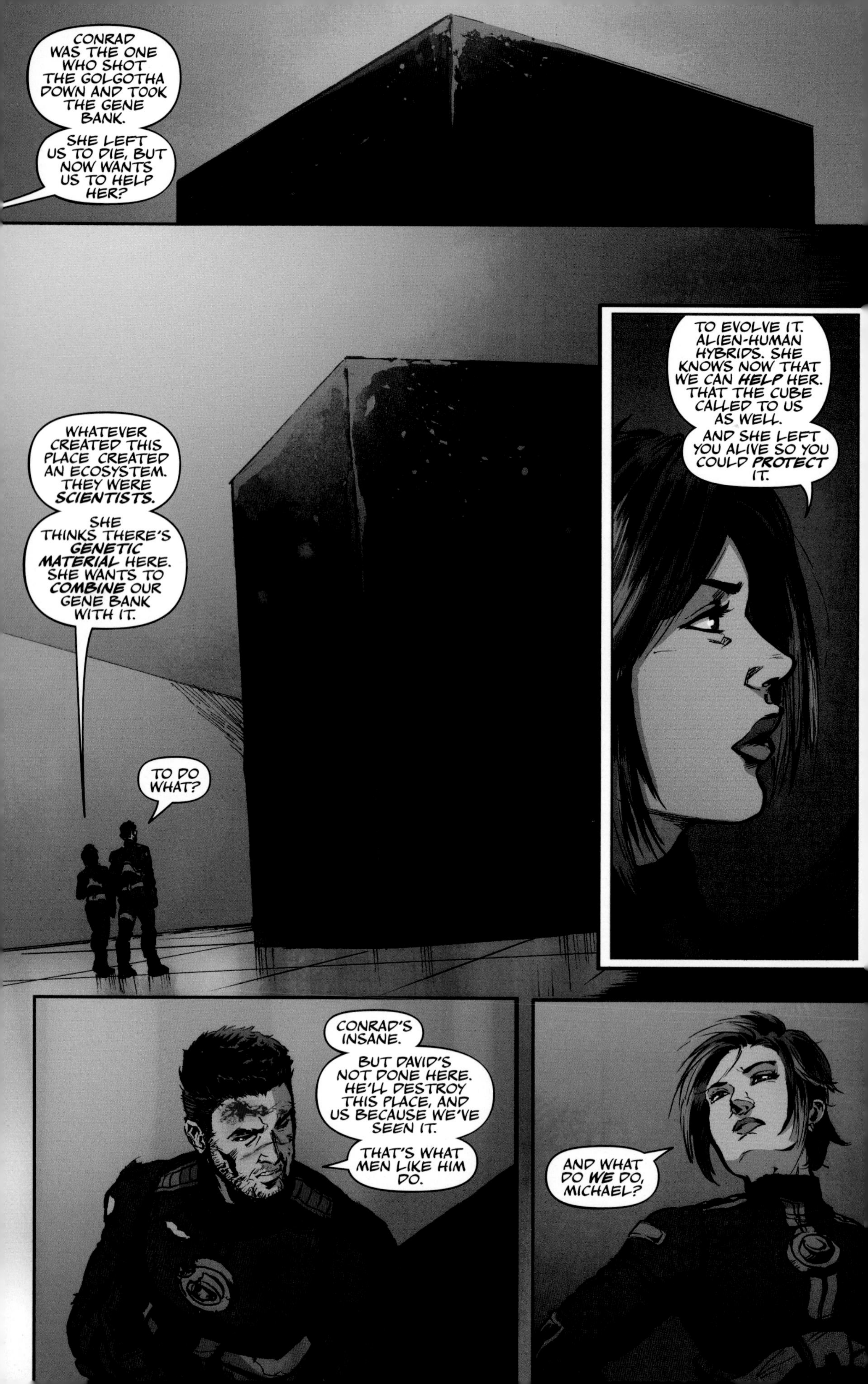
CONRAD WAS THE ONE WHO SHOT THE GOLGOTHA DOWN AND TOOK THE GENE BANK.
SHE LEFT US TO DIE, BUT NOW WANTS US TO HELP HER?
WHATEVER CREATED THIS PLACE CREATED AN ECOSYSTEM. THEY WERE SCIENTISTS.
SHE THINKS THERE'S GENETIC MATERIAL HERE. SHE WANTS TO COMBINE OUR GENE BANK WITH IT.
TO DO WHAT?
TO EVOLVE IT. ALIEN-HUMAN HYBRIDS. SHE KNOWS NOW THAT WE CAN HELP HER. THAT THE CUBE CALLED TO US AS WELL.
AND SHE LEFT YOU ALIVE SO YOU COULD PROTECT IT.
CONRAD'S INSANE.
BUT DAVID'S NOT DONE HERE. HE'LL DESTROY THIS PLACE, AND US BECAUSE WE'VE SEEN IT.
THAT'S WHAT MEN LIKE HIM DO.
AND WHAT DO WE DO, MICHAEL?

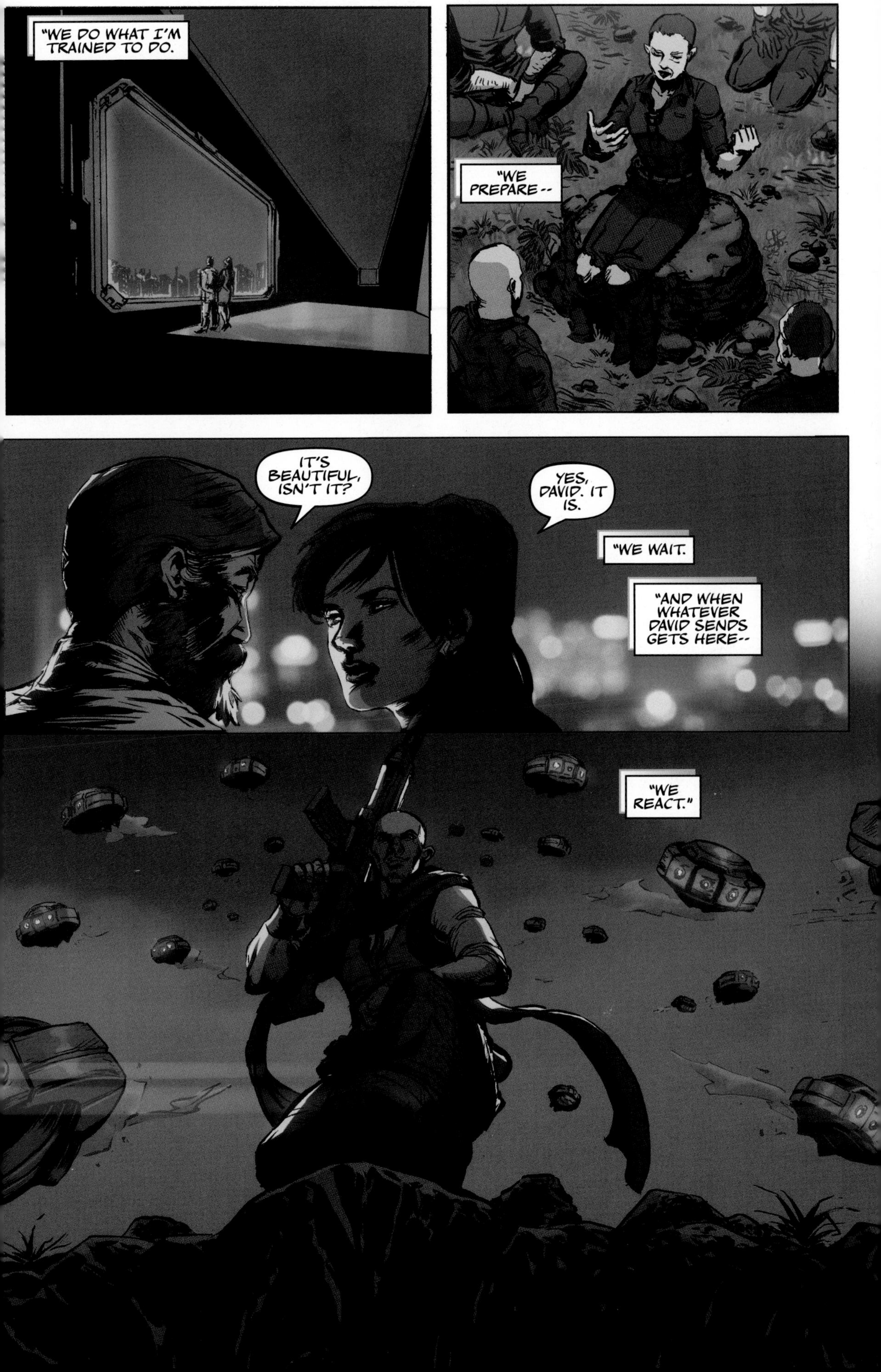
"WE DO WHAT I'M TRAINED TO DO.
"WE PREPARE--
IT'S BEAUTIFUL, ISN'T IT?
YES, DAVID. IT IS.
"WE WAIT.
"AND WHEN WHATEVER DAVID SENDS GETS HERE--
"WE REACT."

From the Journal of Laura Conrad.

" ...only in these private thoughts can I be honest, honest in the face of David's ambition and optimism. I can't help but look at this expedition and the perfection of this world, its lack of human influence and wonder do we have the right to do this? What right do we have to move off of one world and imprint our flaws upon another? Last night, David and I had an argument after I heard him preparing one of his addresses to the colony. It was patriotic, bombastic, all of the things that the people need to hear, but David believes he is entitled to all of this.

I told him that we are not Gods. It didn't find him well, but it's the truth. Mankind isn't owed the universe. It isn't even owed Earth. The goal of this colony is to promote human civilization beyond the boundaries of our born world, but what place deserves all the flaws that mankind will bring?

What has this place done to deserve us making it a home?

No, David. We are not Gods. If we don't learn that lesson on our own, the universe will teach us."

Conrad, Laura

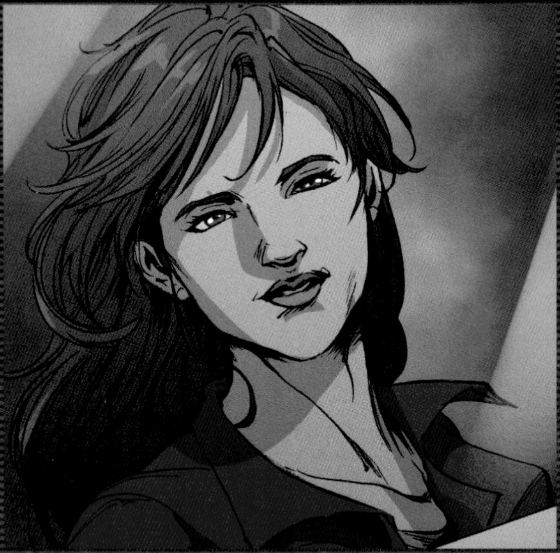

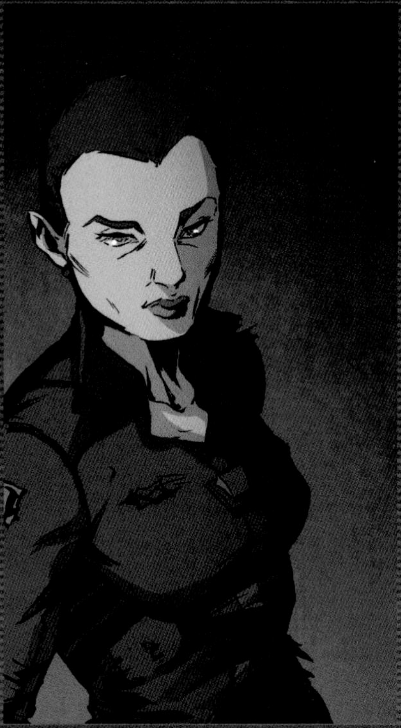

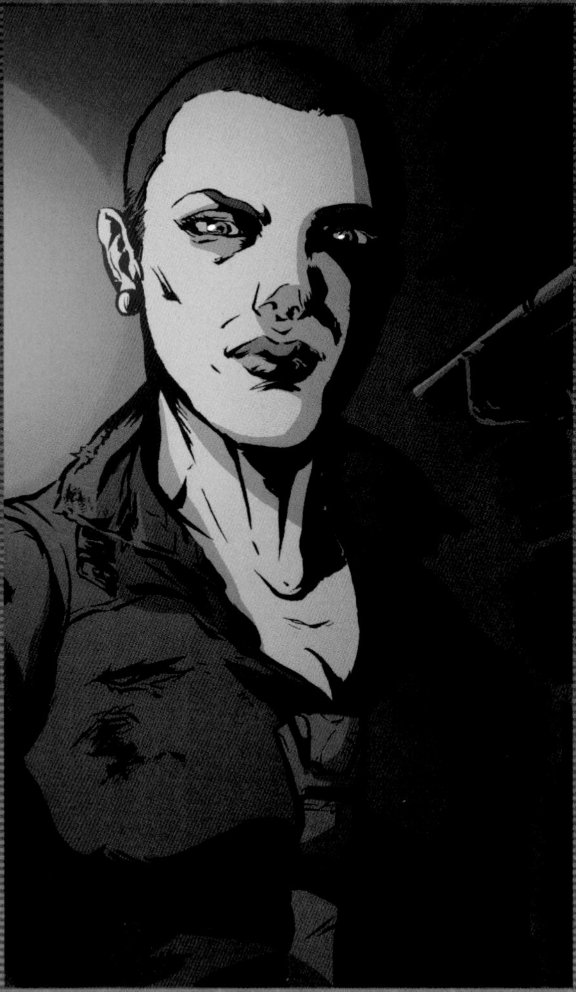

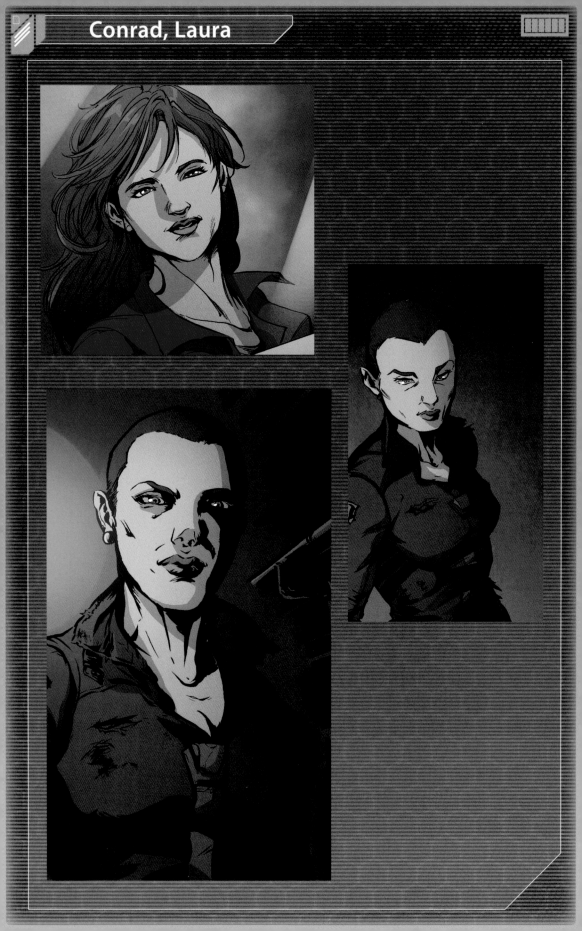

CHAPTER 4

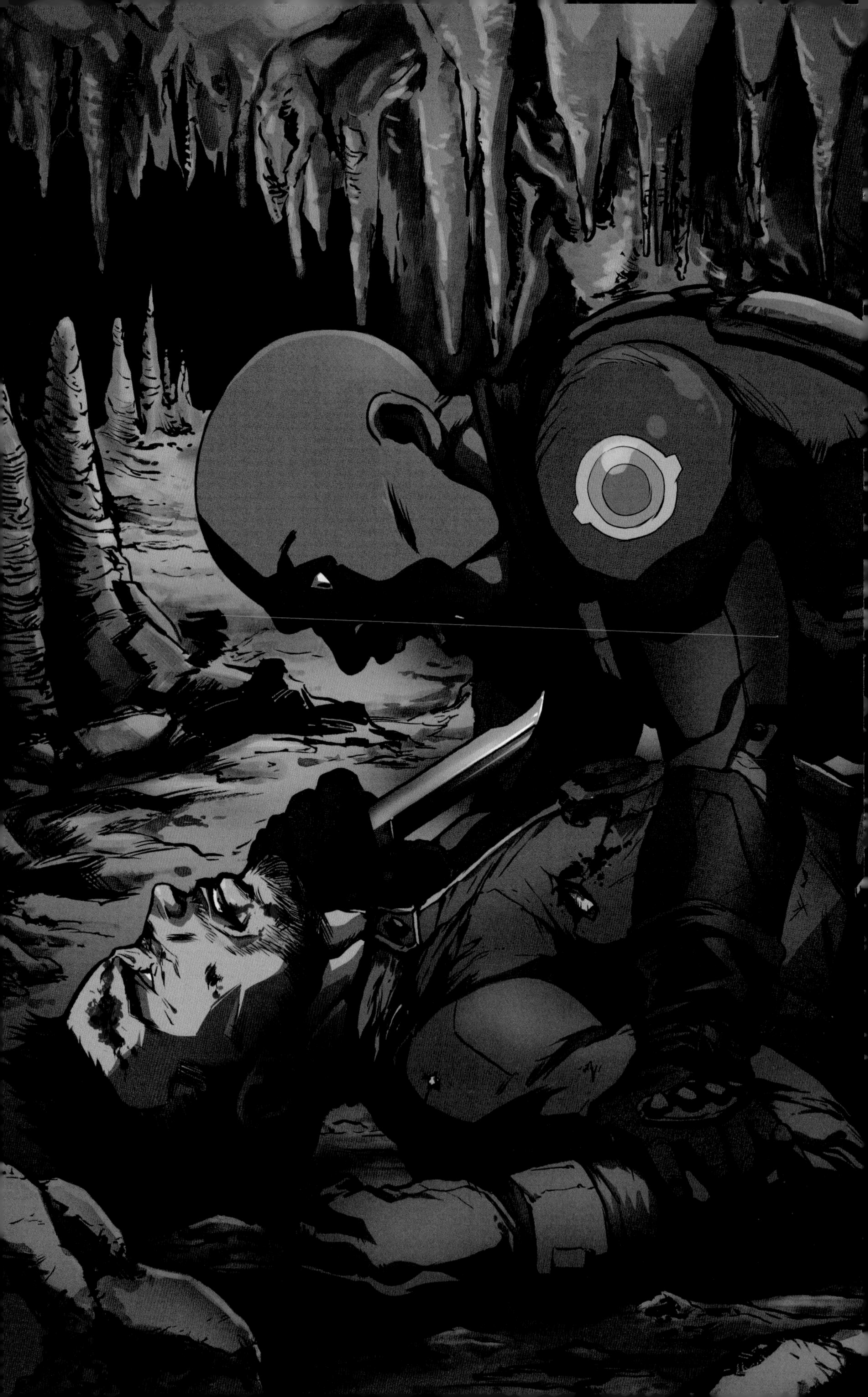

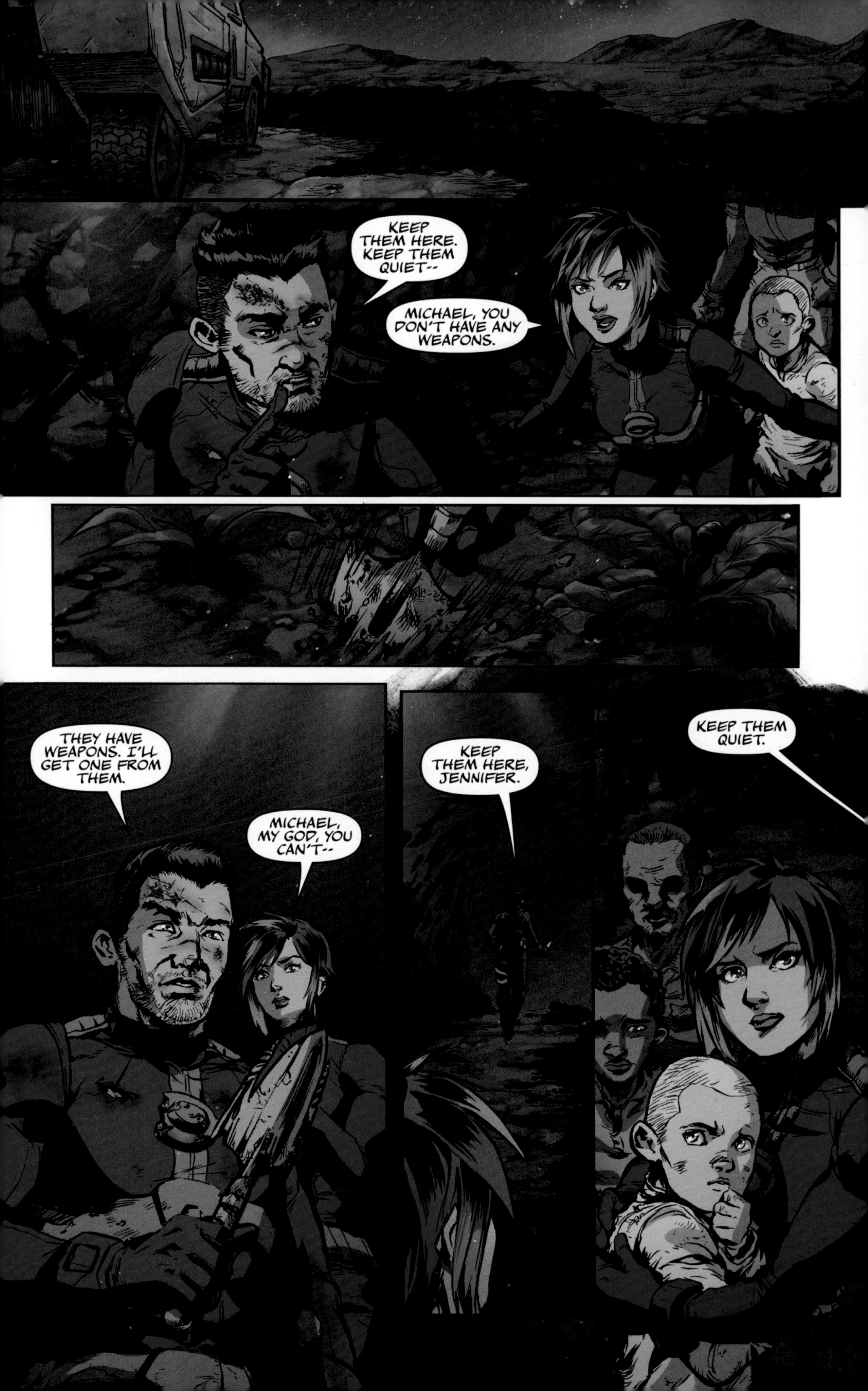
KEEP THEM HERE. KEEP THEM QUIET--
MICHAEL, YOU DON'T HAVE ANY WEAPONS.
THEY HAVE WEAPONS. I'LL GET ONE FROM THEM.
MICHAEL, MY GOD, YOU CAN'T--
KEEP THEM HERE, JENNIFER.
KEEP THEM QUIET.

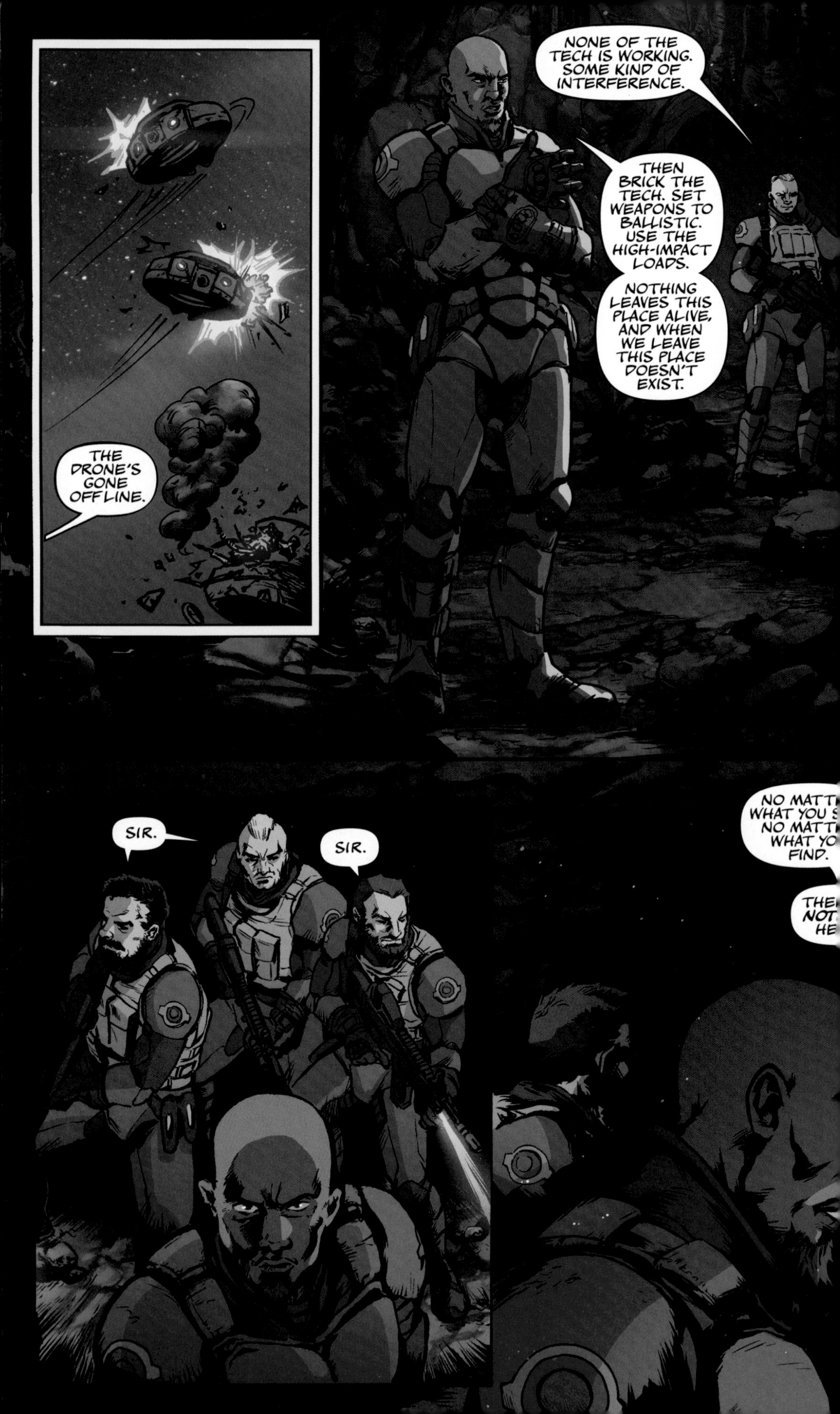
THE DRONE'S GONE OFFLINE.
NONE OF THE TECH IS WORKING. SOME KIND OF INTERFERENCE.
THEN BRICK THE TECH. SET WEAPONS TO BALLISTIC. USE THE HIGH-IMPACT LOADS.
NOTHING LEAVES THIS PLACE ALIVE, AND WHEN WE LEAVE THIS PLACE DOESN'T EXIST.
SIR.
SIR.
NO MATT WHAT YOU NO MATT WHAT YO FIND.
THE NOT HE

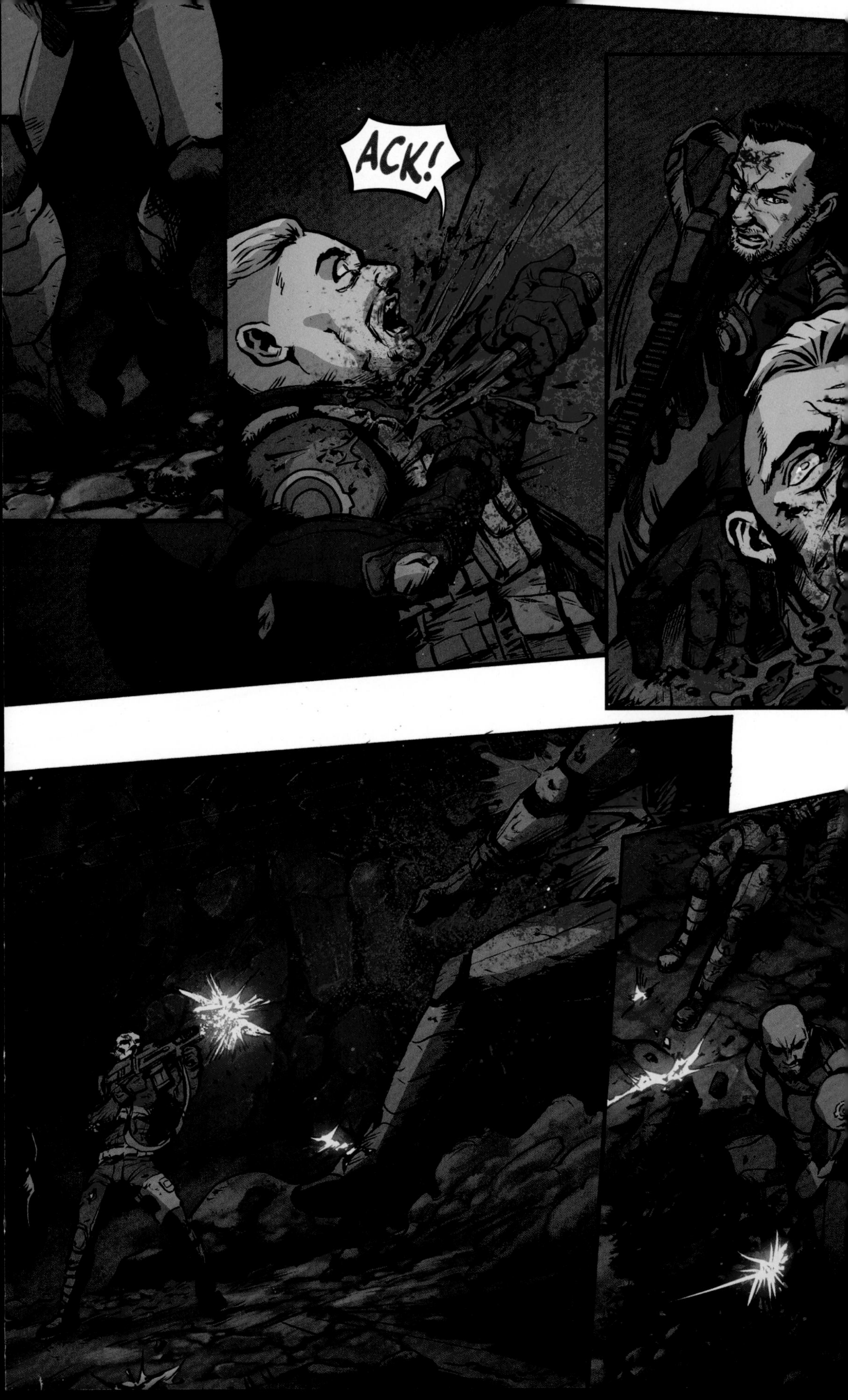
ACK!

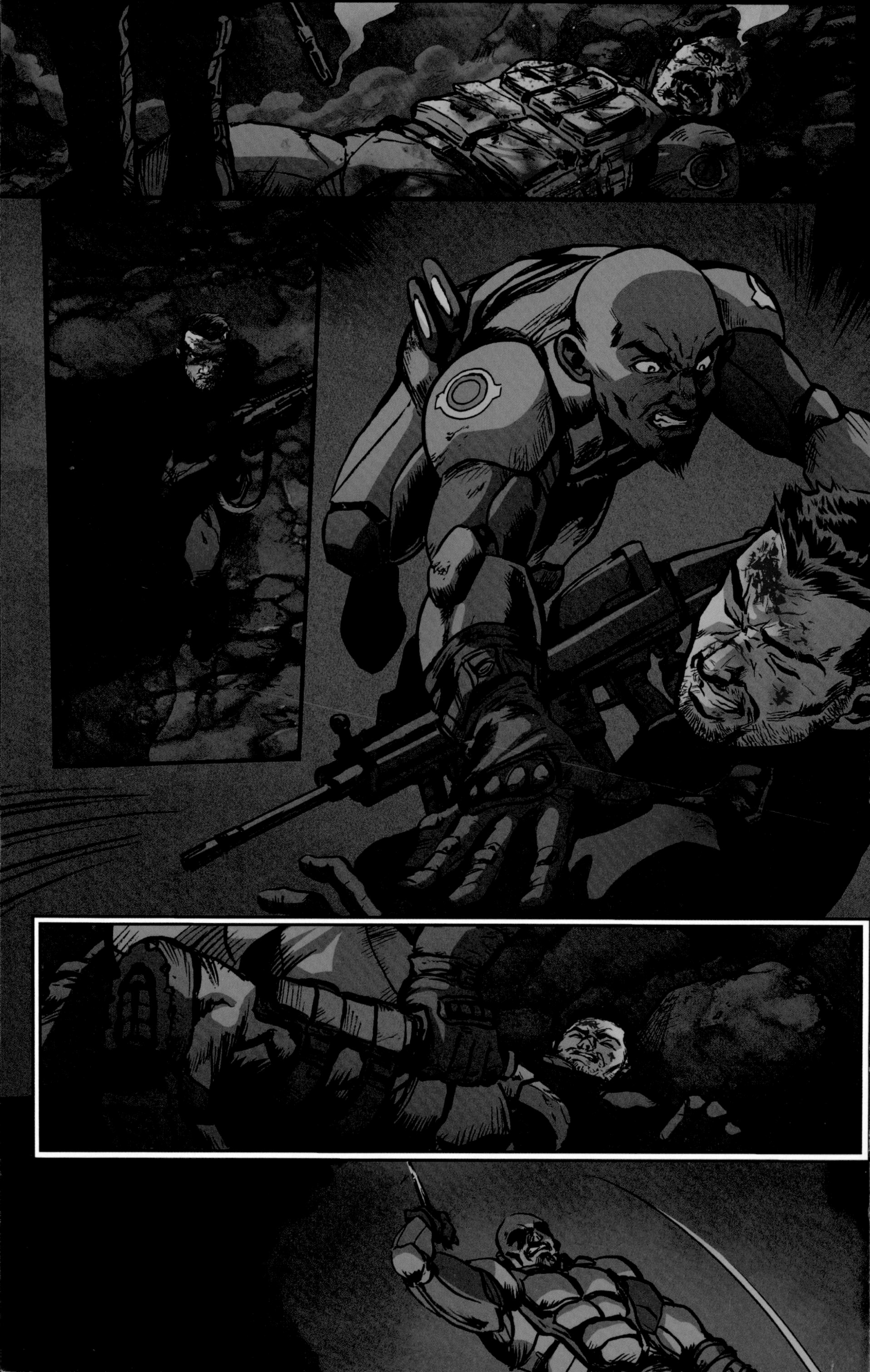

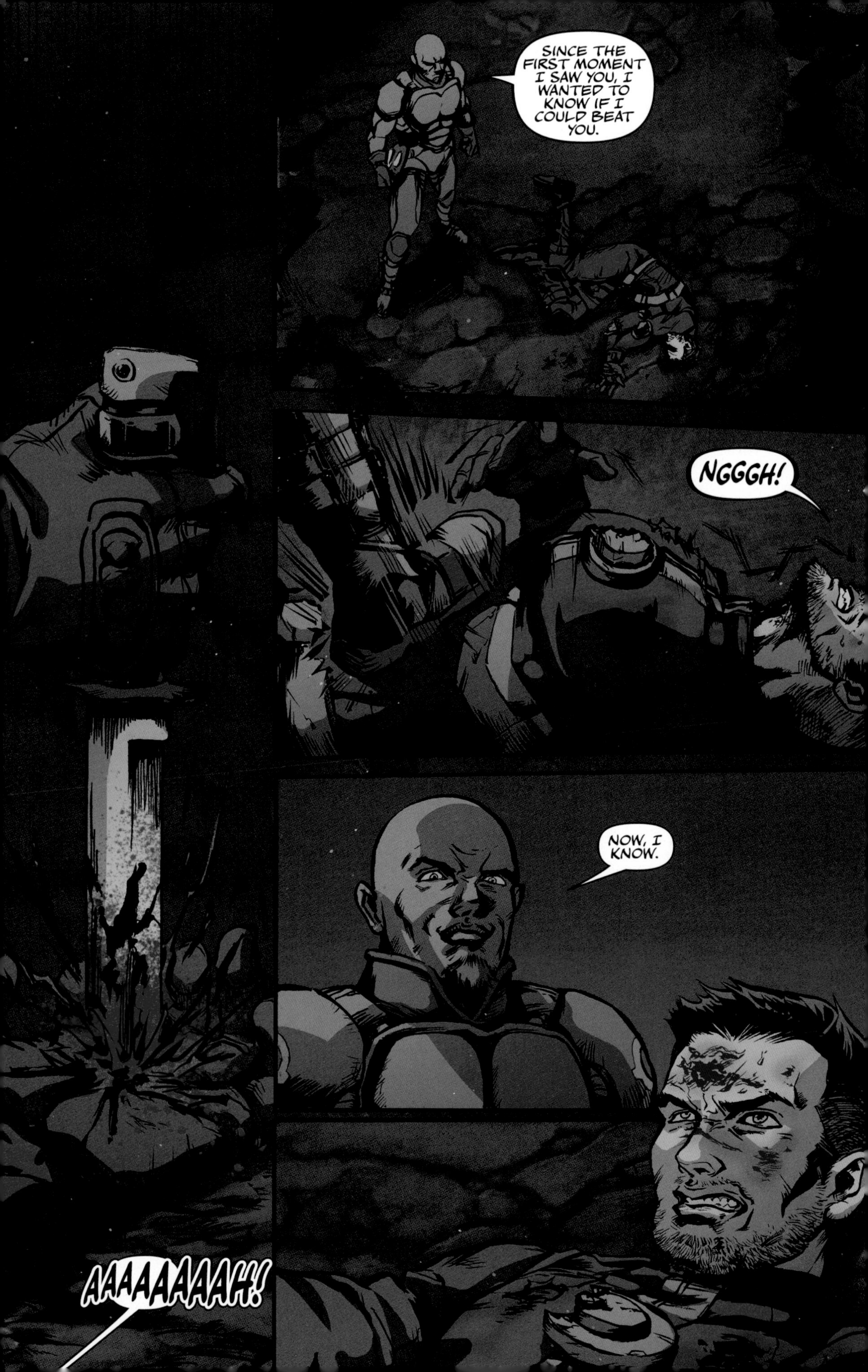
SINCE THE FIRST MOMENT I SAW YOU, I WANTED TO KNOW IF I COULD BEAT YOU.
NGGGH!
NOW, I KNOW.
AAAAAAAAH!

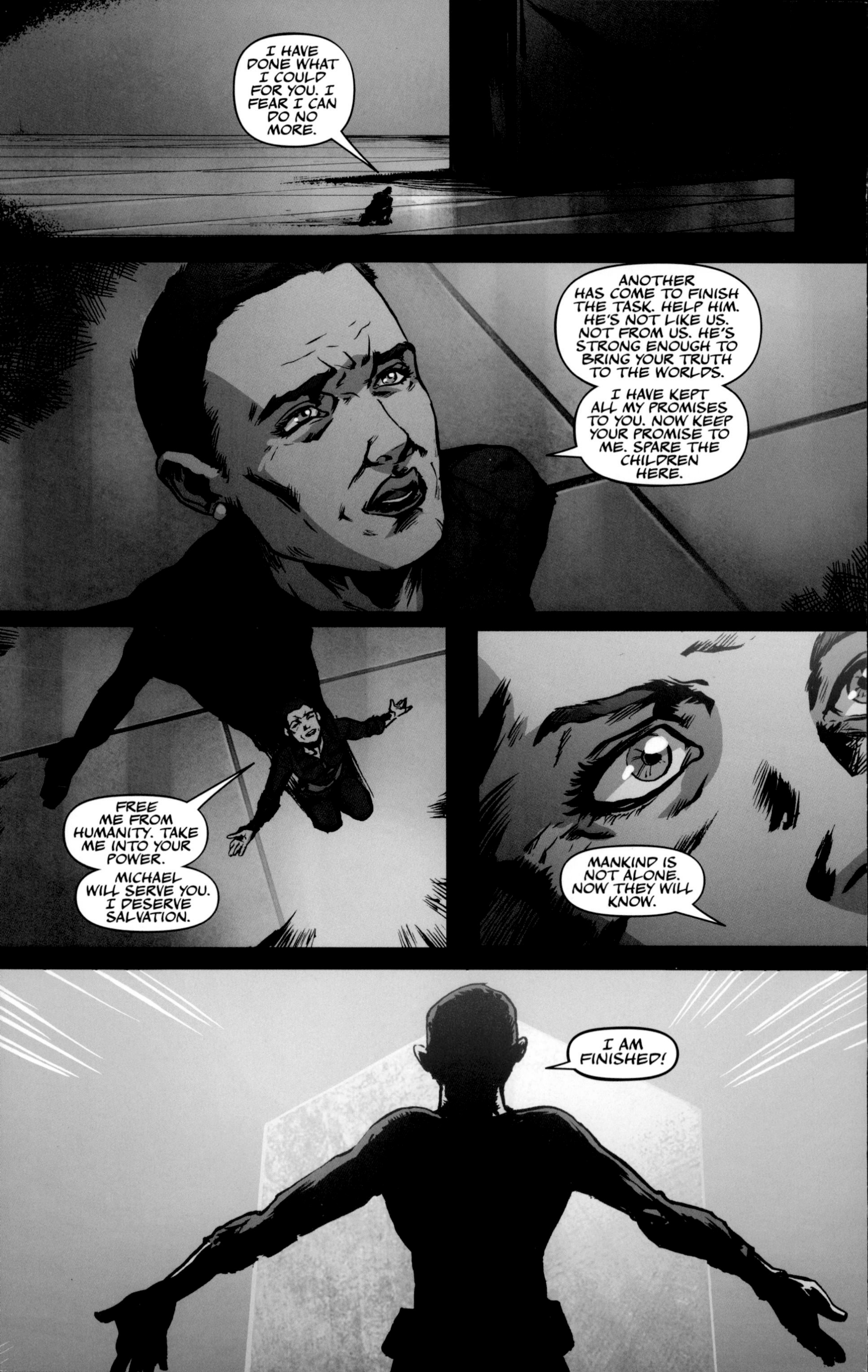
I HAVE DONE WHAT I COULD FOR YOU. I FEAR I CAN DO NO MORE.
ANOTHER HAS COME TO FINISH THE TASK. HELP HIM. HE'S NOT LIKE US. NOT FROM US. HE'S STRONG ENOUGH TO BRING YOUR TRUTH TO THE WORLDS.
I HAVE KEPT ALL MY PROMISES TO YOU. NOW KEEP YOUR PROMISE TO ME. SPARE THE CHILDREN HERE.
FREE ME FROM HUMANITY. TAKE ME INTO YOUR POWER.
MICHAEL WILL SERVE YOU. I DESERVE SALVATION.
MANKIND IS NOT ALONE. NOW THEY WILL KNOW.
I AM FINISHED!

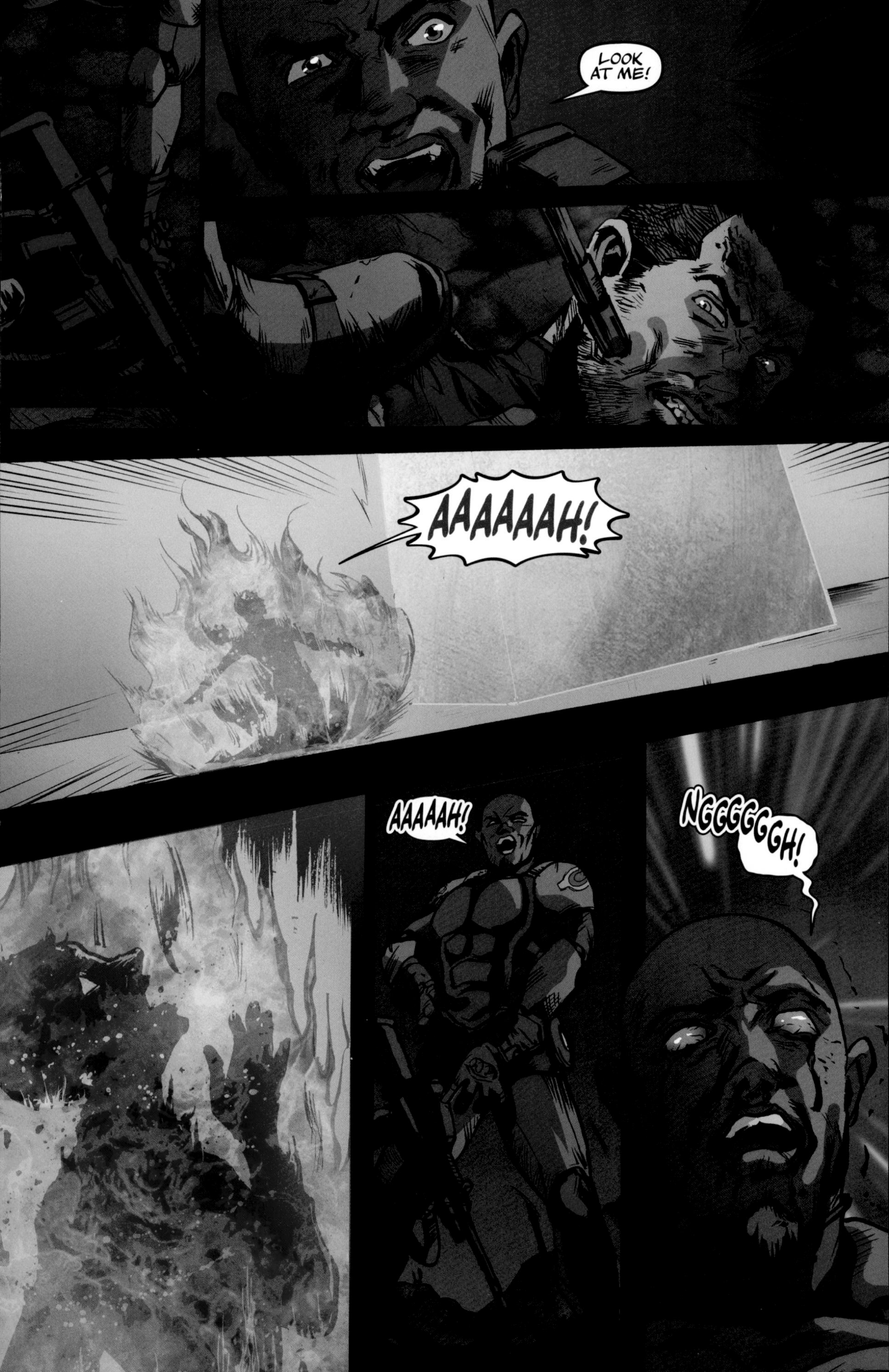
LOOK AT ME!
AAAAAAH!
AAAAAH!
NGGGGGGH!

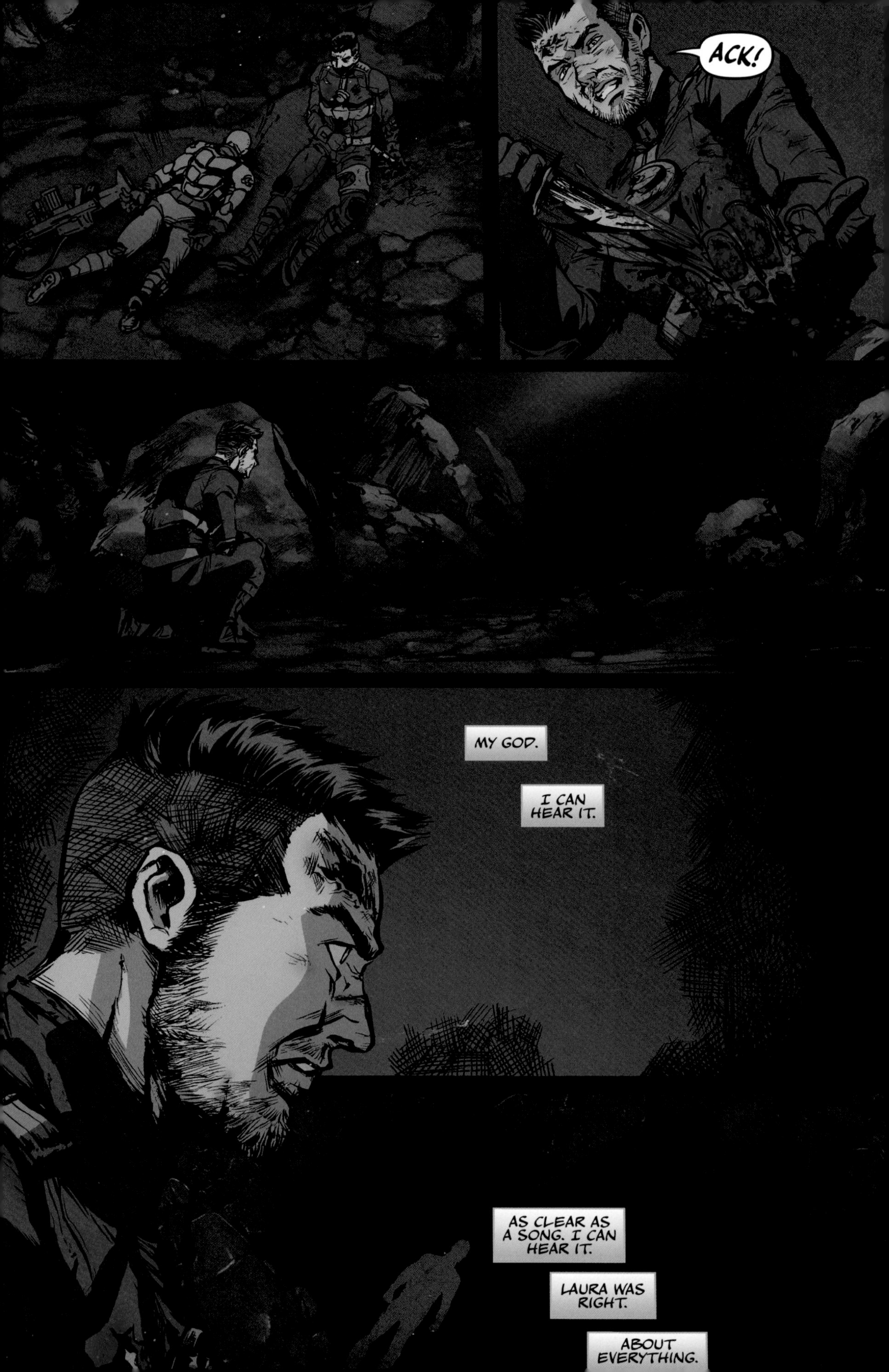
ACK!
MY GOD.
I CAN HEAR IT.
AS CLEAR AS A SONG. I CAN HEAR IT.
LAURA WAS RIGHT.
ABOUT EVERYTHING.

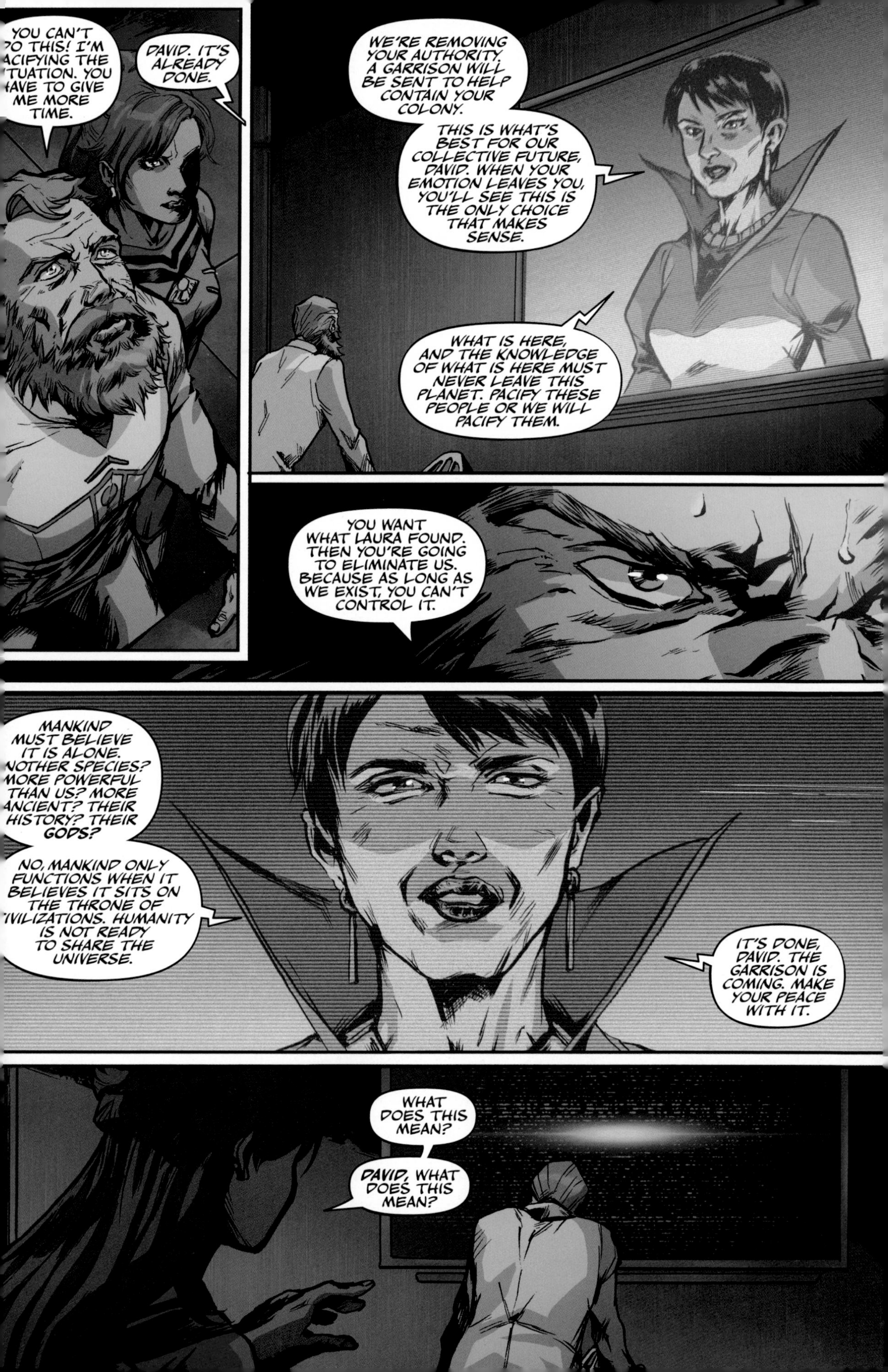
YOU CAN'T DO THIS! I'M PACIFYING THE SITUATION. YOU HAVE TO GIVE ME MORE TIME.
DAVID. IT'S ALREADY DONE.
WE'RE REMOVING YOUR AUTHORITY. A GARRISON WILL BE SENT TO HELP CONTAIN YOUR COLONY.
THIS IS WHAT'S BEST FOR OUR COLLECTIVE FUTURE, DAVID. WHEN YOUR EMOTION LEAVES YOU, YOU'LL SEE THIS IS THE ONLY CHOICE THAT MAKES SENSE.
WHAT IS HERE, AND THE KNOWLEDGE OF WHAT IS HERE MUST NEVER LEAVE THIS PLANET. PACIFY THESE PEOPLE OR WE WILL PACIFY THEM.
YOU WANT WHAT LAURA FOUND. THEN YOU'RE GOING TO ELIMINATE US. BECAUSE AS LONG AS WE EXIST, YOU CAN'T CONTROL IT.
MANKIND MUST BELIEVE IT IS ALONE. ANOTHER SPECIES? MORE POWERFUL THAN US? MORE ANCIENT? THEIR HISTORY? THEIR **GODS?**
NO, MANKIND ONLY FUNCTIONS WHEN IT BELIEVES IT SITS ON THE THRONE OF CIVILIZATIONS. HUMANITY IS NOT READY TO SHARE THE UNIVERSE.
IT'S DONE, DAVID. THE GARRISON IS COMING. MAKE YOUR PEACE WITH IT.
WHAT DOES THIS MEAN?
DAVID, WHAT DOES THIS MEAN?

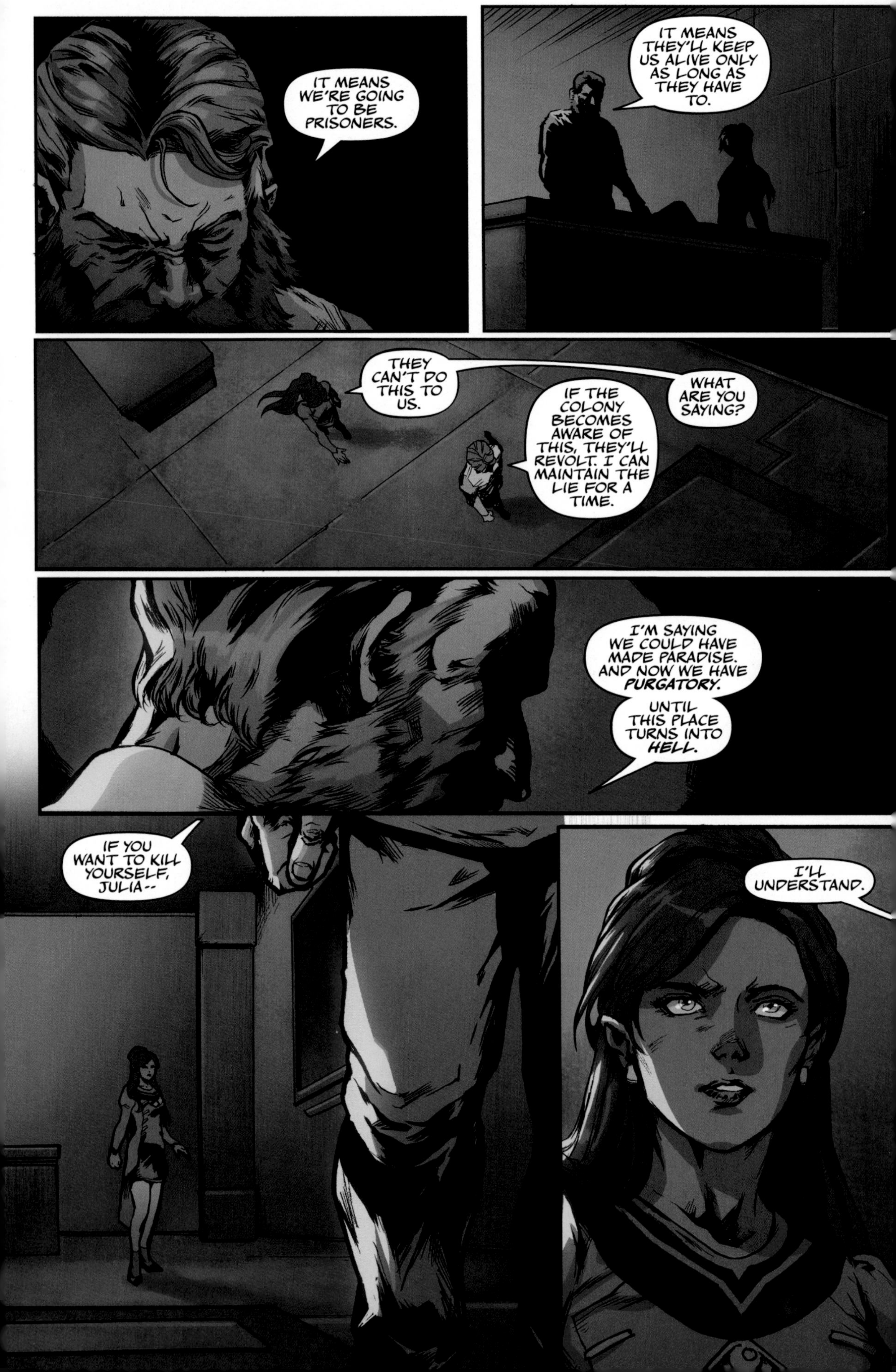
IT MEANS WE'RE GOING TO BE PRISONERS.
IT MEANS THEY'LL KEEP US ALIVE ONLY AS LONG AS THEY HAVE TO.
THEY CAN'T DO THIS TO US.
WHAT ARE YOU SAYING?
IF THE COLONY BECOMES AWARE OF THIS, THEY'LL REVOLT. I CAN MAINTAIN THE LIE FOR A TIME.
I'M SAYING WE COULD HAVE MADE PARADISE. AND NOW WE HAVE PURGATORY.
UNTIL THIS PLACE TURNS INTO HELL.
IF YOU WANT TO KILL YOURSELF, JULIA--
I'LL UNDERSTAND.

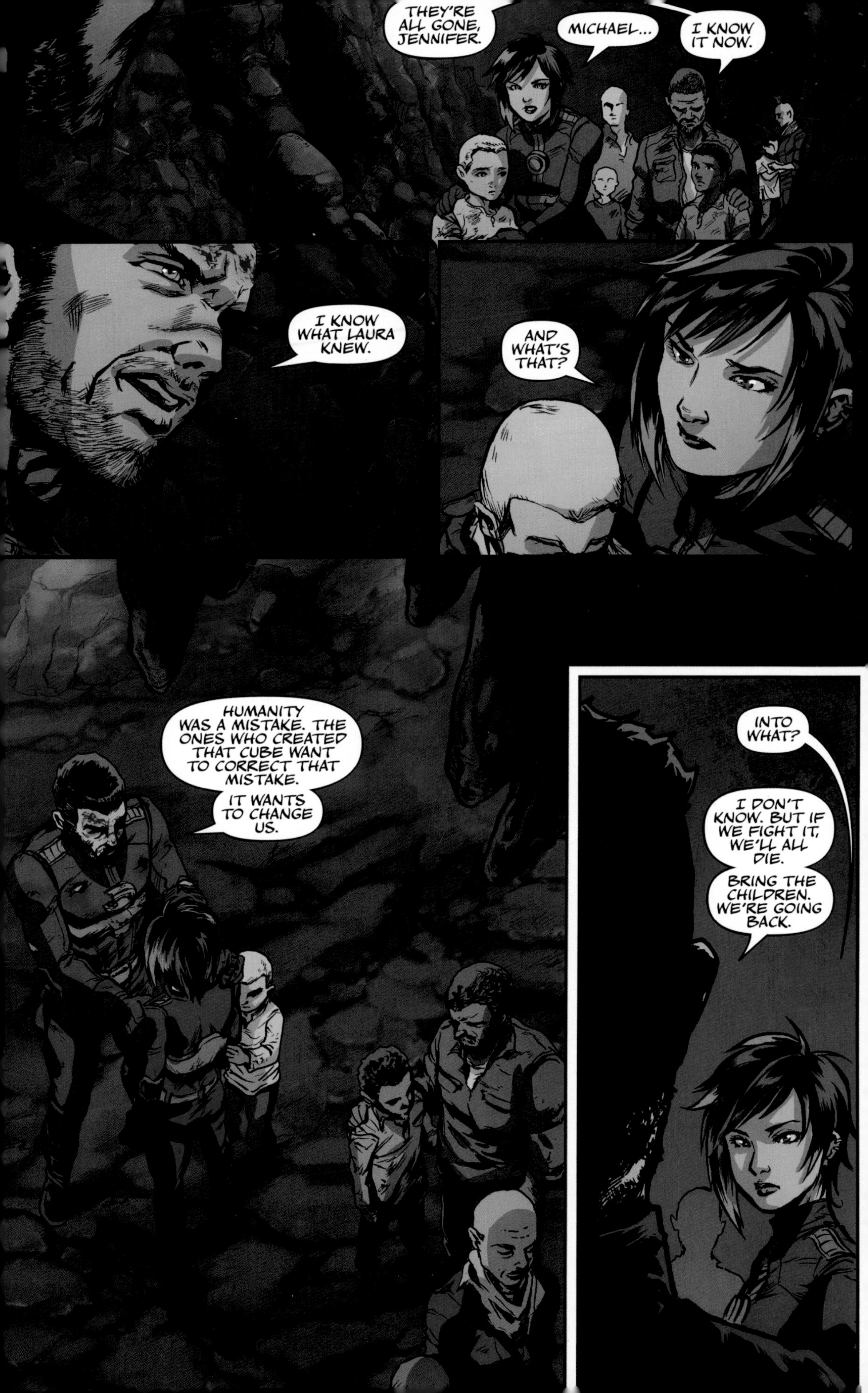
THEY'RE ALL GONE, JENNIFER.
MICHAEL...
I KNOW IT NOW.
I KNOW WHAT LAURA KNEW.
AND WHAT'S THAT?
HUMANITY WAS A MISTAKE. THE ONES WHO CREATED THAT CUBE WANT TO CORRECT THAT MISTAKE.
IT WANTS TO CHANGE US.
INTO WHAT?
I DON'T KNOW. BUT IF WE FIGHT IT, WE'LL ALL DIE.
BRING THE CHILDREN. WE'RE GOING BACK.

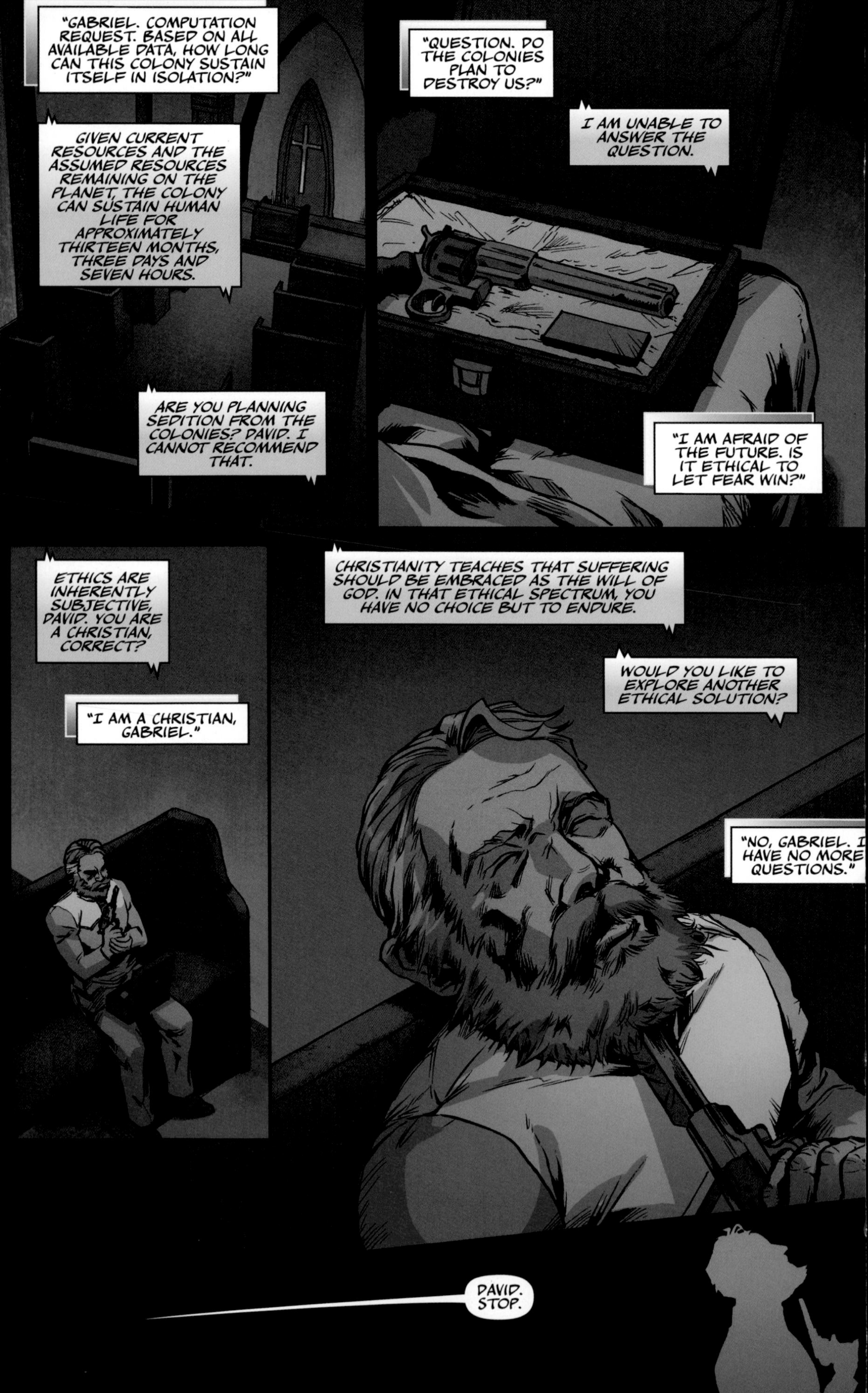
"GABRIEL. COMPUTATION REQUEST. BASED ON ALL AVAILABLE DATA, HOW LONG CAN THIS COLONY SUSTAIN ITSELF IN ISOLATION?"
GIVEN CURRENT RESOURCES AND THE ASSUMED RESOURCES REMAINING ON THE PLANET, THE COLONY CAN SUSTAIN HUMAN LIFE FOR APPROXIMATELY THIRTEEN MONTHS, THREE DAYS AND SEVEN HOURS.
ARE YOU PLANNING SEDITION FROM THE COLONIES? DAVID. I CANNOT RECOMMEND THAT.
"QUESTION. DO THE COLONIES PLAN TO DESTROY US?"
I AM UNABLE TO ANSWER THE QUESTION.
"I AM AFRAID OF THE FUTURE. IS IT ETHICAL TO LET FEAR WIN?"
ETHICS ARE INHERENTLY SUBJECTIVE, DAVID. YOU ARE A CHRISTIAN, CORRECT?
"I AM A CHRISTIAN, GABRIEL."
CHRISTIANITY TEACHES THAT SUFFERING SHOULD BE EMBRACED AS THE WILL OF GOD. IN THAT ETHICAL SPECTRUM, YOU HAVE NO CHOICE BUT TO ENDURE.
WOULD YOU LIKE TO EXPLORE ANOTHER ETHICAL SOLUTION?
"NO, GABRIEL. I HAVE NO MORE QUESTIONS."
DAVID. STOP.

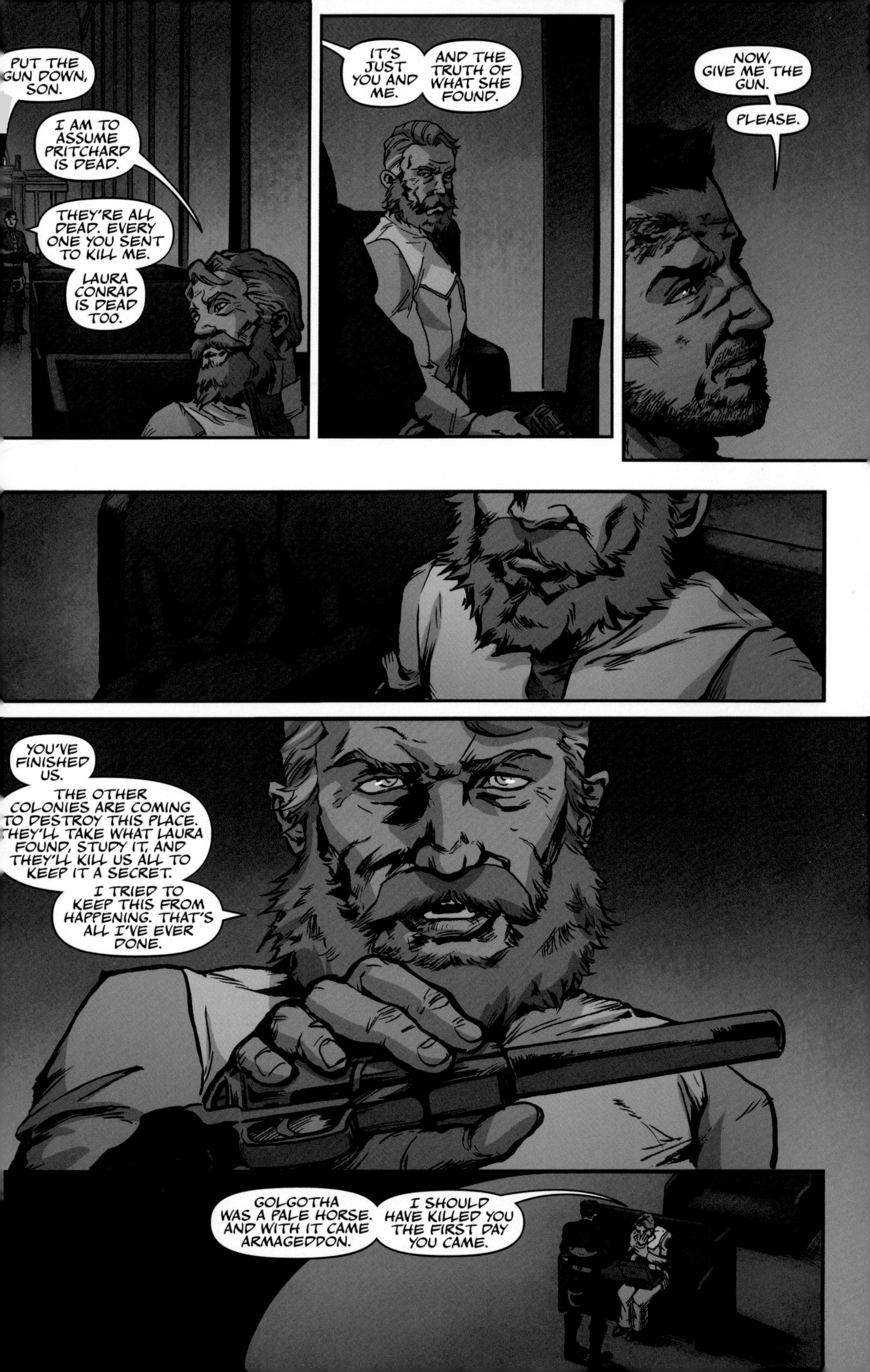
PUT THE GUN DOWN, SON.
I AM TO ASSUME PRITCHARD IS DEAD.
THEY'RE ALL DEAD. EVERY ONE YOU SENT TO KILL ME.
LAURA CONRAD IS DEAD TOO.
IT'S JUST YOU AND ME.
AND THE TRUTH OF WHAT SHE FOUND.
NOW, GIVE ME THE GUN.
PLEASE.
YOU'VE FINISHED US.
THE OTHER COLONIES ARE COMING TO DESTROY THIS PLACE. THEY'LL TAKE WHAT LAURA FOUND, STUDY IT, AND THEY'LL KILL US ALL TO KEEP IT A SECRET.
I TRIED TO KEEP THIS FROM HAPPENING. THAT'S ALL I'VE EVER DONE.
GOLGOTHA WAS A PALE HORSE. AND WITH IT CAME ARMAGEDDON.
I SHOULD HAVE KILLED YOU THE FIRST DAY YOU CAME.

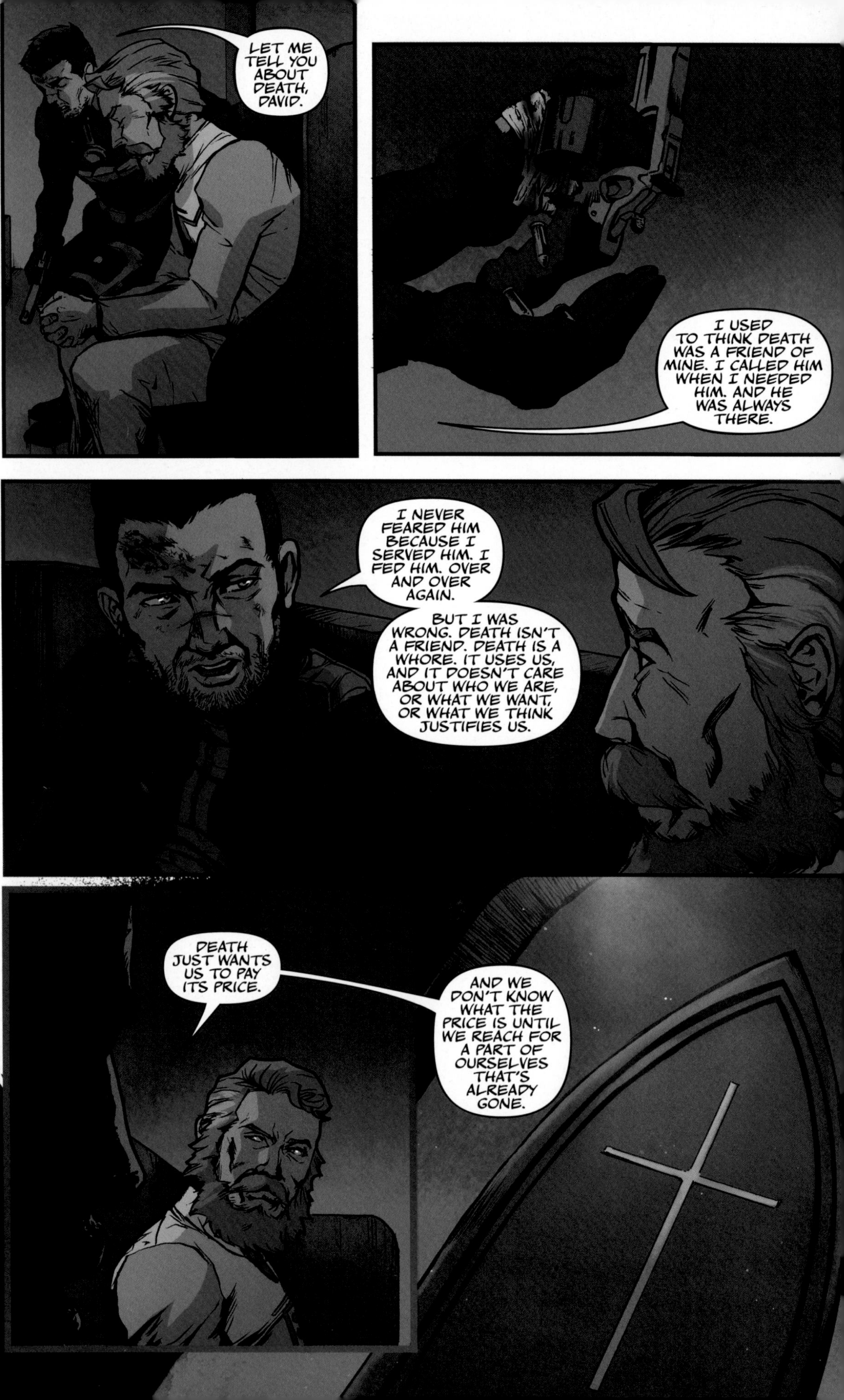
LET ME TELL YOU ABOUT DEATH, DAVID.
I USED TO THINK DEATH WAS A FRIEND OF MINE. I CALLED HIM WHEN I NEEDED HIM. AND HE WAS ALWAYS THERE.
I NEVER FEARED HIM BECAUSE I SERVED HIM. I FED HIM. OVER AND OVER AGAIN.
BUT I WAS WRONG. DEATH ISN'T A FRIEND. DEATH IS A WHORE. IT USES US, AND IT DOESN'T CARE ABOUT WHO WE ARE, OR WHAT WE WANT, OR WHAT WE THINK JUSTIFIES US.
DEATH JUST WANTS US TO PAY ITS PRICE.
AND WE DON'T KNOW WHAT THE PRICE IS UNTIL WE REACH FOR A PART OF OURSELVES THAT'S ALREADY GONE.

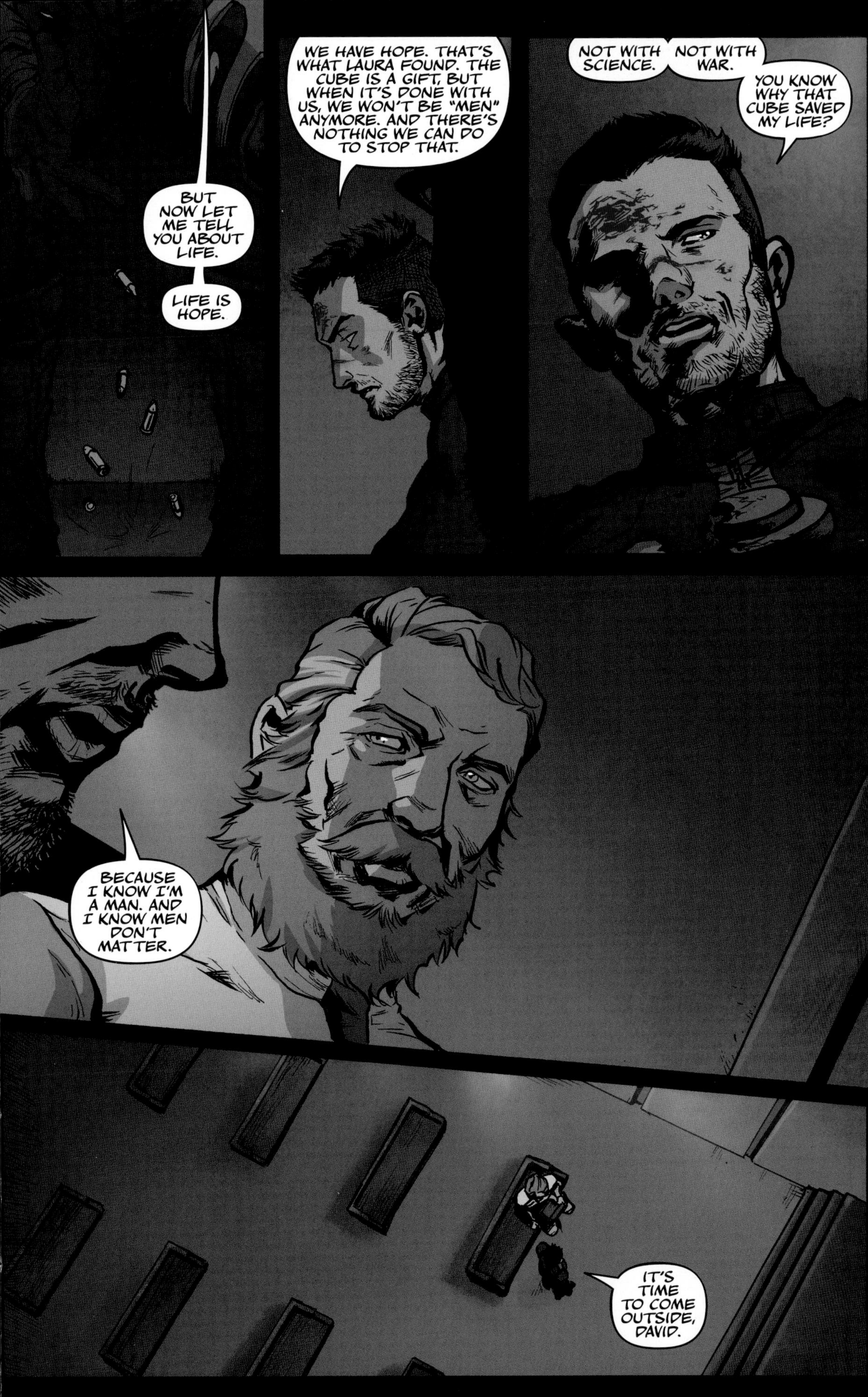
BUT NOW LET ME TELL YOU ABOUT LIFE.
LIFE IS HOPE.
WE HAVE HOPE. THAT'S WHAT LAURA FOUND. THE CUBE IS A GIFT, BUT WHEN IT'S DONE WITH US, WE WON'T BE "MEN" ANYMORE. AND THERE'S NOTHING WE CAN DO TO STOP THAT.
NOT WITH SCIENCE.
NOT WITH WAR.
YOU KNOW WHY THAT CUBE SAVED MY LIFE?
BECAUSE I KNOW I'M A MAN. AND I KNOW MEN DON'T MATTER.
IT'S TIME TO COME OUTSIDE, DAVID.

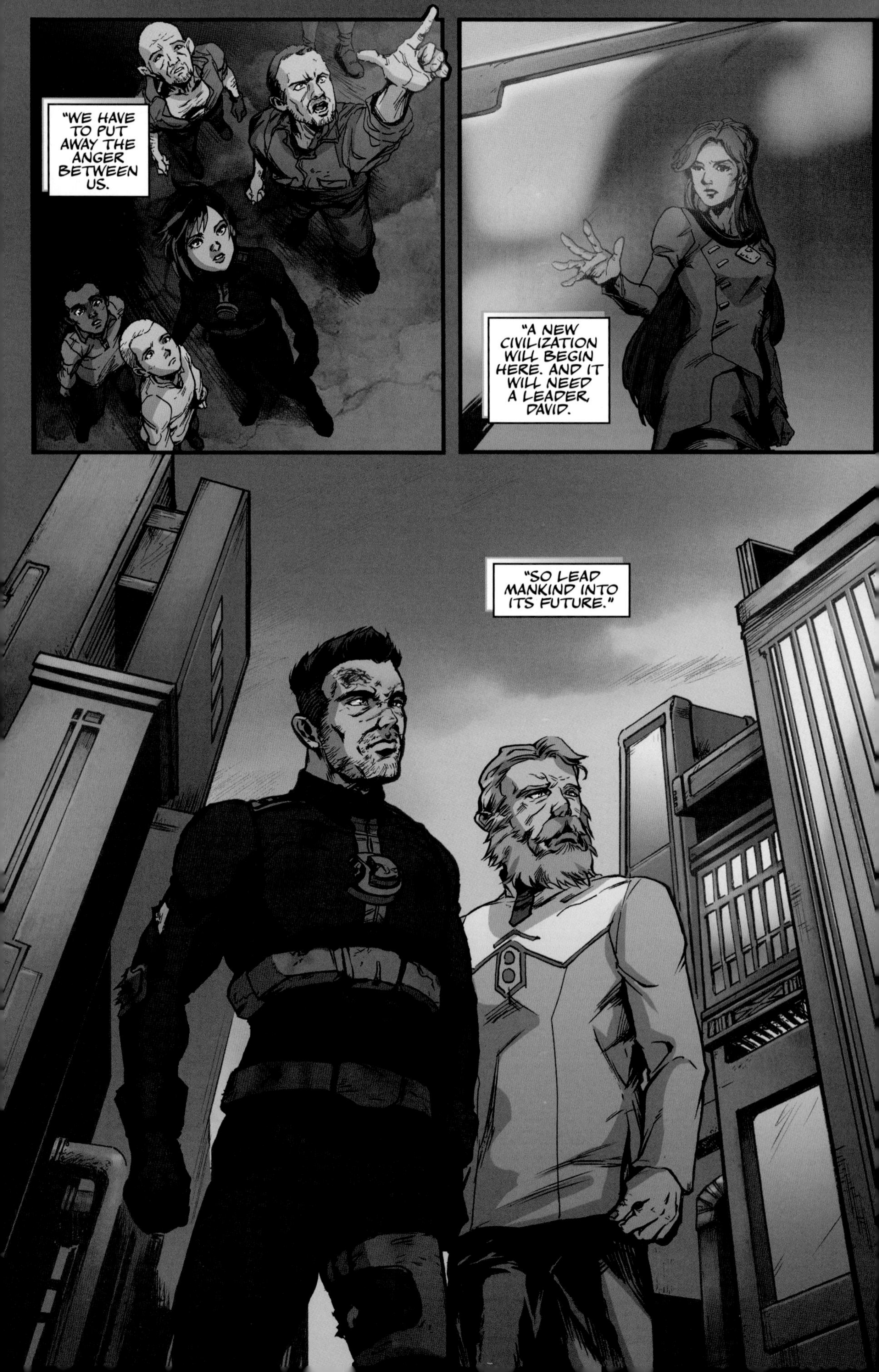
"WE HAVE TO PUT AWAY THE ANGER BETWEEN US.
"A NEW CIVILIZATION WILL BEGIN HERE. AND IT WILL NEED A LEADER, DAVID.
"SO LEAD MANKIND INTO ITS FUTURE."

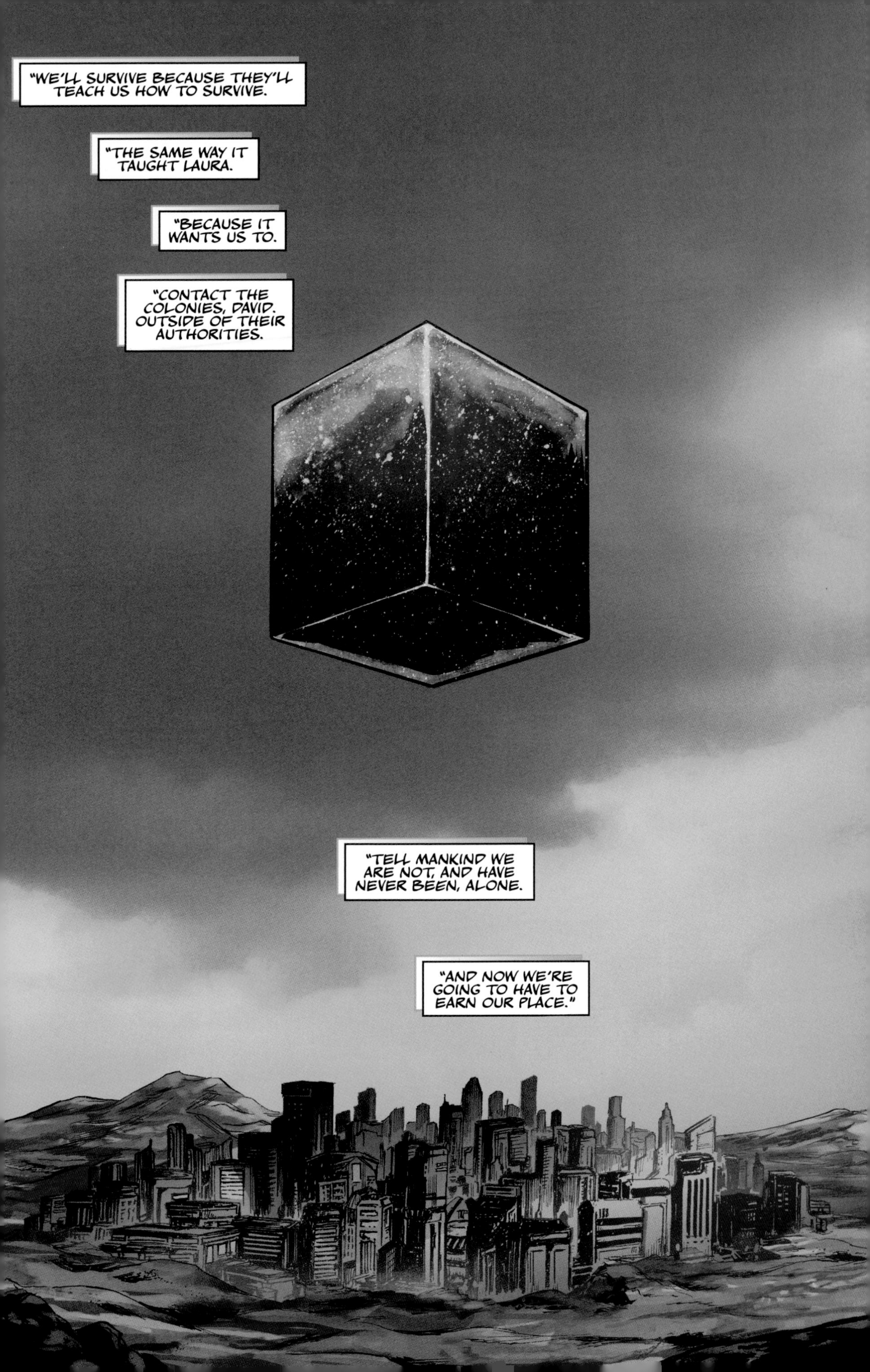
"WE'LL SURVIVE BECAUSE THEY'LL TEACH US HOW TO SURVIVE.
"THE SAME WAY IT TAUGHT LAURA.
"BECAUSE IT WANTS US TO.
"CONTACT THE COLONIES, DAVID. OUTSIDE OF THEIR AUTHORITIES.
"TELL MANKIND WE ARE NOT, AND HAVE NEVER BEEN, ALONE.
"AND NOW WE'RE GOING TO HAVE TO EARN OUR PLACE."

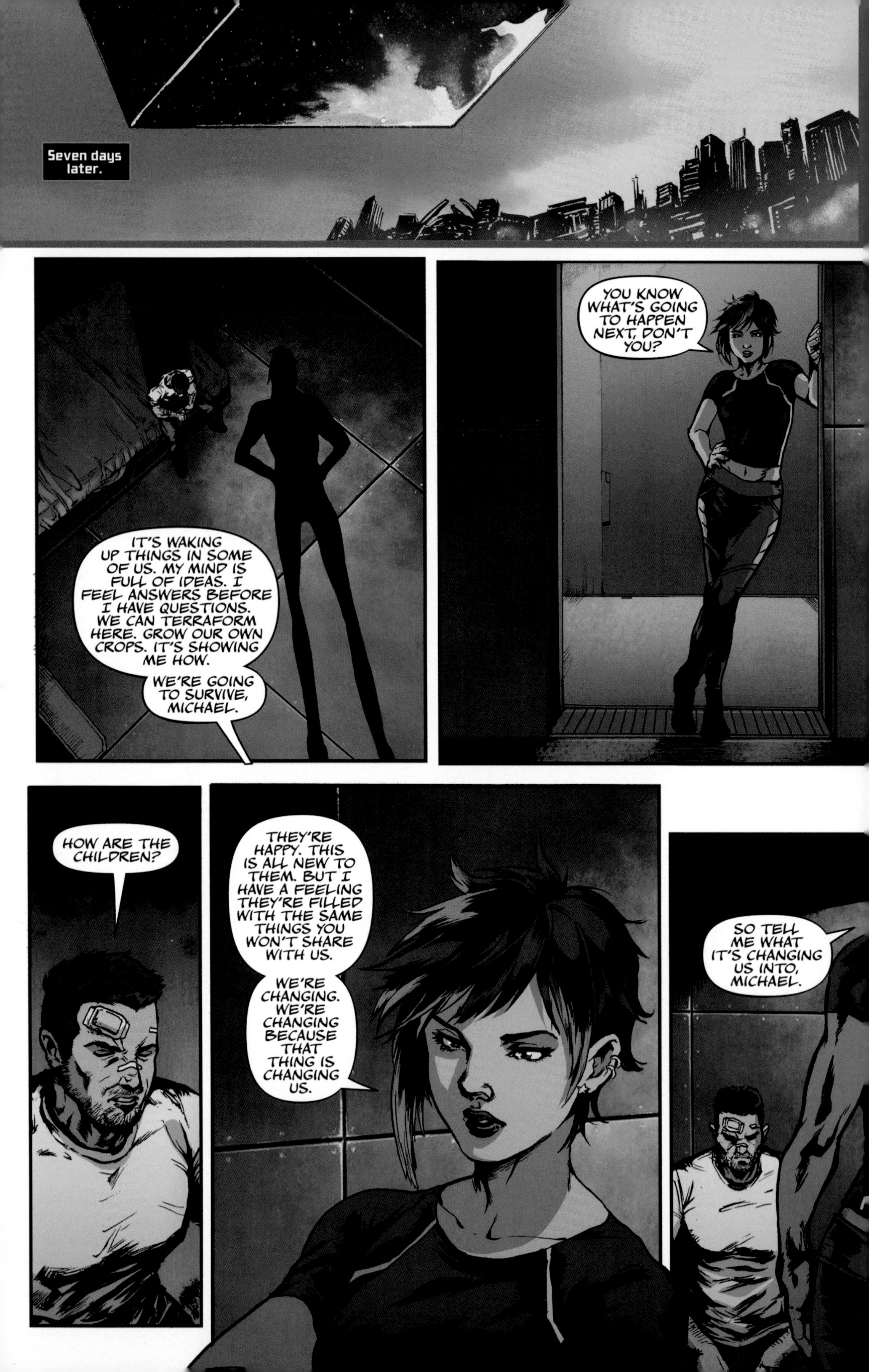
Seven days later.
IT'S WAKING UP THINGS IN SOME OF US. MY MIND IS FULL OF IDEAS. I FEEL ANSWERS BEFORE I HAVE QUESTIONS. WE CAN TERRAFORM HERE. GROW OUR OWN CROPS. IT'S SHOWING ME HOW.
WE'RE GOING TO SURVIVE, MICHAEL.
YOU KNOW WHAT'S GOING TO HAPPEN NEXT, DON'T YOU?
HOW ARE THE CHILDREN?
THEY'RE HAPPY. THIS IS ALL NEW TO THEM. BUT I HAVE A FEELING THEY'RE FILLED WITH THE SAME THINGS YOU WON'T SHARE WITH US.
WE'RE CHANGING. WE'RE CHANGING BECAUSE THAT THING IS CHANGING US.
SO TELL ME WHAT IT'S CHANGING US INTO, MICHAEL.

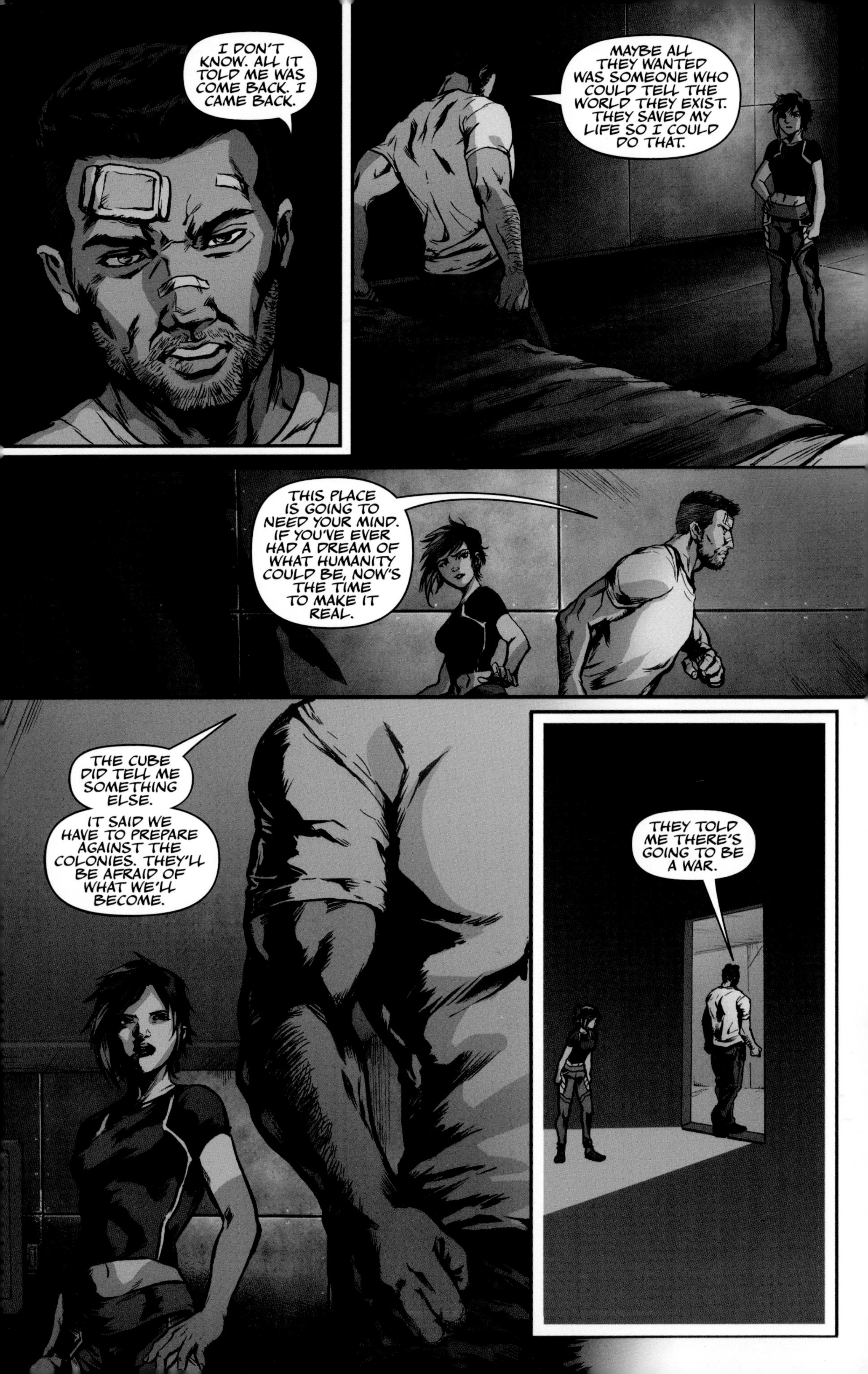
I DON'T KNOW. ALL IT TOLD ME WAS COME BACK. I CAME BACK.
MAYBE ALL THEY WANTED WAS SOMEONE WHO COULD TELL THE WORLD THEY EXIST. THEY SAVED MY LIFE SO I COULD DO THAT.
THIS PLACE IS GOING TO NEED YOUR MIND. IF YOU'VE EVER HAD A DREAM OF WHAT HUMANITY COULD BE, NOW'S THE TIME TO MAKE IT REAL.
THE CUBE DID TELL ME SOMETHING ELSE.
IT SAID WE HAVE TO PREPARE AGAINST THE COLONIES. THEY'LL BE AFRAID OF WHAT WE'LL BECOME.
THEY TOLD ME THERE'S GOING TO BE A WAR.

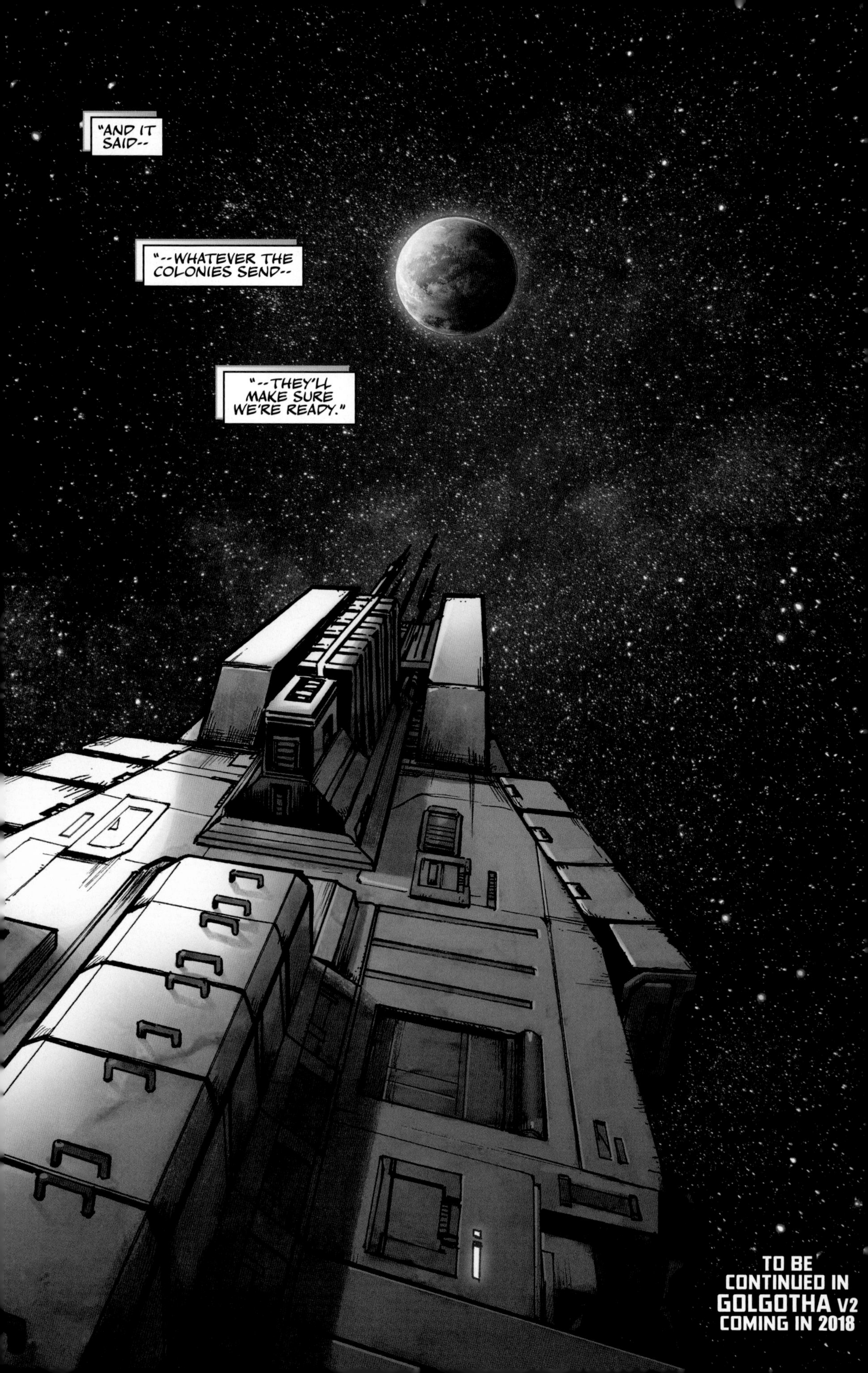
"AND IT SAID--
"--WHATEVER THE COLONIES SEND--
"--THEY'LL MAKE SURE WE'RE READY."
TO BE CONTINUED IN GOLGOTHA V2 COMING IN 2018

SCIENCE CLASS

Golgotha Science Class!

I want to thank you for picking up *Golgotha* and giving it a read. If you dig it, I'd ask that you please recommend it to a friend. Making comics is hard and getting people to try indie books is always a challenge. Personal recommendations go a long way and I thank you in advance for doing so.

If you're unfamiliar with my books *Think Tank*, *Aphrodite IX*, *Symmetry* and *The Tithe,* I always include little articles in the back to discuss and explain certain scientific concepts or thoughts that were in the story. I get a lot of positive feedback on these and people seem to prefer these to endless ads so here we go:

STELLAR DISTANCES

It's actually hard to grasp how far apart planets, stars and other stellar bodies are. Living on Earth, traveling to South Africa last month seemed insanely far. It took me thirty hours door to door to get to my hotel there. Compared to stellar distances that's like a single drop of water in the ocean. With current technologies we're looking at 150–300 days to get to Mars. Voyager I is traveling at 62,000 kph which means it'd circle the Earth in less than an hour and it would take over a billion years to cross the Milky Way galaxy alone.

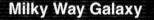
Milky Way Galaxy

Based on current observation from the Hubble telescope, we think there are about 100 billion galaxies out there, but this is likely low and will grow as our technology increases…but you get the point.

Hubble Telescope

https://www.sciencelearn.org.nz/resources/1624-distances-in-space

https://www.nasa.gov/feature/goddard/2016/hubble-reveals-observable-universe-contains-10-times-more-galaxies-than-previously-thought

GENERATIONAL SHIPS

This is one possible answer for the vast distances of space travel. You send out ships that can support life for hundreds or thousands of years. The people that start the transit know they won't live to see it through. They have children and a micro-society inside the ship and multiple generations are needed to complete the mission. We've seen this in episodes of *Star Trek TOS* and in a lot of sci-fi books. Cryosleep and suspended hibernation seems the preferred sci-fi version I'll get to that next. Imagine though, you decide to join an expedition to another world for subsequent generations and will never see it yourself. You either need to be a dreamer, desperate or a combination of both. That first link talks about the morality of it and I found it an interesting read.

https://aeon.co/ideas/would-it-be-immoral-to-send-out-a-generation-starship

https://www.space.com/19047-multigenerational-space-colony-human-evolution.html

CRYOSLEEP

"Cryosleep, a process in which an astronaut is put into a state of suspended animation using a drug or a chamber or something very cold, is a common sci-fi trope. It's one of the main plot points in 2001: A Space Odyssey. *It's how the wormhole-traversing astronauts manage to not age in Interstellar."*

We've all seen it in films, read it in books, but will it actually work? No one has cracked it yet, but some say we're very close. Check some of these links NASA is developing a system that could work as soon as twenty years from now. The advantages of cryosleep suspended hibernation are many; reduced cost, slow aging, less mass to transport and so on. The only way humans are likely to see exoplanets or other galaxies is by being frozen, shipped out and re-awoken. I originally wrote a much longer piece on cryosleep and then found this motherboard piece which was better than what I wrote, so check this first link. Has everything you'd want to know about it.

Realistically, it ain't happening for me in my lifetime. I'll be dead or too old for it by the time it becomes reasonably commercially available. So you young-uns, hope it works for you!

https://motherboard.vice.com/en_us/article/a-brief-history-of-cryosleep

https://www.mnn.com/earth-matters/space/stories/cryosleep-its-not-just-science-fiction-anymore

http://www.mirror.co.uk/science/nasa-planning-suspended-animation-cryosleep-7982029

http://io9.gizmodo.com/5889638/the-economic-problems-with-cryogenically-freezing-your-body

TECHNOLOGICAL ADVANCEMENT IN SPACE TRAVEL

The central part of this story is that Michael Lawton left his life behind to get on an eighty-year journey to start his life over somewhere else. He was looking forward to building something new, being in charge of something…only to get there and have what he was supposed to build already be there. That would suck. Is this a realistic plot device? Yes.

Technology has been advancing exponentially along with the computer chip and computer storage/speed, etc. There has been more technological advance in the last fifty years than there's been in the entire recorded history of humanity. Think about that for a second. We have records that go back roughly about ten thousand years. So we've accomplished more advancement in less than one half of one percent of recorded history.

That's kind of insane but awesome. When I was a kid in the seventies we didn't have computers, the internet, cell phones…and that's just the tip of the iceberg.

"Technology goes beyond mere tool making; it is a process of creating ever more powerful technology using the tools from the previous round of innovation."
–Ray Kurzweil

https://www.technologyreview.com/lists/technologies/2017/

https://singularityhub.com/2016/03/22/technology-feels-like-its-accelerating-because-it-actually-is/

http://news.mit.edu/2013/how-to-predict-the-progress-of-technology-0306

RELIGION IN SCI-FI

In the fifties a lot of sci-fi authors and scientists really thought religion would die out. They believed that the advancement of scientific knowledge and the enlightenment of people would make these relics of the past fade away. I love science. I fancy myself an academic, an amateur scientist who was educated but never did field research. I'm also an atheist, but I struggle with the idea of God, what happens after we die and WTF is the point of it all? These are universal questions science will never answer in an acceptable manner and we will always look for some sort of divine answer either out of fear, love or a narcissistic belief that there should be more for us. Religion isn't going away.

http://www.bbc.com/future/story/20141219-will-religion-ever-disappear

http://www.tor.com/2016/11/01/books-that-explore-religion-in-science-fiction-and-fantasy/

AYN RAND

She was a Russian-American novelist and philosopher who was born in 1905 and died in 1982. Her best-known novels are *Fountainhead* and *Atlas Shrugged*. I went through an Ayn Rand phase in my early 20s where I read these and got obsessed with them. Her philosophy was called objectivism and was about rational individualism. It's probably best explained by her in her own words,

"My philosophy, in essence, is the concept of man as a heroic being, with his own happiness as the moral purpose of his life, with productive achievement as his noblest activity, and reason as his only absolute."

It's worth getting lost in for a few months. I don't believe in this philosophy anymore, it's a bit too selfish and narcissistic for my tastes these days. First link is her own foundation, the second one is a nice skewering of her beliefs.

https://www.aynrand.org/

https://luckyottershaven.com/2015/07/03/the-psychopathy-of-ayn-rand/

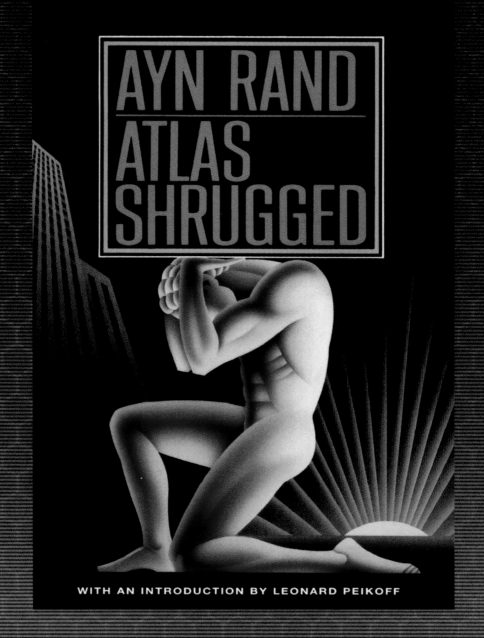

AYN RAND
ATLAS SHRUGGED

WITH AN INTRODUCTION BY LEONARD PEIKOFF

THE CHALLENGE OF STARFLIGHT

SPACE IS BIG. The distance from Earth to the sun is one astronomical unit ("A.U.") Sunlight takes eight minutes to cross this distance. The closest star is 266,000 A.U. away, about 4.4 years' travel at light speed.

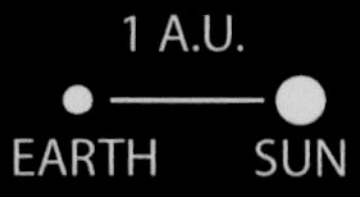

1 A.U.

EARTH ● — ● SUN

The distance from Earth to the black hole at the center of our galaxy is 1.9 billion A.U., about 26,000 years' travel at light speed.

ENERGY: A vast amount would be required

OBSTACLES: The space between stars is full of dust, gas and even rogue planets. Even a tiny particle of matter would cause tremendous damage, when it hits a spaceship traveling at a large fraction of light speed.

THE TIME PROBLEM: A slow-moving starship may take hundreds of years to reach its destination. A higher-technology ship launched years later but traveling much faster will pass them by and arrive first.

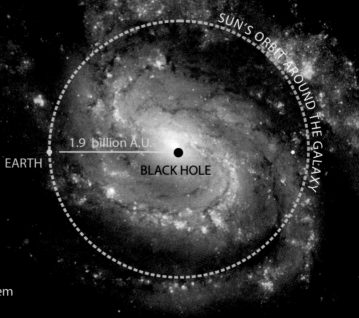

SUN'S ORBIT AROUND THE GALAXY

EARTH

1.9 billion A.U.

BLACK HOLE

SPACE TRAVEL 101: ACCELERATION IN SPACE

To go anywhere in space, astronauts must build up an enormous amount of acceleration. But with nothing to push against, the spacecraft must push against itself, using a rocket engine.

Most rockets in use today are **CHEMICAL ROCKETS**. Fuel and oxidizer are mixed, creating an explosive thrust that causes the rocket to accelerate.

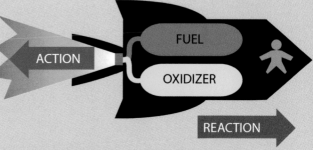

ACTION

FUEL

OXIDIZER

REACTION

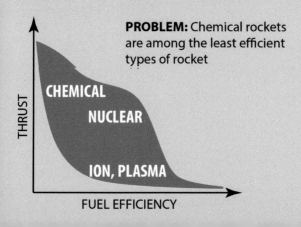

PROBLEM: Chemical rockets are among the least efficient types of rocket

THRUST

CHEMICAL

NUCLEAR

ION, PLASMA

FUEL EFFICIENCY

NUCLEAR ROCKETS heat fuel with a nuclear reactor (or explode nuclear bombs behind the ship to push it)

ION DRIVE uses electricity to accelerate ions (atomic particles). Ion drives have low acceleration but can operate continuously for a long time

PLASMA DRIVE accelerates plasma instead of ions, but otherwise is similar to an ion drive.

SOLVING THE PROBLEM OF FUEL

Using conventional rocket power to reach the stars is out of the question. Most of the mass of any of today's rockets consists of fuel alone. A spacecraft headed for even the nearest star would need a prohibitive amount of fuel, even assuming a travel time of nearly 1,000 years.

FUEL
TANKS

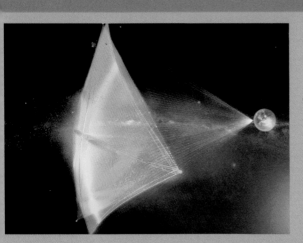

SOLUTION 1: LEAVE THE FUEL BACK HOME

A lightsail craft could be propelled using powerful lasers based on or near Earth. The craft does not need to carry any fuel at all. Limitations include small payload sizes and long travel times. (Shown: Breakthrough Starshot's lightsail concept)

SOLUTION 2: SCOOP UP FUEL ON THE WAY

Although low in density, the space between stars is filled with gases and dust. By focusing magnetic fields, a spaceship could scoop hydrogen gas into its engines to use as fuel for its nuclear fusion engines.

Called the Bussard Ramjet, this concept was proposed in 1960 by Robert L. Forward. Since then, scientists have found potential problems with the idea, such as the varying density of gas in space. (Shown: "Pillars of Creation" nebula, Hubble photo; Bussard Ramjet concept, NASA)

SOLUTION 3: JUST GO SLOW

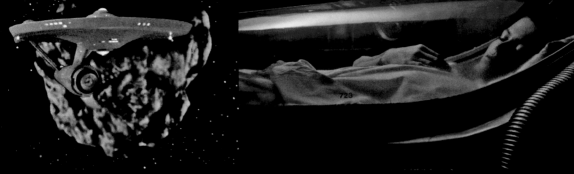

If an extremely long trip time is acceptable, the ship does not need to travel very fast at all. A hollowed-ou asteroid could make the trip, with many generations of passengers born and buried along the way ("Star Trek"). If the human metabolism can be suspended, an individual might make even a centuries-long trip i

Antimatter particles are identical to matter particles but with reversed charge and spin. When particles of matter and antimatter collide, an enormous amount of energy is released, perhaps enough for a star drive. Unfortunately antimatter is rare in this universe and expensive to produce. (Shown: Antimatter rocket concept, NASA)

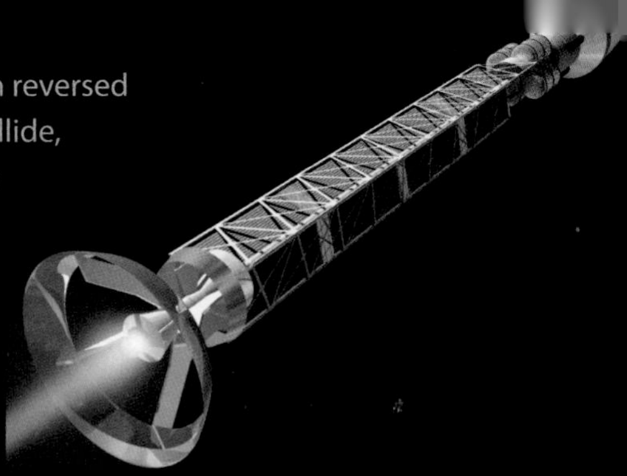

ARTIFICIAL BLACK HOLES

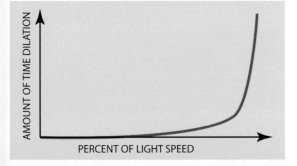

A paper published in 2009 by Crane and Westmoreland suggests that a stardrive using artificially created black holes might be easier and cheaper to make than an antimatter-annihilation drive. Radiation emitted by the black holes would be used for thrust. (Shown: Black hole concept, NASA)

TIME DILATION: SPEED SLOWS DOWN TIME

AMOUNT OF TIME DILATION

PERCENT OF LIGHT SPEED

Einstein found that as speed increases, time slows down compared to stationary observers. The effect is called time dilation. At large fractions of the speed of light, the effect is quite dramatic. If a vessel could travel at a constant 1g acceleration (equal to one Earth gravity), travel across the entire universe would be possible in a single lifetime (although billions of years would have passed back on Earth).

NEW PHYSICS: WARP DRIVE AND WORMHOLES

Physics forbids matter to move at or beyond the speed of light. Theory suggests that if a spaceship can be put inside a bubble of spacetime, the spacetime itself could travel faster than light. Another theory says that if a stable wormhole (tunnel through spacetime) can be held open, travel might be possible faster than light or backward in time. (Shown: Wormhole drive concept, NASA)

Graphic by Karl Tate. Sources: 100-year Starship; Icarus Interstellar; NASA; Allen Everett and Thomas Roman, "Time Travel And Warp Drives"; Paul Gilster "Centauri Dreams: Imagining and Planning Interstellar Exploration"

ORIGINAL GOLGOTHA CONCEPT

COLONY 7
By Matt Hawkins/Top Cow
Slated for Q3 2014 launch, art style color painted (Sejic)

SUMMARY

With overpopulation and climate change increasing exponentially with alarming consequences, a massive international project to establish Colonies on other planets was financed by both public and private funds.

Outcast from his ex-wife and family and nothing to lose, former special forces/ astronaut Michael Lawton volunteers to lead the first interstellar expedition to start a colony on an Earth-like planet found in a neighboring galaxy. With the promise of a new world, unfettered by previous human contact, this specialized team of ten embarks on the eighty-five-year cryogenic voyage.

This initial group's mission is to establish the colony and prepare the way for transport ships that would bring some of their family members and additional colonists to maximize genetic diversity. Technological breakthroughs changed all that when interstellar travel times were cut significantly and what was an eighty-five year transit now took less than five.

Unable to interrupt Lawton's group mid-voyage, they arrive at the new world to discover that a colony has been there for over fifty years and that many of their family members that followed lived and died and their grandchildren are now physically older than they are. Michael Lawton is also shocked to see that his grandson is one of the leaders of this new community.

Lawton's group has mixed feelings about all this, but he is not happy about it at all. Signing on to leave the world behind and do something spectacular by leading the first space colony, he discovers that not only is he not in charge, but this isn't even the first Colony now...but the seventh.

THEMES

The overarching theme is about family and humanity's conflicts being carried into a harsh new environment despite the intent for a fresh start. Additional themes include survival, religion, socioeconomic status, justice all amplified in this petri dish of a small community. A single murder in an environment like this would have massive repercussions unlike Earth where, unless there was a famous person involved, most people wouldn't even notice.

CONFLICT

The largest conflict will be the environment with daily survival of paragon importance. Fights between the people in the Colony, the leadership, between Colonies and between Earth and the Colony all story possibilities. The most important conflict will be inside Michael Lawton's head as he struggles with his identity in this new world and how he relates with his fractured family and what his place is with both.

MAIN CHARACTERS

Michael Lawton – Mid-thirties, ruggedly handsome he led a structured military life where he was never around for his family, always in the field. An affair further isolated him from his family and he volunteered for this mission for a fresh start and to do something extraordinary with his life. Guilt-ridden by his past, but strong and determined. His military background has grounded him in a utilitarian meritocracy with a specific command structure, which places him at odds with the very dysfunctional democracy of the Colony.

David Grymes – Mid-fifties, biologically Michael's grandson who wasn't born yet when Michael left Earth. Loved his grandmother who never had a nice thing to say about Michael. Very liberal socially and believes strongly in a pure democratic environment. Sits on the ruling council, but everything is done here by a Town Hall type vote. Surname is Michael's ex-wife maiden name.

The rest of the original ten all leaving Earth for different reasons, but all wanting a fresh start and running from something. Multi-ethnic, nationality cast. All would be in late twenties to late thirties. Would need a doctor, a hydroponic/agrarian specialist, a geologist, a mechanical engineer, a xeno-biologist (the lady below), a geneticist, couple more muscle, psychologist and a civil engineer/architect.

Jennifer Harkman – Michael's love interest from the original ten, she's about ten years younger than him but has been sent here to keep tabs on the group and him specifically. Call her the internal political officer or spy, but she is a xeno-biologist as well and this is her function to help set up animal species for protein. That's her mission on the surface, but she's also special forces trained. Possible unraveling mystery as she is forced to defend herself or acts instinctively, giving away that she has martial training. Also she could be the woman who was involved in the affair that broke up his family.

The planet – The environment and the world itself will have its own characteristic flavor. Whether we make the world slightly colder or warmer TBD, but its calendar, gravity, day lengths, night view, etc. would all be different from Earth creating interesting details. There would be indigenous vegetation and a pre-existing ecosystem that would be profoundly affected by the Colony. Maybe insects and small creatures but prefer to avoid sentient alien life. Pure desert or ice worlds are not habitable it would need to have waterways and vegetation.

Earth – Complete loss of contact with Earth for unknown reasons or possibly some form of Extinction Level Event happens. They are still somewhat dependent on Earth for supplies and spare parts. With the distances in communication it would take months to years even with enhanced technology to receive messages. Receiving garbled or confusing messages from Earth or the other colonies could spawn conflict. One thought is that perhaps the Colony lost contact with earth about five years before Michael's group landed and the resulting chaos and conflict is the environment they start in.

Resources – With a combination of sophisticated technology and manual labor, they create agrarian society with an interesting mix of low and high tech. Without access to a tremendous amount of spare parts or specialized technicians they have to improvise to repair technologies. Failed crops or damaged equipment could result in rationing and creating conflict.

Leadership – Historically, successful small isolated colonies are utilitarian meritocracies run by a single, strong leader. This one is run as a pure democracy and problems will arise when the group chooses poorly based on propaganda or general misunderstanding.

Unknown viruses/diseases – They'd be hit by new things that we've never encountered before as humans. Similar to the Native Americans with the smallpox it could be very deadly.

Altered ecosystem – One of the human characteristics is that we shape our environment; most other animals don't do that. It has profound effects on the existing ecosystems and lots of story possibilities.

Other colonies – Visitors or fugitives from other Colonies could have profound effects on a small community. The idea that we all have our "groups" and we don't take to strangers in survival scenarios is played out well in *The Walking Dead* series.

Ruins uncovered – I wanted to avoid alien races, but the idea of finding relics of a long dead species that lived here could yield some good story ideas.

POSSIBLE COLONY BREAKDOWN

All seven can be interstellar of TBD placement or a gradated execution like this (either would have story ramifications):

Colony 1 Biosphere on Earth for testing
Colony 2 Orbital colony in low Earth orbit
Colony 3 Orbital platform at one of the Lagrange points between Earth/Moon.
Colony 4 Surface of the moon
Colony 5 Surface of Mars
Colony 6 Surface of Europa
Colony 7 First interstellar

RESEARCH

Possibility of Earth like planets in our galaxy:

http://blogs.discovermagazine.com/badastronomy/2011/02/02/motherlode-of-potential-planets-found-more-than-1200-alien-worlds/#.Um-mx5Tk_D8

http://www.wired.com/wiredscience/2008/10/nearby-solar-sy/

Inner Solar System
Earth
Mars
Jupiter
Asteroid Belt
Inner Epsilon Eridani System
Epsilon Eridani b
Inner Asteroid Belt
Solar System
Asteroid Belt
Jupiter
Saturn
Uranus
Neptune
Kuiper Belt
Epsilon Eridani System
Inner Asteroid Belt
Epsilon Eridani b
Proposed Planet
Proposed Planet
Outer Asteroid Belt
Comet Belt

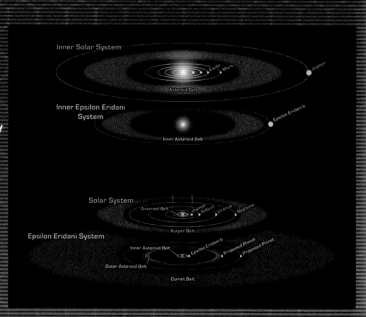

Ethics of space colonization:
http://news.discovery.com/space/astronomy/the-ethics-of-planetary-exploration-and-colonization.htm

Earth like world discovered:

http://www.youtube.com/watch?v=QDB6wxLs1oA
http://www.youtube.com/watch?v=O27uMuXaoV4

Requirements for habitation:
Planet the right size in the habitable zone are only two of the myriad things necessary to promote complex life. You need an oversized moon, a Jupiter-like planet the right distance away to deflect dinosaur killing asteroids, the right mix of elements in the primordial cloud (the Earth is blessed with having come from a particularly violent supernova nebula – where the stellar fusion went way beyond iron). Your star has to be the right size, you have to have a molten core to generate a protective magnetosphere or everything on the surface gets cooked in cosmic radiation. At some point the planet has to have experienced a snowball climate, there must be enough volcanic activity to reverse such a worldwide ice age through greenhouse gases.
   This is just scratching the surface. The odds against multicellular life having the precise chain of events to develop and survive are astronomical and are not normally considered in Drake's equation. Earth is unique for all intents and purposes. any other earth like worlds are likely so far away as to be irrelevant.

There are two main types of space colonies:
  • Surface-based ones that would exist of the surfaces of planets, moons, etc.
  • Space habitats—free-floating stations that would be in orbit around a
    planet, moon, etc. or in an independent orbit around the sun.

Asteroid mining

In 2002, the anthropologist John H. Moore estimated that a population of one hundred and fifty to one hundered and eighty would allow normal reproduction for sixty to eighty generations— equivalent to two thousand years.

Utilitarian meritocracy. Pluralistic society requires educated
Building colonies in space would require access to water, food, space, people, construction materials, energy, transportation, communications, life support,simulated gravity, radiation protection and capital investment. It is likely the colonies would be located by proximity to the necessary physical resources.

After the return to the Moon, in the early 2020s, a special place in space out past it, called 'Sun-Earth Lagrange Point #2,' will be visited by NASA and its allies.

Here are some principles to successfully navigate conflict in your small group:

- Remember that conflict is good. It's what leads to being closer. Shallow relationships never have conflict; growing relationships do.
- You don't have to agree, only reach an understanding you can live with.
- Your relationship is more important than this single issue. Determine that you're going to stay committed to each other while you work through this issue.
- Keep talking to each other. Relationships dissolve when we isolate. Compromise and commitment come when we stay at it.
- Talk to each other, not everybody else. We want to validate our feelings by finding people who'll back our position, but this leads to gossip. Talk out conflict with the people involved, not people who aren't.
- Keep to the facts. Very often conflicts escalate to places that end up being all about hurt feelings and egos, not the actual issues. Recognize your feelings, even voicing them, but remember that the other person has been emotionally affected as well. Keep a cool head, or take a break until you are able to have one.
- It's okay to fight, but fight fair. Stay away from low blows or cheap shots. Respect the other person and speak in a way that expresses your concern without placing blame. It really goes a long way toward reaching a resolution.

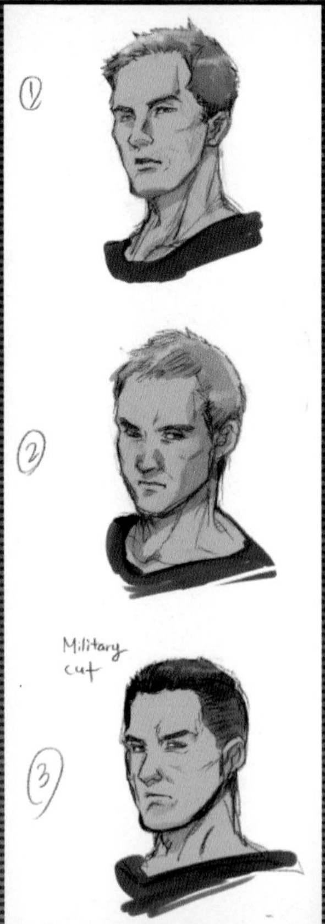
1
2
Military cut
3

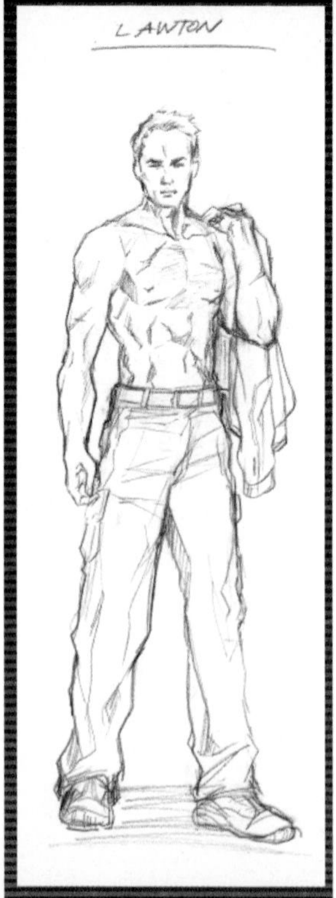
LAWTON

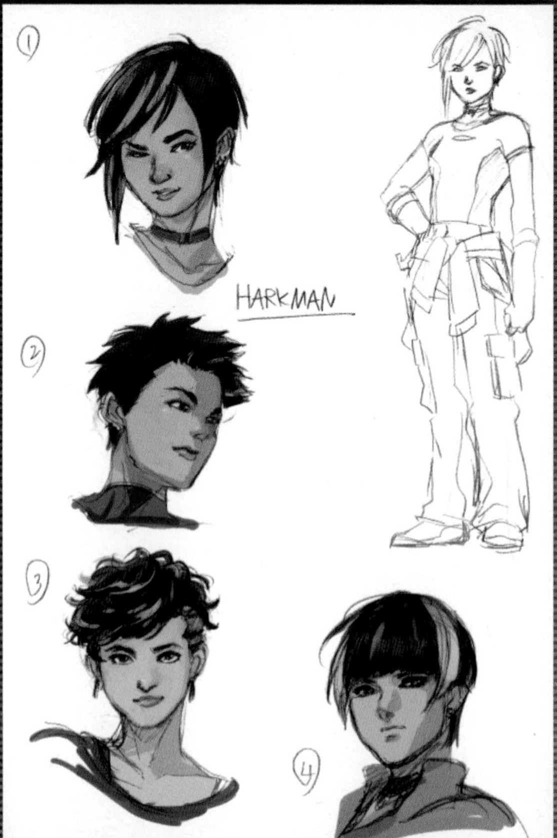
1
HARKMAN
2
3
4

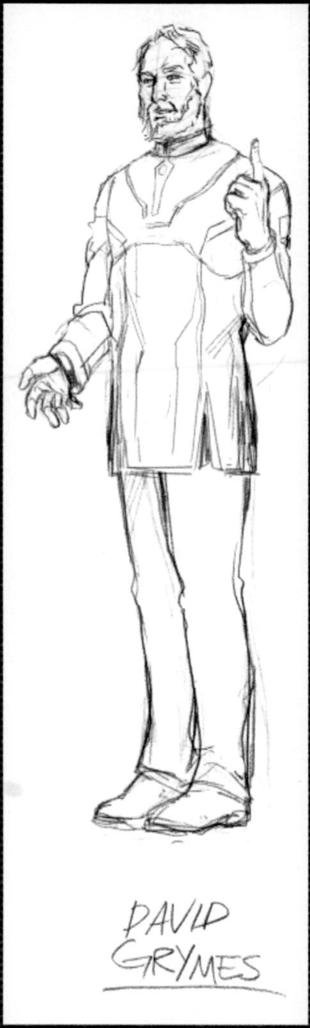
DAVID
GRYMES

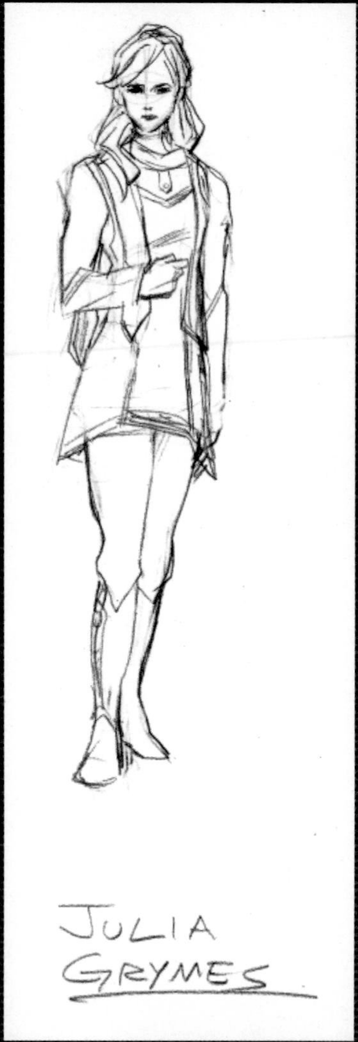
JULIA
GRYMES

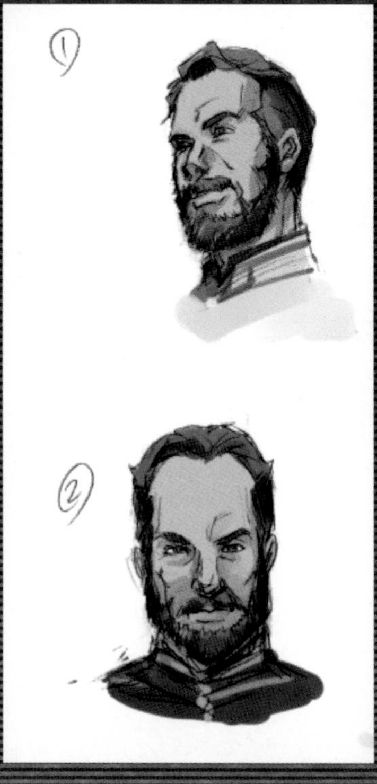
①
②

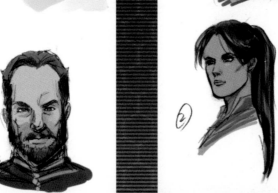

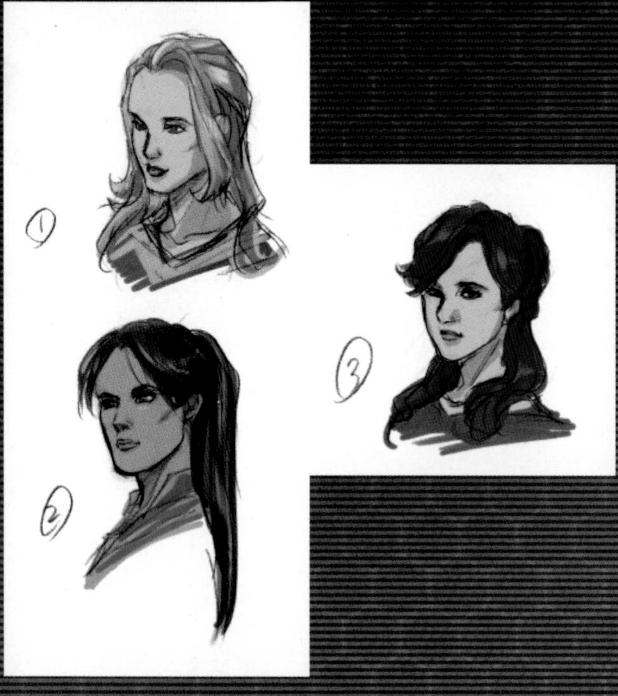
①
②
③

KICKSTARTER THANK YOU

Aaron Higgs
Aaron Keck
Aaron Scholz
Abbigail Wright
Abel Cervantes
Adam Bakow
Adrian Serrata
Aeon Jones
Alan
Alan Alexander
Alan Blank
Alan Smith
alao
Alek Simm
Alex
Alexander Kho
Alexandre Coscas
Alien Lab
Amber Pearce
Amelia
Amit Chauhan
Andrew Biviano Dinges
andrew roth
Andy Kabza
Angela Bowers
Angela Markham
Anthony
Anthony
Anthony Eames
Antoine Gauthier
Bagofrats
Barry Albrecht
Bart Sears
Ben Chadwick
Ben Ferrari
Ben Gordon
Ben Rosenthal
Benjamin Brinkley
Benjamin Slabak
Betsy
Bill Andres
Billy Muggelberg
Black Mast Studios
Bob Eddy
Bobbosce
bobby
Bobby Dean Bentley
Bradley Walker
Brandon Thomas
Brendan Cahill
Brett Bennett
Brett Ruppert
Brian Anderson
Brian Berling
Brian Bolvin
Brian Pierce
Brian Pulido
Brian Weibeler

brkcmd
Bryan Conner
Bryce Boltjes
Byron Hernandez
Carl Rigney
Carlo
Carrie Gan
Chamoxil
chaosprime
Charles Powell, II
Chase Hopper
cheezopath
Chris Callahan
Chris Dresden
Chris Heglar
Chris Marples
Chris Partin
Chris Wyatt
Christian Berg
Christopher Durham
Craig Hackl
Craig jowles
Craig LeBaron
D Kelly
D Michael Martinez
Dale McGarrigle
Dale Wilson
Dalibor Žujović
Dan Courneya
Dan Gibson
Dan Pollack
Dan Rivera
Daniel Brodie
Daniel Buhler
Daniel Corey
Daniel D Hastings
Daniel Eastman
Daniel Petersen
Daniel Pickert
Daniel Schmidt
daniel shorthouse
Danielle
Danielle Michelucci
Dark Shadow
Darketower
Dave Bruno
David
David
David Bateman
David Cantu
David Geye
David Golbitz
David Hildebrand
David Johnson
David Mayo
David Monroe
David Penner
David Pluscauskas

David Rains
David Sheppard
Davyd Martyn Coe
Debbie Crookston
Derek Freeman
dgehen
Dimitrios Lakoumentas
Dirk Manning
DON WALKER
Donald Stewart
Donald W Matanic
DUANE EISELE
Duane Warnecke
Dwain Anderson
Dwayne Farver
Dylan Andrews
Dynamite Entertainment
EAdH
Eileen M.
Eis Annavini
Elzbieta Sawicka
Emil Petrinic
Emily Rain Donovan
Emmet & Jesse Golden-Marx
Eric
Eric Crabtree-Nelson
eric gold
Eric Schwarzkopf
Erica Hussien
Ethan Belanger
Eugene Alejandro
Eva Jarkiewicz
FinalStrigon
FlxCapacitor
Frederick Nduna
Fredrik Holmqvist
Gaëlle Muavaka
Gary Garingo
General Patriot
George O'Connor
Gerald Tichy
Giovanni P. Timpano
Granger Forson
Greene County Creative
Greg
Greg Kane
Greg Rappaport
Greg Scott Bailey
Gregory Lincoln
Guest 1755601816
Gustaf Bjorklund
Hank Barajas
heathpb7777
Hector Rodriguez
HerbtheAnt
Horace
HoverBike
Ian Yarington

insanity prawnboy 23	John Idlor	M G
Inverse Press	John J Ostrosky Jr	m willis
Iran Romaldo	John L Vogt	M'aiq the Liar
J. Michalski	John Nee	Manuel
J.C. Vaughn	John Polanski	Marc Rasp
J.R. Murdock	John Rogers	Marc Whiteley
Jace	john shaw	Marco Catania
Jackie Dill	John Sid	Mari Bolte
Jacob Dill	John Vincent	Maria Craft
Jake Combs	Jon Jebus!	Marilyn
Jake Gentrup	Jonathan Fath	MARIRI KOYAMA
Jake Wendel	Jonathan Gravel	Mark Laramore
Jamall	Jonathan King	Mark Neira
James Ferguson	Jonathan M. Harris	Mark Sasaki
James Hostler	Jonathan Rodriguez	Mark Verma
James Hudspeth	Jonny Hinkle	Markus JÃ¶bstl
james joseph graben	Joseph Rocheleau	Marlena Harris
James Latzer	Joseph Schwartz	Martin Hernandez, Jr.
James R. Crowley	Josh Crews	Martina KutÃ¡lkovÃ¡
James R. Vernon	Josh Gorfain	Marvin Langenberg
James Raynor	Josh Morris	Matt E.
James Turnbull	Josh Rosenbaum	Matt H
Jaroslaw Ejsymont	Josh Southall	matt kund
Jason Bennett	Joshua Bowers	Matt Lowe
Jason Canary	Joshua Winters	Matt Perrine
Jason Crase	Juan campos	Matthew Childers
Jason Gabari	Justin Tebo	Matthew Crowe
Jason Reid	Justin Yang	Matthew Gasero
Jason Snyder	Kasper Jorn	Matthew Hazelbaker
Jay Lofstead	Kelly Keach	Matthew Wang
JD Hardin	Ken N.	Mauro
jeff aronoff	Kenneth Leyden	Megan & Z Krick
Jeff Coelho	Kenny Porter	melissa wright
Jeff Graham	Kevin	Micah Stevens
Jeff Griffin	Kevin Cuffe	Michael Farah
Jeff Henson	Kevin Tyce	Michael Haack
Jeff Tan	Ki Sa	Michael S Sturgis
Jenn West	KickFurn	Michelle Arington
Jennifer Wick	Kirk Lund	Michelle Marsh
Jennifer Zenduck Lewis	Knight of Words	Miguel Apodaca
Jens A. Watson	Kory Colon	Mika Köykkä
Jeremiah Gleim	KOV	Mike
Jeremy	Kris Kulin	Mike Montes
Jeremy D King	Kunal	Mike Scigliano
Jeremy Hachat	Kurt Prünner	Mike Thurlow
Jerry Avitia	Kyle	Mike Twiggs
Jesús R. Cantú	Kyle Worthington	Mikel Muxika
Jim Emmons	Larissa Paluca	Mikkel Thomas
Jim Rittenhouse	lars	Miranda Zabaneh
Jim Sigler	Leon Ramage	Names
JLC	Leonard Johnson	nate wright
Joanne C. McLaughlin	Lewis Brown	Nathan Kelly
Joe Mulvey	Lewis Lawrence	New Paradigm Studios
Joe Ramos	Lisa Lambert	Nicholas Tibbetts
Joe Rawlings	Liza Vercruyssen	Nicholas Vieth
Joerg Mosthaf	Lóri P Bob	Nick Nafpliotis
John Davies	LOUISE johnston	Nick Thornley
John Flynn	Lusipher Diablo	Nick Zamora

KICKSTARTER THANK YOU

Niels Christensen
Nikita Hellsing
Nixon Saget
Nor Azman
nydol
oathbreaker
Oliver Mertz
Olivier ARON
Olivier Devert
Omar Morales
Omar Spahi
otomo
Panagiotis Drakopoulos
Patrick
Patrick Burns
Patrick Montero
Paul Bradford
paul jarman
Paul Quick
Paul Spence
Paul Spencer
Paul Yeates
Pavan Anand
Perry Clark
Peter Rebiskie
Peter Strömberg
Philip R. Burns
Philip Walpole
Phoenix Dreams
Publishing
plueschkissen
Poop Office
Preston Mcbaine
pund
R
R.Soares
Ralph Lachmann
Ramon Geronimo
Rebecca Fraser
RecklessFable
Reilly Blumenthal
Rene Hinterberger
Rhel
Rhiannon
Richard C. Meyer
Richard Foster
Richard Paugh
Richard Vela
Rick Mave
Rickard von Essen
Rita Blaisdell
Robert B II
Robert Lee Jefferson
Coffil
Robert McCoy
Robin Catesby
Rocky
Ron Lauman
Ron Peterson

rwalling
Ryan
Ryan Cady
Ryan Lenig
Ryan Percival
Ryan Sanford Smith
Ryan Woods
SableFox
Salvatore Puma
Samuel Shuskey
Sandra Marie Hinojosa
Scott Morrison
Scott Uhls
SCOTT W SCHUMACK
Sean Arteaga
Sean Bodnar
Sean D Sullivan
Sean Gruosso
Sean McClure
Sean Milliner
Sebastian H.
Sequential Art Gallery
Seth Coleman
Seth Park
Shannon J Hager
Shawn Sexton
Shawnee Myers
Simon Shaw
Siobhan
skarsol
SM
Space Goat Productions,
Inc.
Stacey Figore
Stefan Burns
Stefan Lütjen
Stefan Melnick
Stelio Kontos
Stephan Schober
Stephanie P.
Stephen Buzzell
Steve Foxe
steven baltz
Steven Brunson
Steven Callen
Steven Hoveke
Steven Leitman
Sune Kristensen
SwordFire
T Frank Lugaresi
TAGG
ted contreras
Thomas Gernert
Thomas Johnson
Thomas P. Forehand
thomas severn
Thomas Tellefsen
Thomas Wittig
Tim Fontaine

Tim Smyth
Timothy W. Haskins II
Tobias Jaeger
Tom Akel
Tomasz
Tony Di Schino
Tony Lebel
Tor Andre Wigmostad
Travis Heath
Travis Jones
Trent Dugas
Trent Sessoms
Ty "the SEGA Guy"
Hornbeck
Tymothy
vivek goel
Wally Haworth
Walt Robillard
Wayne Hall
Wendy B
Wendy Cheairs
Wesley Ashkinazy
Will Lum Brogdon
William Anderson
William boyles
William De Micheli
Wulf Bengsch
www.gnut.co.uk
Yun Koo
Zac Elliott
Zack Holterhaus
Zayfod

MISSION STATEMENT

ISOCSS Golgotha.
Fleet number 18739840(09).
Modified Drawnheim MC-69B Taurus E-Class Vessel.

MISSION PARAMETERS:

Attempt to create the first human, mining colony beyond Earth.

DESTINATION: IAU-ACHILLES.

TIME TO DESTINATION: Est. 80 years.

ESSENTIAL CREW:

CARILLO, Anabelle.
(AEF. HUM-INT.)

Born: **Chicago, Illinois.**

Decorated pilot in both sea and Earth Orbit operations.

Graduate of ISOC Naval Academy.

Unmarried. No children.

MEAD, Lancaster.
(Engineer)

Born: **San Diego, California.**

Graduate of MIT.

HIV Positive (Remission). Unmarried. No children.

ESSENTIAL CREW:

LIPPENCOTT, Charelene.
(PhD. Agrophysics)

Born: **Joplin, Missouri.**

Graduate Johns Hopkins (B.A. Applied Sciences), PhD Cornell University (Agrophysics.).

Unmarried. No Children.

CHENG, David.
(Chaplain. AEF.)

Born: **New Orleans. Louisiana.** Base Chaplain, Flynn Air Force Base.

Graduate Saint Louis University (B.A. Religious Studies).

Widowed. Laura Cheng (Deceased). No Children.

ROSENTHAL, Moshe.
(Rabbi. AEF.)

Born: **Haifa, Israel.** Dual Citizenship United States of America. Naturalized.

Graduate University of Haifa (B.A. Hebrew Literature and Language, Political Science).

Base Rabbi Rumsfeld Air Force Base.

Unmarried. No children.

GAFANI, Abdul-Ghafaar.
(Imam. AEF.)

Born: **Istanbul, Turkey.** Dual-Citizenship-United States of America. Naturalized.

Graduate Harvard University (B.A. Philosophy). Founder North African Sunni Islam Mosque.

Served USMC, honorable discharge. Rank: Captain (declined).

Unmarried. No children.

ESSENTIAL CREW:

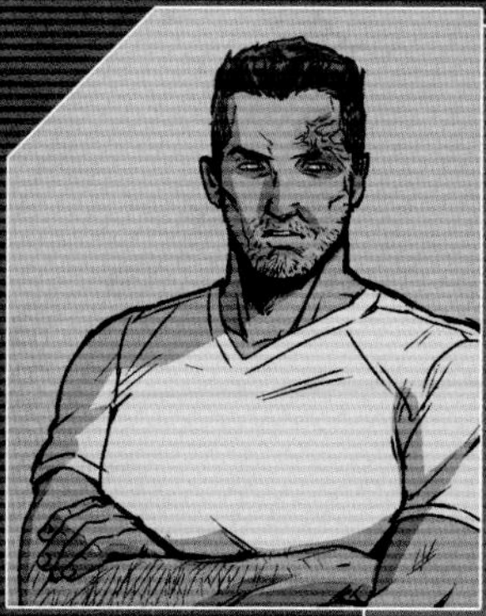

LAWTON, Michael.
(Cpt. 31st Special Forces Group. ISOC.)

Born: **Kansas City, Kansas.**

Graduated Wyandotte High School. No post graduate education.

Enlisted Marines. Served two tours Marine/Resource Coalition Conflict. Promoted to Special Forces.

Duty status: Active.

Married to Jennifer Lawton.
Expecting first child.

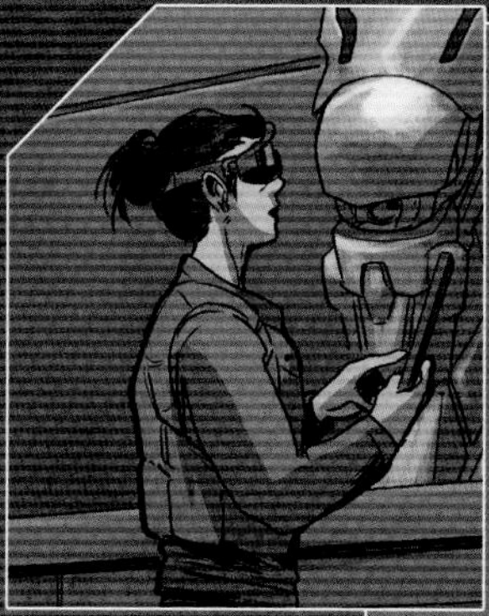

BARDOT, Clemènce.
(Applied Robotics. Kinematics. Control Dynamics.)

Born: **Brooklyn, New York.**

Graduated Cornell University (B.A. Applied Robotics, M.S. Applied Robotics).

Winner Nobel Prize (Team Awarded).

Unmarried. No children.

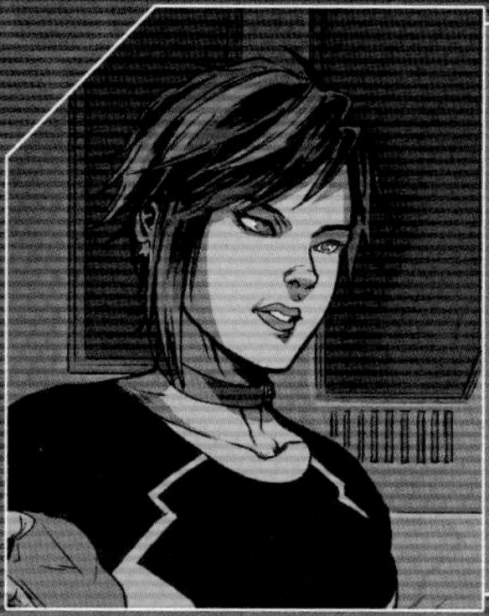

CARPENTER, Jennifer.
(PhD. Xenobiologist.)

Born: **Los Angeles, California.**

Graduated UCLA (B.A. Biosafety) Graduated USC (PhD. Xenobiology).

Divorced. No children.

CREATOR BIOS

MATT HAWKINS

A veteran of the initial Image Comics Launch, Matt started his career in comic book publishing in 1993 and has been working with Image as a creator, writer, and executive for over twenty years. President/COO of Top Cow since 1998, Matt has created and written over thirty new franchises for Top Cow and Image including *Think Tank*, *Necromancer*, *VICE*, *Lady Pendragon*, *Aphrodite IX* as well as handling the company's business affairs. **@topcowmatt** | **facebook.com/selfloathing narcissist**

BRYAN HILL

Writes comics, writes movies, and makes films. He lives and works in Los Angeles.
@bryanedwardhill | **Instagram: bryanehill**

YUKI SAEKI

Yuki is a comic artist and illustrator born in Japan and raised in Taiwan. She has enjoyed working in a variety of web/mobile technology startups while consistently producing independent comics over the years. As a former internship member of Helioscope (formerly Periscope Studio), she was trained under an unique group of artists and writers based in Portland. She was also involved in costume design for the Hollywood adaptation of *Dragonball: Evolution*. She is currently based in Oregon with her husband Ken and two very spoiled cats.

BRYAN VALENZA

Bryan is a comic book colorist based in Jakarta, Indonesia. He currently occupies his time coloring various projects, including Mythopoeia's *Skies of Fire*, Aftershock's *InSexts*, Mythopoeia's *Glow* and Boom! Studios' *Mighty Morphin Power Rangers*. **Instagram: bryan_valenza**

POSTAL

Written by Bryan Hill & Matt Hawkins
Art by Isaac Goodhart

POSTAL brings readers into the fictional town of Eden, Wyoming, a place founded by criminals for criminals. A place where, despite its inhabitants, no crime is allowed. Local postman Mark Shiffron has Asperger's, and through his peculiar eyes we see a town struggling to keep its fragile peace, a town on the constant brink of chaos. When a murdered woman's body is found on Eden's main street, Mark's need to solve her crime leads him into darkness and truth about the town he's known his entire life and the hidden realms of his own psychology.

ISBN: 978-1632153425
Diamond Code: APR150614
Download issue #1 free here:
http://topcow.com/files/PO001_loreader.pdf

THE TITHE

Written by Matt Hawkins
Art by Rahsan Ekedal

A heist story unlike any before! Mega-churches are being robbed for millions of dollars by a crusader hacker group known as Samaritan who is giving the money to causes they deem more worthy. This modern day "Robin Hood" is being pursued by two FBI agents who actually admire their quarry but want to stop the theft before it escalates.

ISBN: 978-1632153241
Diamond Code: JUN150588
Download issue #1 free here:
http://www.topcow.com/files/TI001_loreader.pdf

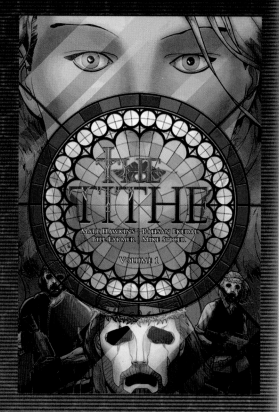

APHRODITE IX: REBIRTH

Written by Matt Hawkins
Art by Stjepan Sejic

Hundreds of years after a cataclysmic event scorched the surface, Earth and its inhabitants have been forever altered and a new landscape and political struggle has taken hold between two distinct factions fighting for control. Aphrodite IX is both anachronism and advanced technology in a world that she no longer recognizes. To survive in this future, she must choose sides in a war that she wants no part in.

ISBN: 978-1607068280
Diamond Code: SEP130520
Download issue #1 free here:
http://topcow.com/files/AIX01_reader_lo.pdf

SYMMETRY

Written by Matt Hawkins
Art by Raffaele Ienco

Utopia is here. Hunger, sickness, work... all relics of a long forgotten past. All individuality, creativity, and negative emotions have been genetically bred out and medically suppressed. The population is limited to segregated areas, but when a natural disaster disrupts the status quo and Michael and Maricela from two different worlds meet and fall in love, their relationship sparks a revolution. Will their love cause the salvation or destruction of mankind?

ISBN: 978-1632156990
Diamond Code: FEB160640
Download issue #1 free here:
https://goo.gl/Zchfpx

ROMULUS

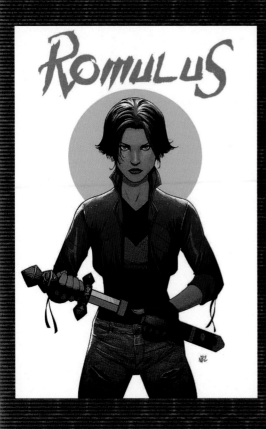

ROMULUS

Written by Bryan Hill
Art by Nelson Blake II

Our world isn't free. All of us, for generations, have lived under the secret control of The Ancient Order of Romulus. One young woman, raised by them, trained by them, betrayed by them, must push through her fear to take a stand against the silent evil that masters our world.

Diamond Code: JAN170811

SAMARITAN

Written by Matt Hawkins
Art by Atilio Rojo

A woman with a vendetta decides she's going to take down the largest military contractor in the world and has the means and a plan that just might work. How do you bankrupt one of the richest, most technologically advanced and successful companies in the world? You steal all their research and give it away to everyone. Can she survive long enough to pull it off with the entire U.S. government trying to kill her?

Diamond Code: MAR170694

SAMARITAN
VERITAS
#1
MATT HAWKINS • ATILIO ROJO

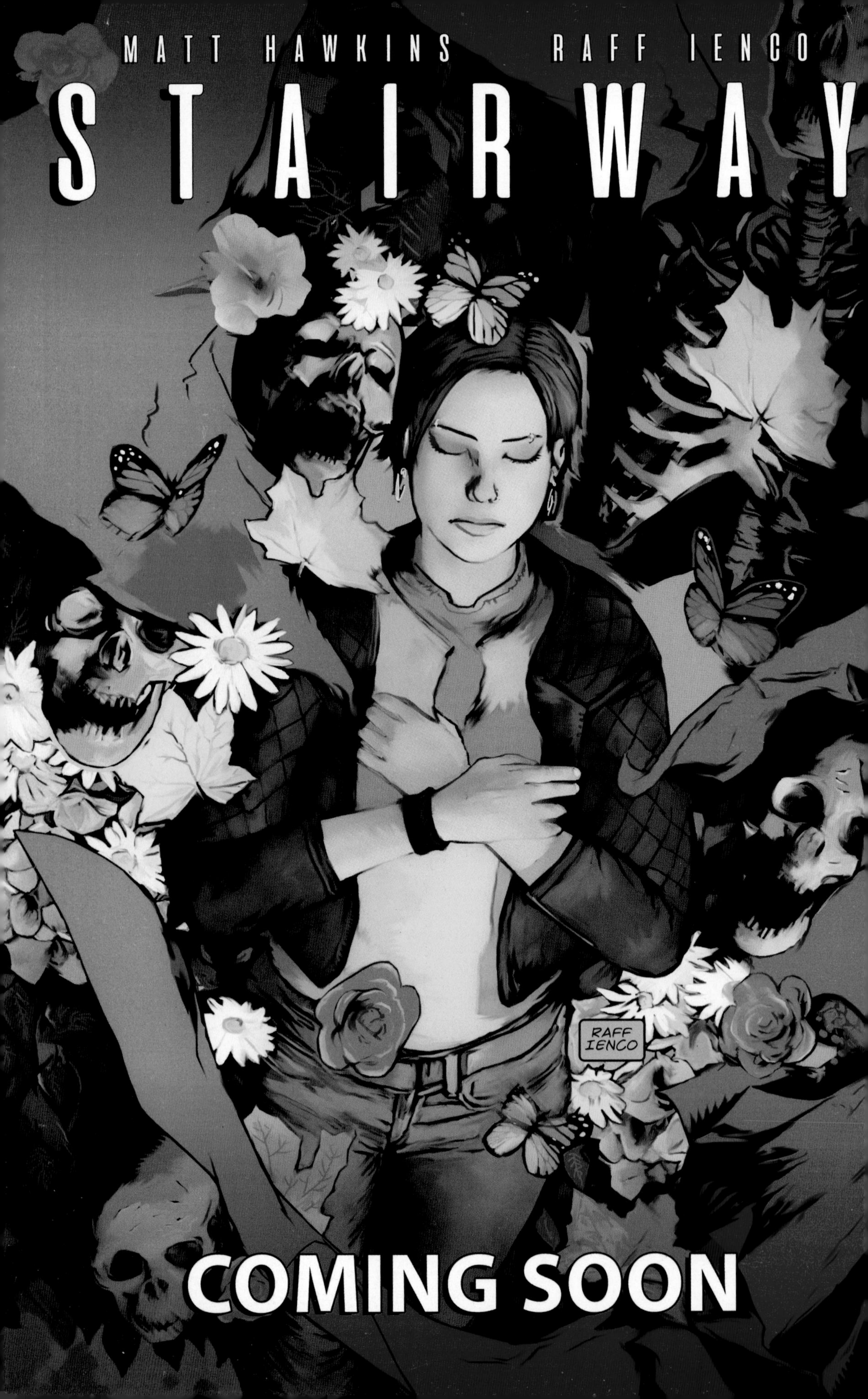

MATT HAWKINS
RAFF IENCO
STAIRWAY
RAFF IENCO
COMING SOON